HOW TO GET A NEIGH WITH MURDER

ELLEN RIGGS

BOUGHT-THE-FARM
MYSTERIES

FREE PREQUEL

Can this sleuthing sheepdog solve a riddle in time to save a missing cat?

Edna, Ivy, Gertie team up with Keats and Percy to outwit a wily catnapper in this EXCLUSIVE Bought-the-Farm story.

Purrrfect for animal cozy mystery readers who love face-paced adventure, laugh-out-loud humor and characters who feel like family.

Join Ellen Riggs' author newsletter today to receive *The Cat and the Riddle* FREE at **Ellenriggs.com/opt-in.**

How to Get a Neigh with Murder

Copyright © 2021 Ellen Riggs

ISBN 978-1-998742-05-9 Paperback - D2D
ISBN 978-1-989303-78-8 eBook
ISBN 978-1-990613-24-1 AudioBook
ASIN B08ZL767XX Kindle
ASIN 1989303773 Paperback
ASIN B0D38DPKQN AudioBook

Publisher: Ellen Riggs
www.ellenriggs.com
Cover designer: Lou Harper
Editor: Serena Clarke
2501221759

CHAPTER ONE

Jilly and Keats both stared at the side of my head as I took the turnoff to Twin Points, one of the smaller and prettier towns in hill country. It was squeezed between two high crests in the rocky range, a topographical limitation that also kept the local council's ambitions in check. Since our mutual neighbor Dorset Hills had transformed into Dog Town with great economic success, nearly every municipality wanted in on the action. Even my hometown of Clover Grove kept grasping for more, getting tackier with each desperate attempt. It was something my best friend Jilly Blackwood and I wanted to counter with our Culture Revival Project. Despite being derailed a few times, we hadn't given up hope.

"What?" I said, as Jilly's green eyes bored into me now. "I haven't said anything to deserve a stare like that. Not for at least an hour."

"You're ruminating, Ivy," she said. "And after rumination comes an eruption you live to regret."

I didn't bother arguing. Things did tend to get lively when I had too much time to think. I was a woman of action, not all of it wise.

Diversion was a better tactic when Jilly was on the case. "And here I thought Janelle was the mind-reader," I said.

Two days ago, we'd left Jilly's cousin Janelle Brighton behind at the Briar Estates, the gated retirement community where their grandmother lived. We'd gone to handle a savage swan and stayed to solve a couple of murders.

Just your typical vacation.

Everything worked out fine in the end, at least for us. Janelle decided to stay to sort out the shady politics on the condo board. Whether or not her many talents included mind-reading was a subject of great debate. Jilly was a rather hostile skeptic, but I prided myself on keeping an open mind.

A snort from the back seat revealed my other passenger's opinion.

"I don't believe in that nonsense," said Edna Evans, my octogenarian neighbor, who'd arrived in the south just in time to save us from a sinister attack. Shaking her index finger, she sent a ball of orange fluff toward my nose. Percy, my marmalade cat, was curled in her lap—the only truly relaxed creature in the vehicle. "It's a crock of baloney."

"Does baloney come in crocks?" I asked. "I thought it was just big rolls of delicious processed meat."

Jilly took the bait I threw down. "Do not call bologna meat. It offends my culinary sensibilities."

"It delights Keats' sensibilities," I said.

The wriggling in her lap confirmed it. My border collie wasn't as highly motivated by food as many dogs, but bologna bits had been welcome rewards during our early training classes. Later I learned treats had never been necessary. Keats performed for the sheer joy of working and pleasing me. In fact, he'd pretty much trained himself and I had wondered even at the time if *he* was a mind-reader. It couldn't have been easy then, because my thoughts had been scrambled by the concussion I got while saving him.

While we saved each other.

Keats gave a little whine and rested one white paw on my thigh.

Our new life at Runaway Farm was an incredible gift that came out of that incident, but we'd paid a high price for it.

I reached for his soft black ears while continuing to focus on the twisty road. I sensed my dog's brown eye pouring sunshine and reassurance into me, while his cool blue eye kept me on the alert. This wasn't a sightseeing mission and Jilly wasn't wrong to worry about how I'd handle myself. That's why my friends had insisted on joining me, despite being exhausted from the long drive home. There was plenty of work waiting back at the farm but I had a more pressing matter to resolve first.

"If you must ruminate, do it out loud so that Keats isn't the only one in the know," Jilly said.

That made me laugh, or at least give it a fair try. "I cannot believe that woman had the audacity to try to steal my horse in broad daylight with half a dozen people on site. I keep going over it and over it."

"The very definition of rumination," Jilly said. "No good comes of that. We'll have more information soon."

"It's my fault and I'm sorry," Edna said. "If I'd stayed in my role of Chief Farm Officer it wouldn't have happened."

"You don't know that," I said. "Whereas I do know that if you hadn't shown up when you did I might not be here to ruminate today."

"I'm the one who should be apologizing," Jilly said. "My family's legacy got us in over our heads in that murky swamp."

"Enough," I said. "This truck is a no-apology zone today."

Jilly's heritage was intriguing, to say the least. On the way down to the Briars, we'd been tailed by some suspicious characters that were apparently part of a crime syndicate. Jilly's grandmother, Bridie Brighton, claimed it was a magical threat that stemmed from old grudges in the lower hill country town of Wyldwood Springs. True or not, I was glad to be back in an area where magic began and ended with an unusually prescient sheepdog. The trip had posed some interesting questions but there were enough mysteries in my life already.

Like why a renowned dog trainer would try to steal Clippers, my miniature horse, out from under the nose of another highly skilled trainer. Trelise Sutcliffe may have regretted that decision after discovering my farm-sitter was Cori Hogan, leader of the fierce Dog Town Rescue Mafia. Or maybe she liked a challenge, and she certainly got one. Evie Springdale had filmed the encounter while Cori beat down the older woman with fists of fury. The orange middle fingers of Cori's trademark gloves flashed in the video, which circulated widely before I got home. Trelise had left the farm howling threats about returning for Clippers.

That's why I hadn't bothered unpacking or visiting my livestock before heading out to confront Trelise. This needed to be nipped in the bud, pronto.

"More ruminating?" Jilly said, grinning.

"I'm thinking I'll feed her to the pig," I said. "Sorry you asked?"

"A sick pig we do not need," Edna said. "Luckily, I distributed my gear evenly between your brother's truck and yours before our trip home. No cause for alarm, girls."

Edna's gear was potentially more cause for alarm than the wannabe horse-thief. There was a fine collection of blades, cross-bows, handguns and rifles, as well as more exotic weapons. She claimed to have left the explosives in Asher's truck. If true, that left him in a compromising position. My brother was a Clover Grove police officer, working under Kellan Harper, chief of police and keeper of my heart. Asher couldn't afford to be pulled over by a state trooper with a full arsenal, but his brain went on vacation the moment he slipped a beautiful emerald engagement ring on Jilly's finger. The former high school starring athlete had never won a better trophy than my best friend.

"Let's have an engagement party," I said, mostly to decoy Jilly. My friend oversaw Runaway Inn's kitchen, having mostly delegated day-to-day operations to my eldest sister, Daisy, and Jilly loved a party. "I was thinking smart cocktails on the patio, since the nice weather is finally here to stay?"

"A cocktail party?" Jilly sat up straight and then slumped just as fast. "We'll talk more on the way home if you and Edna elude arrest. Asher says the Twin Points police are notoriously crusty. Maybe you should take him up on his offer to talk to them about Clippers. There's video evidence of Trelise trespassing and—"

"Horse rustling," Edna chimed in. "There's nothing lower than a horse thief in hill country. Except a murderer of course."

The entire region was built on a foundation of corruption, although I hadn't known that until my return last fall. Since then, there'd been a variety of crimes that were difficult to rank in order of severity. It was no wonder Edna, a committed survivalist, liked to be armed. It was more a wonder that I didn't. I still had faith that Keats and Percy would help me use my own wits to stay one step ahead of trouble. Trelise was no match for them.

We all fell silent as we turned into the Sutcliffe Academy, a large training facility. Trelise either had a very successful operation going, or a generous backer. Were there enough dogs in need of training in hill country to finance a place like that? Dog Town had obviously created an appetite.

"Looks like business is good," I said, pulling the truck into a parking spot beside a dozen other vehicles. "What does she want with Clippers?"

"That's what we're here to find out," Jilly said. "And we're more likely to learn that if no one blows up." Her eyes left me as she craned around to pin Edna with a stare. "Figuratively or literally."

Ignoring her, Edna hopped out of the back with an ease that always astounded me. I wasn't as limber as she was at less than half her age. Maybe she'd cover that in her survivalist course, to which I had yet to be invited. It had taken restraint not to bring it up on the drive home from the Briars but despite Jilly's opinion, I was capable of waiting for the right moment.

Sometimes.

"I'll be nice," I said. "Or as nice as I can be when I'm exhausted."

"Exhausted? You slept all the way home," Edna said.

Her voice was smug because she'd actually driven most of the way, despite being unlicensed. She was a highly skilled driver with too many tickets on her record—likely from daredevil antics that predated our acquaintance. I didn't surrender the wheel to her often, but it had seemed safer than nodding off myself.

"Ivy, how about letting me do the talking?" Jilly said. "You're understandably emotional about your animals."

"A hothead, you mean." I let my friends move into position on either side of me. "A loose cannon."

Percy and Keats trotted ahead to the double front doors, vying for the lead and getting faster and faster. We started to trot, too, just to keep up.

"Let's see if we can pool our resources and charm answers out of her," Jilly said.

"Never waste charm on a horse thief," Edna said. "They'll come back for the rest of your herd."

"If she gets near my property again, I'll hire a professional security guard," I said.

Edna pulled open the front door. "Good, because I could use some extra cash. Properly equipping a bunker is expensive. The pension from my nursing career can't begin to cover it."

Jilly blocked her in the doorway. "I'm sure the Blackwood touch will work in this swanky facility. Meanwhile, Ivy needs to dig deep into her HR toolbox and pull out the fake smile and serene tone that used to earn the big bucks."

I forced my lips into position. That smile came harder the longer I was away from the business world. I made a mental note to practice daily. My corporate fakery skills were extremely useful not only in handling difficult guests at the inn, but suspects in the crimes that seemed to hover around us like a flock of crows. A murder of crows. That was the collective term.

Murder, I thought, walking inside. Why did my thoughts so often come back to that?

Keats turned to shoot me a look with his blue eye and offer a vague warning in his strange mumble-talk.

"I don't like the sounds of that," Jilly said.

I blew out a sigh. "This might be more than fake smiles can handle."

"Hence the heavy artillery," Edna said, using her backpack as a battering ram to force her way in front of us. "If it comes to that, girls, I brought ear protection."

CHAPTER TWO

I nside the academy, a group of about a dozen men, women and dogs of various placid breeds surrounded Trelise Sutcliffe in the middle of a large oval arena. I recognized her both from the video and from my online searches, although she actually looked better in person than in her professional publicity shots. She was probably in her late fifties and had let her hair go entirely gray. Her sleek angular bob gleamed under the lights in the center of the arena. It was a humid late spring day and Jilly, Edna and I all sported haloes of frizz. How did Trelise avoid that? And why did her smile look sincere, when she most certainly knew who I was and my reason for coming? Unfortunately, my face had appeared in every small paper in hill country and some bigger ones beyond. Murders—even solving them—had a way of gaining press. On top of that, I'd had a brief brush with reality TV fame when a production house had tried to co-opt my city-to-farm experience. That hadn't ended well, either.

As we approached, the small crowd opened a runway for our landing at their leader's feet. No one looked nearly as pleased to see us as Trelise did. There were as many scowls as I saw around Daisy's kitchen counter during a Galloway family meeting. It was as if I were the bad guy, when I'd been out of state when the incident happened.

Trelise's face was smooth and unlined, and her amber eyes sparkled. Despite the rage percolating in my belly, I could feel her natural charisma tugging at me. She wasn't just a trainer but a performer, who had fans hanging on her every word and social media post.

Her hand came out and flipped palm down. Did she actually expect me to kiss her fingertips? I'd rather kiss a pig, and had done so on numerous occasions. Instead, I maneuvered my palm under hers and gave her hand an awkward upward slap that might have been cool coming from someone, well... cooler. I was born a nerd and would die one, since "cool" couldn't be learned.

"Ivy Galloway," Trelise said, in a rich, pleasant voice that deserved an accent, or at least a podcast. "What a pleasure to welcome you to the Sutcliffe Academy. You and Keats have come for training, I presume? It's high time, since this dog seems to run roughshod over you."

I had imagined a few scenarios, none of which involved Trelise dissing my relationship with my dog. Keats didn't take kindly to her tone, either. He gathered himself to lunge at her pant cuffs and I snapped my fingers. "Don't, buddy. You're playing right into her hands."

The smirks that raced like wildfire around her entourage told me I was the one who'd been played.

"How adorable," she said. "You really *do* chitchat to your sheepdog as if he were capable of understanding complicated concepts."

"Contempt isn't that complicated," I said. "Clearly that's what you're showing us, and Keats senses it. Sheepdogs are brilliant." I glanced around at the dogs in the class. All labs and golden retrievers —typical therapy and service breeds. Border collies had too much energy for the average person. That's what made Keats the perfect emotional support dog for this corporate refugee who liked to stay busy. What's more, he had plenty of extra support for those in my circle. Therapy came in many packages, some of them black, white and furry.

"Contempt?" Trelise said. "What do you mean? I welcome you to my academy."

"But I didn't welcome you to my farm," I said. "You came when I was out of town and tried to make off with my horse. That's contempt."

Jilly stepped forward. "We don't know that's what Trelise was doing. Maybe she has another explanation."

"She had both hands on his halter while hauling him toward a trailer," I said, watching Trelise closely. Her smile was stiff and her forehead barely mobile. Was she shot up with Botox?

"If her hands had been free she wouldn't have taken such a pummeling," Edna said. "Cori is half this lady's size."

"And fights like a wolverine," I said, pointing to the fierce red welt on Trelise's left cheek. "That's a glove burn, I bet."

The trainer's smile waned and her fingers, which had been dangling awkwardly, touched the war wound. "That little... wolverine, as you called her... wouldn't listen to reason."

"She was watching over my livestock at my request and had every right to toss you out of that pasture. For your own safety alone. The camelids are grumpy. Donkeys, too."

Now her fingers dropped to her arm where I suspected Drama Llama had left a souvenir, too. "No one's safe at Runaway Farm," she said. "It's downright treacherous."

"It's perfectly safe with knowledge or appropriate supervision," Jilly said, dropping her polite façade. "You had no right to be there."

Edna crossed her arms with a flourish. "Let's talk about treachery. You know all about it."

Keats paced in front of us protectively, and Trelise and her students took a step back—even the placid dogs. Meanwhile, Percy climbed up onto my shoulder and took his pirate's parrot pose. Once settled, he offered a loud hiss.

Trelise managed to hoist her eyebrows a little. "Clippers really isn't safe in your care, Ivy. It's a good thing I'm taking custody of him."

"Pardon me?" Jilly said. "You can't take custody of Ivy's horse."

"That's just the thing," Trelise said. "He's not Ivy's horse, but mine." She pulled out her phone and fiddled with it. "There. I sent a copy of the contract."

"Contract? What contract?" I asked. "This horse was given to me by his owner, Bailey Miller, on Christmas Eve."

"He wasn't hers to give. Vinnie Swenson signed Clippers over to me before he passed. Then the horse disappeared before I could take possession." She shook her head. "I thought he'd pulled a fast one on me until I heard you'd added a miniature horse to your menagerie alongside the yodeling donkey."

Jilly saw that I was too stunned to speak, and jumped in. "Clippers was a gift from Vinnie to Bailey when they were a couple, so the horse was rightfully hers. He took him back and neglected and isolated both animals for months. Are you really going to argue over who had Clippers' best interests at heart?"

"No, I'm not going to argue about that," Trelise said. "Or anything else. Because I have a contract."

Edna had fallen silent and her head swiveled as she evaluated the facility. "Why on earth would you go to such lengths to get this horse?" she finally asked. "Clearly, you have plenty of money to buy your own. And while I'm hardly one to throw the word 'reputation' around, that video reflects very poorly on a professional trainer."

Trelise stared at Edna, perhaps trying to wither her without enough facial flexibility for the job. It was a waste of energy anyway, as Edna was completely unwitherable.

"That video brought a lot of attention to the Sutcliffe Academy and the good work I do here, so I can live with it," Trelise said. "I was merely collecting an animal I purchased nearly a year ago to join my therapy training program."

"Therapy program? It's a horse," Edna said. "A small horse that dumps a surprisingly big pile. I know, because I've cleaned up after him. And for your information, he nips, too."

"He doesn't," I said, finding my voice again.

"Sure, he does," Edna said. "Ripped my best fatigues. I'll add that to your tab, by the way. My point is, he'd make a terrible therapy horse, if that's even a thing. Sounds like a silly, newfangled notion this horse thief has invented."

"It's neither silly nor newfangled," Trelise said. "There's a demand for service horses in rural areas. Clippers is destined to help a woman who's waited for years for the right horse. It takes a special blend of traits to make a good service animal, regardless of species, and Clippers has what it takes. I could tell before I made my offer. Obviously, he's gone downhill under Ivy's care, as is typical at Runaway Farm, but I'll turn him around in no time."

Jilly picked up the communication baton. "If you really did have a contract with Vinnie— the deceased and abusive criminal—a lawyer can resolve the matter."

Edna prodded me with a sharp finger. "Do *not* let this horse thief buy you off, Ivy. Next thing she'll be seizing Drama for her therapy llama program, or some other cockamamie idea."

The group of students surrounded their leader and swam into focus for me. They were all in her age range or older, probably because retirees had more time for training. Nearly everyone, male and female, wore a purple baseball cap emblazoned with the Sutcliffe Academy logo. Sycophants, every one of them. I recognized the gleam in their eyes from my days of training new hires at Flordale Corporation. This was the cult of Trelise.

She emerged from her protective circle wearing the same smile. "I can't be bought off, ladies. My work is beyond price because I change lives. Perhaps you've read some of the testimonials on my website. People with disabilities who've been housebound for years are finally getting out in the world with their Sutcliffe Academy service animals." She stared me right in the eyes. "Through me, Clippers has the chance to make a great contribution. Even if you had a legal leg to stand on, would you want him grazing in your pasture while someone suffered?"

My head spun and not just from fatigue. Warm furry ears arrived under my fingertips at just the right moment to set me back on track. I glanced down at Keats' warm brown eye and smiled as he shot comfort into my veins. The way before me was obvious now.

There was no need to look at the contract. If Trelise had made a deal with Vinnie, it would take time to sort out with lawyers. Years of dealing with contentious issues in HR had taught me it would be better to negotiate a win. I was very good at that then, but it was harder to be clinical when there was an animal I loved hanging in the balance. Clippers was a cheery soul who loved to shuffle a little dance as I sang. We needed his energy at Runaway Farm to balance some of the less resilient personalities—particularly his best friend, Bocelli the donkey.

Finally, I gathered my thoughts. "Even if *you* had a legal leg to stand on, Trelise, I'm sure you wouldn't be so inhumane as to part Clippers from his constant companion, the yodeling donkey."

"Of course not," she said. "I'll take the donkey, too. Although they're useless in service work. Far too stubborn."

"Ivy, you can't let this villain seize your livestock," Edna said. "I'm the first to say you have too many animals, but you don't want to set a precedent of letting people grab and dash."

"Oh, I'm not giving her Clippers," I said. "Or Bocelli."

"My lawyer will settle this with your lawyer," Trelise said. "You *do* have one?"

I turned to Jilly, who shook her head. "We'll find one," I said. "Things have a way of working themselves out."

Edna's face turned a furious shade of puce. "Ivy, the longer you lie down and—"

"No one's lying down," I said. "In fact, joining the Sutcliffe Academy will take plenty of work."

"You don't have time for that," Jilly said.

"I'll make time, because I know the value of service animals better than most," I said. "Maybe Clippers is destined for this calling, but I'll be the judge of that and he won't leave my care till I know. Trelise, you have a chance to convince me, as well as Clippers and Bocelli."

"I don't need to convince you of anything. The contract is proof enough."

I waved her comment away. "Contracts are made to be broken. So get ready to cast your spell over us like you have the others. If you try any funny stuff, I'll send my cop brother with Clippers instead."

Edna couldn't help snorting at this. "Asher Galloway is a total pushover. He has no business training anything."

Jilly gave Edna a frosty stare. "I'll thank you to speak kindly of my fiancé."

"I'm not the villain here," Edna said.

"Nor am I," Trelise said. "I stand behind my work and you can expect a call from my attorney."

I turned and beckoned my friends. "And you can expect my trailer to pull up tomorrow. I'll let my horse explore his potential because I strive to keep all of my animals happy. It'll be his decision, Trelise. Take it or leave it."

Without waiting for an answer, I let Keats herd me back the way we'd come. Percy jumped off my shoulder and held back. When I turned, he was making scraping gestures with one fluffy orange paw on the laminate floor.

Jilly and Edna saw it, too, and our eyes widened. Percy's patented litterbox sweep always occurred around a death. If I had to make a prediction, I'd say someone in that arena was likely to die before too long. And probably not from natural causes.

I just hoped my team, all of us so weary from dealing with recent murders, could stay well out of trouble.

Keats looked up at me with his eerie blue eye and panted ha-ha-ha. His message was clear: fat chance of that.

CHAPTER THREE

W e were silent for the first leg of the drive back. Soon we would come to a turnoff that required a decision, and as much as I hated to disturb the relative peace, it was time.

"Should we run over to Dorset Hills and talk this through with Bailey Miller?" I asked. "See if she knew anything about Vinnie's arrangement with Trelise?"

"I vote yes," Edna said. "She might have some pull, given the horse was a gift to her."

"I say we go straight to a lawyer," Jilly said. "Trelise obviously isn't open to negotiation. She doesn't even care that there's a video circulating of her getting tossed off your farm by Cori. That can only mean her followers—"

"Sycophants," Edna interrupted.

"—are willing to put up with her outrageous behavior," Jilly continued. "I think you did the right thing in playing along, Ivy, because Trelise would—"

"Probably come back fortified, and her people look dead-eyed," Edna interrupted again. "Like zombies. Something's rotted their brains."

"—use social media against you," Jilly carried on, unfazed. "She's got millions of followers across the country. Her service animals have been profiled on every major news outlet."

I held up my hand to stop Edna's barrage of interruptions. "So that's why Cori barely badmouths her despite what happened with Clippers."

"Evie Springdale said Trelise is a training guru," Jilly said. Keats turned in her lap to stare at her and she added, "Not as good as Cori, of course."

"Cori chose not to turn her gift into big business," I said. "Probably so she could focus on rescue. They're both doing good work but Trelise has fallen for her own hype."

Jilly laughed. "I never thought I'd say something like this, but Trelise makes Cori look humble."

I smiled, too. Cori was known for her daring exploits to extract and rescue animals, yet she was nearly beaten at her own game by a horse thief. "It must be hard to be Cori right now. I suppose that's why she wasn't around when we got home."

"Attending to her bruised ego," Edna said. "But it's like the severed leg of a tadpole. Always grows back."

"Is that even true?" I asked, slowing as we neared the turnoff and then pulling onto the shoulder. I hit the flashers and turned off the ignition to give the discussion my full attention.

"Of course, it's true. I'm a nurse and I know these things."

Jilly craned around. "You learned that in nursing school?"

"Education was just a formality for me," Edna said. "I'm largely self-taught. With my family, you had to stay a step ahead to stay alive. Did you know I built my first bunker at age nine? I sensed I'd need it one day. Then I learned how to live off the land, and a good thing, too. After my sister burned down the house, I had someplace to go till she skipped town."

I turned to look at Edna, too. "I want to hear more about this, Edna. Truly, I do. But for the moment we need to decide on a course of action."

"I vote we drive to town and visit Teri Mason's grandmother and then find a lawyer," Jilly said. "Asher said Teri was beside herself that you might not make it home in time."

"I can't imagine what Imogen Pigeon wants with Ivy," Edna said. "She was an irascible woman and the town breathed a sigh of relief when she lapsed into a coma."

Jilly gasped. "Edna, that's a terrible thing to say."

Four sets of eyes stared at Edna, and then Percy vacated her lap with a meow of disgust.

Imogen Pigeon had taken over the school vaccination program when Edna was forced into early retirement by the sheer volume of complaints about her gleeful inoculations. Since Imogen was about 15 years Edna's senior, it was an even tougher blow to our friend's pride. There was no way to save face, and while Edna had mostly recovered, some bitterness evidently remained.

She waved a dismissive hand now. "Oh, everyone would say the same. You'll see."

"Teri adores her grandmother," I said. "The fact that Imogen's come out of the coma like her old self is incredible."

"It's actually quite common for people to have a few hours or days of clarity before they pass," Edna said. "The formal name for it is 'terminal lucidity.' I saw it often in bedside nursing."

"Really? Why does that happen?" I asked.

"No one knows, but there's research underway," Edna said. "I try to stay current so that I'm as well prepared as possible for the dissolution of society."

"Apparently, Imogen had dementia before she failed," I said. "For her to become lucid again sounds like a miracle to me."

"Scientists agree with you there," Edna said. "They can't figure out how the mind could clear in such cases. Unfortunately, the phenomenon gives families false hope. It's called 'terminal' for a reason. But it can give people a chance to say their goodbyes and resolve any differences."

"That's so interesting," Jilly said. "I love the idea of a final curtain call to sort things out."

Edna pursed her lips. "There are no guarantees it will happen. That's why I speak so frankly in the present. We might suddenly go poof without a chance for last words."

I turned the key in the ignition, rolled back onto the highway and then took the turnoff to Clover Grove. "I'm surprised Imogen would want to share any of her last words with a complete stranger like me, but it sounds like we may not have long. So we'll see her first, and deal with Clippers afterward."

"Clippers is safe," Jilly said. "He's got protection twenty-four seven."

"For the moment. We'll need to be vigilant till a lawyer puts Trelise Sutcliffe in her place," I said. "In the meantime, it wouldn't do Clippers any harm to learn some manners. He's starting to think like a donkey and it's a waste of his potential."

"Please promise me you won't let her have him," Edna said.

"Trelise is unethical and I'd never put one of my animals in her care," I said. "But I also made a commitment to do all I can to make my animals happy. If Clippers shows an aptitude for this work, and a person with a disability could live a better life because of his service, I'd consider training with someone else." I sighed as we took another turn to Imogen Pigeon's house. "It would break my heart to lose him, but rescue work isn't about my comfort."

Keats touched the hand that rested on the gear shift with his nose and a wave of sweet comfort flowed up my arm. That's exactly why I had to entertain the notion of parting with my little horse. If Clippers was called to service and wanted to deliver, someone else could experience the magic of an animal's companionship, just as I had.

"We're a long way from that happening," Jilly said. "One step at a time."

"One step into Trelise's toxic spider web of an arena," Edna said. "Do be careful, Ivy."

"I'm always careful." We all laughed, except Percy. I glanced back and found his green eyes wide and unblinking. "I sure hope Percy was just predicting a natural passing. Some of Trelise's followers were getting on in years."

"There wasn't a face over seventy," Edna said. "They have years of valuable contribution ahead if they can escape her sphere of influence. And get into mine."

We laughed again as we turned into the long lane that led to the old Pigeon manor.

"How does Imogen manage to live alone given the circumstances?" Jilly asked.

"Round-the-clock caregivers, according to Teri," I said. "It's what her grandmother wanted, and luckily, can afford."

Edna tutted from the back seat. That wasn't the way she'd want to go. Her vision of a worthy death was more in line with a Viking's: in battle or by her own sword.

Keats stood up on Jilly's lap and cast a wary blue eye my way. "What's going on, buddy? Something we should be worried about?"

The dog's noncommittal mumble suggested there was no immediate cause for alarm. Maybe he was as uneasy about the idea of terminal illness as I was. What did you say to someone who was so close to the end, and a stranger at that? I'd faced many challenging situations over the past year, but this felt unusually daunting. My human resources skills and armor might not help me here.

The nose poked my arm this time and I realized I had more to fall back on than clinical distancing. My dog would get me through this awkward situation. I needed to stay centered and remember it wasn't about me. It was about Imogen, Teri and the rest of their family.

"It'll be fine," Jilly said, patting my arm. "I'll be with you to help and Edna will be in the truck waiting for us when we're done."

There was an indignant snort behind us. "I will not be left behind like a handbag at your convenience."

"Edna, you've already shown us your baggage about Imogen," I said. "I doubt she came out of a coma to resolve things with you. If she did, we'll send Keats and Percy to get you."

"Percy is going in and I can't?" she asked.

"Yes, Percy's coming." I let both pets climb over me and out the door. "I don't know if Imogen is a dog person or a cat person yet. One of these two might delight her."

Jilly jumped out and joined me in front of the truck and we walked arm-in-arm up the porch stairs after the animals. The sound of Edna's muttered complaints reached us, so she must have rolled down the back window to make sure the sound carried.

I considered pressing the doorbell but worried it would wake Imogen if she were sleeping. Instead, I lifted the knocker, which was in the shape of a bird.

One tap did the trick. The door cracked open and a woman in turquoise surgical scrubs peeked out at us through thick glasses. Her short gray hair was in the sensible cut of most older women in our town. My sister, Iris, made a decent living off repeating that cut over and over at Bloomers, the salon she ran with Mom.

After introducing Jilly, Keats, Percy and myself, I told the caregiver that Teri had sent us to visit Imogen.

"Ima's not taking callers outside immediate family," the caregiver said. She looked over my shoulder and saw Edna in the truck. "Certainly not the likes of Edna Evans."

"I heard that, Prudence Hoggins," Edna called. "I'm not in your fan club, either."

"Edna isn't coming in with us," I said. "Teri confirmed Mrs. Pigeon would welcome Jilly and the pets."

"I don't believe you," Prudence said.

"Teri said she spoke to you directly, and followed up with a text," I said. "Shall we call her together?"

"Do you have any idea how sick this woman is?" Prudence asked. "You can't, or you wouldn't think about barging in here to... do what you do."

I crossed my arms. "What is it you think I do, Ms. Hoggins?"

"Cause trouble. You touch down like a tornado and leave devastation in your wake."

A snuffle of laughter escaped me at the mental image and Jilly gave my arm a little pinch. "Ms. Hoggins," she said. "We have no idea why Mrs. Pigeon asked to see Ivy, but she did. We owe her the respect of meeting her request, don't you think? It's not for any of us to question her reasons."

The door opened a little more so that she could take our full measure through both thick lenses. It seemed like she was going to cave, but then her eyes dropped to Percy, who was repeating his sweeping litterbox maneuver on the welcome mat. I hoped my cat was just making a statement about the death of hospitality here. Regardless, it seemed to rub Prudence the wrong way and her frown deepened.

She tried to close the door and found my steel-toed boot wedged in the gap. "This isn't the right time for a Galloway circus," she said. "Try another day."

"I understand you're looking out for Mrs. Pigeon's welfare," I said, "but I gave her my word through Teri that I'd visit and I'm here to meet that obligation."

"Meet it later," Prudence said. "After Ima's nap." The door opened just a little more and a white sneaker swung forward with enough force to eject my boot from the doorway. Just before it clicked shut, she added, "If she ever wakes up again."

CHAPTER FOUR

E dna chuckled in the back seat as we headed off to Dorset Hills. "Imogen and Prudence are the perfect pair. Prudie isn't even an RN but she acts like she's chief scrub nurse at a big city hospital."

"She's a little overprotective," Jilly said, fingers flying over her phone. "Teri needs to deal with her grandmother's gatekeeper so that we can swing back after talking to Bailey."

I let out a gusty sigh that practically blew Keats' ears back. Either that or those fluffy black triangles had other reasons to flatten. "All I wanted to do today was putter in the barn and pastures," I said. "I missed the farm so much."

"All I wanted to do was take inventory at my bunker and see what gaps need filling," Edna said, adding her sigh to mine. "The end of days feels closer now that I know about the criminal underworld in Wyldwood Springs."

Jilly sighed, too, probably thinking about her family's rather sinister past. "All I wanted to do was check every cupboard in the kitchen and make sure everything was as I left it."

"Bet our farm-sitters messed up your alphabetized spice shelf," I said, "But I'd be happy to be proven wrong about that."

She slipped the phone into her purse and twisted her fingers together. "I need order, Ivy. We have a large group of guests coming in two weeks, remember."

"I remember. That's why I was thinking we should throw your engagement party this weekend."

"This weekend? Are you crazy?" Jilly's voice spiked. "Events like that take careful planning. I want it to be just right."

"You've organized many a party in less time," I said. "Including several last week at the Briars."

"True, but this is different," she said. "The stakes are higher."

I noticed she was twisting the emerald ring on her finger. We hadn't really had time yet to talk about the proposal because she'd traveled home with Asher while I rode with Edna. I hoped she wasn't regretting her decision. My brother would be utterly heartbroken if she called things off.

After we got some rest, I'd bring it up tactfully and see how she felt. Now certainly wasn't the time to—

"Are you getting cold feet, Jillian?" Edna asked. "One could hardly blame you. That Galloway ruffian has quite a history. It's not too late to back out, you know. Many a bride has realized the folly of her ways after the paperwork was signed, and it's a legal hassle you don't need."

"No one's backing out of anything," Jilly said. "On the contrary, I'm looking forward to the party and shaking off what happened at the Briars."

"What about the marriage itself?" Edna pressed. "Can you tolerate the prospect of spending decades in a bunker raising little Ashers?"

"Yes, Edna, I can," Jilly said. "Except for the bunker part, there's nothing I'd love more than raising little Galloways." There was a pause and then she added, "As long as I don't have to give up my kitchen at Runaway Inn."

"Aha!" Edna sounded victorious. "I knew you'd regret giving away your freedom so soon."

"Edna, I turn thirty-four this year. My time for producing little Galloways is running short."

Reaching through the seats, Edna gave Jilly's shoulder a poke. "There's an old expression: marry in haste and repent at leisure. Be careful, or you could end up like Dahlia."

"Excuse me?" Jilly's voice overlapped with mine but I was the one to continue. "Edna, come on. Jilly is nothing like my mother. *Nothing.* And Asher is nothing like his father."

"Really?" Edna was bemused. "I wouldn't be so sure about that."

I geared down, pulled the truck onto the shoulder again and pressed the flashers. Then I turned and gave Edna the full force of my glare. "Okay. Here's how this is going to go. Stop giving my best friend a hard time about something so personal and important, or hitch a ride home."

"I've hitched plenty of times," she said. "Although my thumb does have a touch of arthritis these days. I've been overdoing it with the fencing and swordplay."

I stared at her but her eyes were shifty. "I doubt you'll catch a sweet ride in those fatigues, Edna. But if you want to miss what happens next with Bailey and Prudence, that's your choice. Otherwise, you can apologize to Jilly."

She waited long enough to let us know it was a tough decision before saying, "I misspoke, Jillian. You'll make a lovely bride and no doubt a blissfully happy wife."

"That's better," I said. "Unlike his father, Asher will work his butt off to take care of Jilly and their family. And Jilly, your job as chef at the inn is permanently open for you. We can set up a play area for the little Galloways. No bunker for my nieces."

"And nephews," Jilly said. "I'd like a boy first."

"It took Mom five tries to get Asher, but anything is possible," I said. "I'll do my best to make sure none of your offspring are bitten, trampled or spit on."

"Good luck with that," Edna said. "You pamper those animals too much."

Keats gave a mumble of agreement. His instincts told him livestock should be treated as such rather than as valued members of my family. He wasn't permitted to use the force he sometimes deemed necessary in doing his job.

Regardless, I was happy Edna was picking on me instead of Jilly. We were all overtired from our so-called vacation, and probably needed some space. Instead, we were confined in a vehicle again, worrying about fractious people.

I wasn't thrilled about seeing Bailey Miller again. She hadn't impressed me much in our only exchange on Christmas Eve. Mind you, at that point she wasn't long out of a relationship with Vinnie Swenson, the biggest crook in Clover Grove. Ultimately, Bailey had done the right thing for Clippers by shoving the little horse into my truck. She was glad to put the Vinnie experience in her rearview and now we had to bring it up again.

"Let's keep this short," I said, as we parked in front of Bailey's house.

"Do I have to stay in the truck here, as well?" Edna's jutting lower lip proved no one was ever too old to pout.

"On the contrary," I said, releasing the dog and cat and then getting out myself. "We need an enforcer. You had to menace Bailey's new boyfriend, remember?"

"You just use me when you need me," Edna grumbled as she preceded us up the walk. "If you mastered weaponry, I'd be relegated to my recliner again."

"Edna, we love you," Jilly called after her. "You just saved my life from a bigger enemy than you can imagine. So if you want to diss Asher and me, I give you full permission."

Turning at the bottom of the stairs, Edna found a smile. "Permission takes the fun right out of it, Jillian. I'll find something else to mock."

"Suit yourself," Jilly said, linking arms with our favorite crusty octogenarian. "We're a team, and my engagement doesn't change a thing."

"I wish that were true," Edna said. "But once you're accountable to others you can't take as many risks. That's why Ivy keeps turning down Chief Hottie McSnotty. She isn't ready to give up her daredevil lifestyle."

I shook my head as I linked arms on Edna's other side. "I wouldn't turn down Kellan, just so you know. Hopefully one day we'll *all* be married and still fighting crime. Janelle said she had a perfect guy for you, Edna."

My senior friend's eyes bulged in their sockets. It was very difficult to shock her, and I was inordinately proud of succeeding.

"Dagnabit, Ivy, you can't throw out grenades like that and expect me to stay on my game." She shook off my arm and pulled a canister of pepper spray out of her pocket. "Comments like that will get you turfed from my bunker without appeal."

Keats gave a pant of amusement as he headed up the stairs and I laughed, too. "I just want my friends to be happy. All species."

No one answered my knock but Keats' right paw lifted in a point. Someone was inside and likely applying an eyeball to the peephole. We were unwelcome everywhere today.

"Bailey?" I said. "I just wanted a quick word about Clippers, the miniature horse. Someone tried to steal him from my farm this week."

Keats' paw dropped and the door cracked open. Vinnie's ex-girlfriend looked paler and sadder than the last time we were here. I could only guess that her bald and brawny boyfriend wasn't turning out to be much better than the last one.

"I miss Clippers," she said. "What happened?"

I told her the story about Trelise. "This trainer says Vinnie signed a contract surrendering Clippers into service. Do you know anything about that?"

Bailey shook her head. "No, and it doesn't sound like Vinnie. Good deeds weren't his style. Maybe if she offered big money. Vinnie was always trying to make a fast buck."

Jilly gave her a kind smile. "Do you think he might have done it to spite you?"

"And give up his leverage? No. Something sounds off about this."

Hope swelled in my heart. "Maybe the contract is fraudulent."

"Show her the signature," Jilly suggested.

I pulled out my phone and enlarged the image for Bailey.

"It doesn't look right," she said. "Vinnie's handwriting was nearly illegible."

"No surprise," Edna muttered, and Keats added his mumble of agreement.

"Do you have anything with his signature on it?" I asked. "Something I could show a lawyer to disprove Trelise's claim?"

Bailey glanced over her shoulder into the house and then pulled the door closed behind her. "I kept some old cards and notes," she whispered. "I don't know why, when Vinnie turned into such a creep. But I did and they're hidden right now. Give me a day or two." Then her expression brightened. "There was a lawyer here in Dorset Hills who helped me get most of my stuff back, and get the restraining order. Maybe he'd sort this out for you. I'll send his name, too."

"That would be great," Jilly said, as I slipped my card into Bailey's hand. "I hope you're happier now."

Bailey's shoulders rose and fell. "Like I said, I miss Clippers."

"Couldn't you get a dog?" Jilly asked.

The young woman's blonde curls swished a negative. "My boyfriend doesn't like pets."

Edna dropped the mumble and spoke her mind. "Out with the old boyfriend and in with a pet, Bailey. You've got your whole life ahead of you. Don't waste it on another deadbeat."

Keats' ruff rose just as the door opened with a jerk. *By a jerk.*

Bailey's big brute of a boyfriend pulled her inside so abruptly that Edna reached for her pepper spray.

"Don't, Edna," I said. "Bailey knows she can call us anytime if she wants to see Clippers."

The brutish boyfriend shook his head in the doorway. "She doesn't and she won't. In this house, we look forward, not back."

"Good policy," I said, in a mollifying tone. I didn't want our visit to put Bailey in a worse position. "But in my experience, the past keeps repeating itself if you don't take a close look at it."

He snorted. "Don't look back as you drive off my property."

I was reasonably sure the house belonged to Bailey, but I signaled Keats to stand down and he rounded us up to leave.

Bailey had my contact information. Hopefully one day she'd use it and the Rescue Mafia could extract its first human.

None of us spoke on the way back to Imogen Pigeon's house. Our usual banter had faltered under the weight of that exchange, even though things looked more promising in relation to Clippers.

As we turned into Imogen's driveway, Jilly checked her phone again. "Teri spoke to Prudence but it sounds like we might be better waiting for the caregiver shift change. I can't imagine why Teri doesn't fire her."

"Good caregivers are hard to find in Clover Grove," Edna said. "Prudence doesn't have much going for her personally, but she is reliable."

"I want to get this over with," I said, as we sat in the truck outside the old manor. "Keats, what do you think?"

I asked him directly because the dog was clearly uneasy. His ears flattened as fast as his ruff rose. He mumbled a warning that seemed overly cautious for the caregiver threat, but I paid attention.

"Now I'm nervous," Jilly said, as Keats shifted in her lap to paw at the passenger door handle.

"Me too, but it looks like we're going in," I said.

When the doors opened, both pets shot out like comets and raced toward the porch, equally puffed and ready for... something.

"I suppose I'm permitted to come this time?" Edna said. "As muscle?"

"Yes, please," I said, hopping out. "The pets are way more worried than they were about that deadbeat in Dorset Hills. I hope nothing's happened to Imogen while we were gone. Maybe the moment of terminal lucidity passed."

"Or maybe Imogen herself," Edna said, slipping her arms into her backpack of fun. "That's the definition of terminal."

Grabbing the winged door knocker, I rapped sharply several times. "I'll be furious if we lost our only chance to speak to her because of Prudence."

Keats mumbled again and it sounded like he was telling me to keep it down. Now he was on full alert, from flared nostrils to bottle brush tail. Percy's back had arched, but he still managed to claw at the welcome mat with the feline reaper paw.

"Oh no," Jilly said. "Something's obviously happened to Imogen."

"Prudence probably smothered her with a pillow," Edna said.

"Don't joke, Edna," Jilly said. "The pets are signaling this is serious."

I knocked again, and this time Keats' ears flickered. Putting my own ear to the heavy door, I heard faint shouting. "Someone's inviting us in," I said.

"Really?" Jilly asked.

"Well, I hear shouting and that qualifies as an invitation in my books. Imogen must be in trouble."

Perhaps she was, but when we walked into the spacious front hall, Prudence was in far worse trouble. The shouts weren't coming from her. In fact, judging by the way she was sprawled head-down on the stairs, she wouldn't be raising her voice again. Ever.

Her thick glasses lay broken on the hardwood at the bottom, and

I motioned for Percy and Keats to stay well back from the bits of glass that gleamed under the overhead lights. Edna stepped around us and crunched forward on heavy combat boots.

"You don't need to be an RN to diagnose something terminal here," she said. "The only question is whether Prudence fell or was pushed."

CHAPTER FIVE

I looked down at Keats and Percy for the answer to Edna's question. Both animals were still stiff, puffed and wary, suggesting Prudence's sensible sneakers had been kicked out from under her, just as she'd hoofed me earlier.

"It must have been Imogen," I whispered. "Her dementia probably came back and she lashed out."

"A plausible explanation," Edna agreed, beckoning for us to follow her up the stairs.

"Why is it that plausible is so often unlikely?" Jilly asked, bending to scoop Percy up.

I followed suit with Keats, who squirmed over the indignity of being carried in a critical situation. "Take the ride," I said. "We've got enough trouble without sliced paws."

Edna held an index finger to her lips and waggled the can of pepper spray. At the top of the stairs, she stopped and we all waited in silence. There was a murmur behind the door directly across the landing. Was Imogen speaking to someone... or no one? Either possibility sent a chill down my back.

Keats wriggled again and I set him down. If he were called to defend himself or us, he needed paws and teeth available. Jilly did the same with Percy, and both pets marched toward danger, rather than away. Together, they pawed at the door until a quavering voice called, "Come in, already. If you're going to kill me, be done with it. Although why you'd bother when one foot's out the proverbial door, I don't know."

I cracked open the door and poked my head inside. "Mrs. Pigeon, it's Ivy Galloway."

"Well, it's about time." Imogen sounded as crochety as Edna had said. "I've been asking for you for days."

"I was out of town till this morning. We came by about an hour ago and Prudence wouldn't let us in."

"I know, and we had words about it," Mrs. Pigeon said. "She knew very well I was waiting for you. That you and Teri are the *only* people I want to see."

"You've got more company than you want, Ima," Edna called out from behind me. "And less, I'm afraid."

"Is that Edna Evans?" Imogen said. "She's definitely not on my welcome list."

"You're not on mine either, Ima," Edna said. "But here we are."

"And there you go," Imogen called back. "I have little time left on this earth, Edna, and I don't plan to waste any of it on you."

"I feel the same, Ima," Edna said, "but if you want to hold onto the time you've got, you'd better keep me around."

"What is she yammering about, Ivy?" Imogen asked. "Obviously I don't have time for puzzles. Or much else."

I stood in the partially open doorway collecting myself. It was quite possible that Imogen had been in an altered state and shoved her caregiver down the stairs. From what Edna said earlier, lucidity could come and go.

Keats had no such qualms about Imogen's state of mind. His ears came up and his hackles settled, suggesting she wasn't a threat. At least, for the moment.

"Mrs. Pigeon, I'm afraid there's been an accident," I said.

"What kind of accident? I heard a scuffle and I've been yelling for Prudence for ten minutes. I can't get out of bed on my own."

Taking a deep breath, I stepped into the room to deliver the bad news at closer range. "Prudence fell down the stairs and... well, she's gone."

"She quit? I hope I don't need to find someone else at this late stage of the game. I'm hardly in the mood for interviewing caregivers."

"She either quit," Edna called, "or was terminated."

"Edna, please," I said. "Allow me to deliver the staffing news in my own way. I have more experience with that than you do."

"Don't pussyfoot around a dying woman," Edna said. "And a retired nurse at that. Ima can handle the truth."

Imogen's hand went to her throat and then covered her mouth. Her fingers were gaunt, as was her face, but her eyes were bright and alert. For a moment I worried Edna was wrong—that Imogen could not handle this horrible truth. But then her hand dropped into her lap and she laced her fingers.

"Well, Ivy?" she said. "Did Prudence slip or was the scuffle I heard more serious?"

I glanced at Keats and his eerie blue eye held no doubt. "It seems that in the hour between our visits, someone else came by and..." My voice drifted away as Percy used the reaper paw beside my boots.

"Killed Prudence?" Imogen asked. "Is that what you're trying *not* to say?"

Edna had been right that Ima Pigeon was a practical woman. There was a tremor in her hands and her voice but that could have been because of her condition.

"Yes," I said. "At least probably."

Percy left his reaping maneuver in favor of bedside care. He landed beside Imogen and her frail hand instantly reached out to stroke his back. I could hear the purr from where I stood. That cat knew when to rev the motor.

Jilly had stayed well back in the hall, and now her quiet, clipped voice told me she was speaking to the police.

"Still alive in there?" Edna called.

"I'm afraid so," Imogen said.

"I'm so sorry you have to go through this," I said.

Imogen's shoulders rose and fell under a colorful quilted bed jacket, and then she shivered. The room was warm—stuffy, even—but not to her.

"No need to apologize when it's not your fault, Ivy," she said. "Although murder does seem to follow wherever you go." I opened my mouth to argue, and she shook her head. "That's actually the reason I summoned you. Teri told me about what I've missed since you got home, and I want you to help me."

"With this Prudence situation?" I said. "Did you see it coming?"

Her nicely coiffed white curls swished a no. "Prudence treated me well and I'm sorry she's gone, but we'll leave that to the police to sort out. She had a few enemies, I'm afraid. Hopefully the investigation won't obstruct *our* investigation."

"What do you mean?" I asked, coming closer.

"Well, I hear that boyfriend of yours is as diligent as he is handsome."

"True," I said. "How will that obstruct your, uh, side project?"

"We'll all be suspects in Prudence's death, that's how." Her brow furrowed, perhaps wondering if my sleuthing skills had been overrated. "You'll be on the security cam arguing with Prudence, I presume. And they'll assume I lost my faculties again and gave her a hard shove." Imogen gave me a surprisingly youthful smile. "I expect you thought the same."

My face burned in confirmation. "I'm sorry. This is all very new for me."

"And me," she said. "No one anticipates this last gift of clarity, even though I saw it happen time and again. I'm sure Edna did, too."

Now standing in the doorway, Edna nodded. "I was telling the girls earlier that it can be such a gift to families."

"And in my case, something more," Imogen said. "It's a chance for redemption. I have a secret I've never revealed to anyone, Ivy, and I need you to put it to rights before I pass."

My stomach sank and I shook my head. I wasn't ready to hear Imogen's secret. Might never be ready for the next thing Clover Grove threw at me. When I left for college, I had no idea what lurked in the valleys and forests of this hilly region. Would I have stayed in Boston if I'd known?

Apparently, my head kept shaking because Imogen reached out with one skinny hand. "Don't deny a dying woman's last wish. Help me to do some good before I go."

Edna gave me a nudge from behind and my legs met the mattress. "It's a noble cause, Ivy," she said.

I glanced down at Keats and his compassionate brown eye seemed to confirm it. "Okay. I'll help if I can, Mrs. Pigeon."

She gestured to the chair beside the bed, while peering at Edna and now Jilly, in the doorway. "Could we have a moment alone before the police arrive? Just Ivy and this so-called genius of a sheepdog?"

This time my head shook on purpose. "Jilly, Edna and I come as a package deal along with the pets, Mrs. Pigeon. You can trust all of us."

Her fingers had plenty of life as she flicked them in Edna's direction. "I wouldn't trust Edna Evans as far as I could throw her."

Edna laughed. "Don't blame you one bit, but I've changed since you've been... away."

Taking in Edna's attire, Imogen pursed her lips. "Looks like you enlisted in the army. Their admission requirements have gotten lax since I've been... away."

There was a little pause and then both women laughed. Cackled, actually.

"The state of the world has declined, Ima," Edna said. "You'd do well to exit stage right before you go out the hard way."

Imogen turned her blue eyes on me. "What's she talking about? Edna's always been eccentric, but it looks like she's been preparing for an apocalypse."

I nodded. "The zombie threat is closer than we know, Mrs. Pigeon. And so are the police. So perhaps you'd better say what's on your mind."

"While I still have a mind," she said, sighing. "There's no telling when my faculties might drift again, so you're right. I only hope the good Lord gave me this reprieve for a reason and will keep me around long enough to right my wrongs."

I perched on the edge of the chair and Keats moved under my fingertips, knowing I'd need those soft ears to cushion whatever news Imogen had to deliver. "Tell us and we'll do our best to get to the bottom of it."

Edna crossed her arms. "I never fancied you much, Ima, but I'm hard pressed to believe you did anything too atrocious."

"I did my best, Edna, but as nurses, you know we faced hard choices sometimes," Imogen said. "Hindsight isn't always kind." Her eyes narrowed. "I'm sure you have a few decisions you regret."

I expected Edna to deny it but she gave a grim nod. "I started reviewing my regrets early. Needed extra time to get through my list."

They gave another joint cackle and then Imogen sighed. "Ivy, my work made me privy to a few deathbed confessions just like you're about to hear now. Most were harmless enough, at least by the time people shared them. Lies, affairs, illegitimate kids and the like. Rarely something I felt obligated to share with those left behind."

Sirens screamed now, and Edna raised a hand and spun it. "Keep it moving, Ima. Time really is of the essence."

"Murder," Imogen blurted. "A patient told me with his dying breath that he strangled a man and buried him at Bluffers Ridge."

"Who?" Edna said, coming closer. "Did I know him?"

"Perhaps," Imogen said. "It was Morris Tubbs."

"Morris? He was one of the kindest old men in our community. Never had a harsh word for anyone and always helped those in more need." Edna sighed, too. "There was plenty of need in those days. Very hard times."

Imogen nodded. "That's why I didn't believe him at first. Didn't want to believe him, I guess. I knew about the Swensons and the Milloys. Nothing would have surprised me with them, and I had to visit their homes, too. But Morris Tubbs? It was unthinkable."

"Perhaps he was confused," Edna said. "That's far more likely to happen at the end than what you're experiencing right now."

"I know, but it had the ring of truth. He asked me to put it to rights and I never did. I couldn't bear to tell his family because they adored him. What was done was long done, I figured. But to give him the peace he craved on his way out, I had said I would look into it. And now, on *my* way out, I realize how important that promise was. I nearly broke it, expecting I still had time." She locked eyes with Edna. "Don't we all think we have more time?"

"I used to," Edna said. "But I had a terrible shock last fall that changed everything. I'm compressing my timelines just in case."

"She certainly is." Jilly spoke for the first time. "And the police are here, Mrs. Pigeon."

"Call me Imogen," she said. "Or Ima."

"Details, Ima," Edna said. "Spill them fast."

"I don't have much more to go on," she said. "Find out if Morris was telling the truth about the body he buried at Bluffers Ridge."

"Who was it?" I asked. "He must have given you a clue about who he killed and why."

Imogen reached for my hand and I let her take it. Her fingers were cold but energy pulsed through them. "All he said was that the man had it coming. That it was for the good of the town. And because I respected Morris, I chose to believe him."

"Then why was he so fussed about ridding the world of a pest?" Edna asked.

"Like anyone facing the end, Morris had doubts about how he'd handled it. He said the police of the day wouldn't have made the man he killed pay for his sins. Morris volunteered tirelessly and gave away every cent he had, but he never felt a moment's peace afterward. He put himself in a prison of sorts."

"The cops were corrupt back then," Edna said. "He was probably right about that."

I squeezed her hand. "What more do you have to go on?"

"Nothing. I truly don't know who Morris killed or why." She shook off my fingers and reached for Keats' ears. "He'll know more."

"Who? Keats?" I stared down at the dog and found him directing his blue eye at Imogen. It seemed like he was downloading files from her memory banks, and the thought made me shiver.

She leaned back on the pillows. "I've heard about this genius dog. Let him lead you." She gave Percy a feeble pat and closed her eyes. "And this fine fellow, too. You're in good paws." Her lids cracked open for a second and then fluttered shut. "Do you promise, Ivy?"

"I promise to do what I can," I said.

"Make it fast. I don't have long."

A smile played on her lips and then suddenly the energy shifted in the room.

"She's gone," Edna said.

"Gone, as in dead?" I asked. "No!"

"Not *that* gone." Edna was grinning. "Just asleep. But in her condition, you never know whether she'll wake again. Or wake lucid."

The sound of boots on the stairs made me turn.

"Well, it looks like I just made a deathbed promise, too," I said.

Keats' tail gave an enthusiastic swish. Someone was more excited about the new project than I was. Edna was smoothing her fatigues briskly, too.

Only Jilly seemed to share my misgivings. "It would have been nice to have a little break," she said.

"Jillian, no one likes a whiny bride," Edna said. "And you can't just take a honeymoon from murder."

CHAPTER SIX

Imogen Pigeon's bedroom door swung back hard enough to make the hinges creak and Kellan Harper charged into the room ahead of his men. I could tell by the look on my boyfriend's handsome face that he'd heard Edna's words. Seeing a dead caregiver on the stairs was bad enough, but finding us up here chitchatting about murder like it was commonplace might even be worse.

Unfortunately, it was more commonplace in our lives than it should be. Kellan and I hadn't seen each other since I got home and it wasn't the romantic reunion either of us likely envisioned. I had pined for him, and I wasn't ashamed to admit it. The trip had been scary—all the more so because I was off my familiar turf and without my uniformed hero. It made me understand I wasn't as fiercely independent as I'd believed, which in turn led to some long-distance conversations that seemed to move our relationship into new territory. A new crime probably wouldn't keep it there.

Nor would the sheepdog diligently applying his teeth to Chief Harper's ankles. I knew Keats was just trying to bring us together but Kellan held back at the cost of his uniform cuffs. Then I realized he was likely holding back out of respect for Imogen Pigeon. His dark blue eyes flicked to the bedridden woman and then dropped.

"She's asleep," I said. "We told her about what happened to her caregiver."

His lips pressed together for a moment. "What *did* happen to her caregiver? Do you have any idea?"

I shook my head. "We found her that way. Imogen said she'd heard a scuffle and that Prudence Hoggins had some enemies. In fact, she didn't seem particularly surprised, which is strange, come to think of it. You'd think she'd want a caregiver without a history."

"Everyone has a history in Clover Grove," Edna said. "Prudence was no better or worse than most, and like I said, she was reliable. But I expect you'll have this sorted out in no time, Chief. Imogen had so much faith in you that she fell asleep as you pulled in."

Kellan's eyes shifted to Edna and narrowed, before moving back to me. "Please explain how you happened to be here, Ms. Galloway."

Ms. Galloway? That's how it was going to be? Again? Well, fine. I could be as formal as he could and then some.

"As I mentioned in one of our phone calls, Chief Harper, Teri Mason let me know through Asher that her grandmother wished to speak with me. Mrs. Pigeon doesn't have much time, so we came by nearly as soon as we got back. Prudence Hoggins wouldn't allow us in on the first visit." I gave up the formal front and sighed. "She couldn't keep us out on the second."

"And what happened in between?" he asked. "How long were you gone?"

"Just over an hour, I believe. We drove to Dorset Hills to speak to Vinnie Swenson's ex-girlfriend."

"What? Why?" He was startled enough to sound more like my boyfriend. Raking fingers through his thick, dark hair, he even *looked* more like my boyfriend.

"Apparently Vinnie Swenson signed paperwork to surrender Clippers, my miniature horse, into a service animal program before—"

"He got terminated," Edna supplied, with a mischievous grin.

She enjoyed irritating Kellan nearly as much as Keats did. Now the dog gave my boyfriend's cuff a little shake with a mock growl.

"Keats, stop," I said. "The chief is here in a professional capacity and needs his full focus."

Kellan looked down, as if he hadn't actually noticed the dog's antics. "True. Be off, dog, while I figure out what your owner isn't telling me."

"What makes you think I'm not telling you something?" I asked.

"Years of interrogation experience," he said, "with a recent specialty in questioning Ivy Galloway."

"We know nothing more about what happened to Imogen's caregiver," I said. "However, you'll see on the security camera that Prudence and I had words when she barred us from visiting."

"Wonderful," he said. "It would be strange not to have at least one Galloway on the suspect list in any local murder."

"Very funny," I said. "I was merely here to fulfill a dying woman's request to—"

"See Keats, the wonder dog," Edna said. "And Percy, who pulled his litterbox prognostication. He's become the grim reaper of cats."

"Edna," I said, "Kellan needs to know exactly what happened. I won't—"

"Say another word about your commitment to a dying woman."

We all jumped because the voice came from the bed behind us. Apparently, Imogen had awoken with such lucidity that she wanted me to lie to my boyfriend, the chief of police.

"Mrs. Pigeon," Kellan said, "with all due respect, I need to know everything *you* know about the current situation."

"Of course," Imogen said. "Ivy, you'd better get going and let the police do their work. Chief Harper, I'll tell you about every grievance I know about between Prudence and the good people of Clover Grove, and beyond. It'll take a while. I suggest you sit down."

"I'll stand, thank you," Kellan said, gesturing for his officers to leave the room.

"Suit yourself," Imogen said. "If you can afford to lose your cuffs, that's fine with me."

Kellan saw the sense in what she was saying and took the chair as I vacated it. The dog made sure that our hands brushed together as Kellan passed. It was enough for the usual sparks to fly, at least on my end. I wanted nothing more than to hug my boyfriend and tell him about the strange and ominous details of our trip that were better conveyed in person. Now the previous mystery had to take a back seat to the latest one. It seemed like we never got enough time to catch up properly.

"Ivy, you can go," Kellan said. His eyes met mine to confirm he'd felt the spark of connection, too. "I'll come by the farm as soon as we're done here."

"I'm sure that will take some time," Imogen said. "Prudence and I had a long history together. Very long."

"We can discuss it in stages," Kellan said. "You must be very tired, Mrs. Pigeon."

"You have no idea, young man," she said. "I'm in God's waiting room, nearly ready to pass through the turnstile. I've been... elsewhere... for some time and came back with my brain firing on all cylinders. I have no idea how long this will last. Hours or days, perhaps." She looked over at Edna. "What's the longest you ever witnessed?"

Truth and tact fought a rare battle on Edna's face. Finally, she said, "A week perhaps. I'm sorry, Ima."

"I'm not sure I follow," Kellan said.

"It's called terminal lucidity," Edna said. "Some people return from the brink for a short period as sharp as they ever were. But it doesn't last, unfortunately, so you'd better settle in for a good chat while you can, Chief."

Kellan's eyes had widened. "Well, then. I'll let my team do their work while Mrs. Pigeon and I talk."

"A wise decision," Imogen said, flicking her fingers to send the rest of us on our way. "I'll do my very best to stay awake and alert. And in answer to the first question you'll ask, no, I didn't kill Prudence myself."

"With all due respect," Kellan said again, "You may not have been fully lucid in that moment. I'm not sure how all this works."

"I'll tell you how it *doesn't* work," Imogen said, as we edged toward the door. "You don't sit in God's waiting room and then decide to kill someone so close to your number being called. That wouldn't make much sense, would it young man? Even if I could get out of bed by myself."

"I—I suppose not," Kellan said. It was rare for him to sound nonplussed at a crime scene but Imogen was enjoying her moment.

Edna desperately wanted to stay for the show but Keats was trying his teeth on her fatigues to get her moving.

"Stop that, you cur," she hissed.

Before Edna could retaliate with fancy footwork, Jilly and I grabbed her by each elbow and shoved her ahead of us out the bedroom door.

I expected Kellan to say something more, but instead heard Imogen ask him to take her hand. She was planning to lead him on a long and merry chase that would give us time to head up to Bluffers Ridge and look for another body.

CHAPTER SEVEN

No one was thrilled about setting off on yet another mission, except the team member in the furry tuxedo. Jilly found the dog's energy annoying enough to send him into the back seat of the truck with Edna, and Percy came forward to luxuriate on Jilly's lightweight wool coat. After the tropical weather at the Briars, we felt a bit of a chill in the damp spring breeze in Clover Grove. Perhaps not Edna, who seemed to thrive in her camo gear regardless of temperature. A prepper doesn't whine about the weather, she said, because she's grateful just to be on her feet and fighting. That mindset was something she shared with Keats, although I never said so. I considered it high praise to be compared to my dog, but not everyone agreed.

"Do you think Imogen's story is legit?" Jilly said, trying to brush some of the fur off her coat and succeeding only in moving it around. "Maybe she's delusional as the end nears."

"She didn't seem delusional," I said, gearing up as we hit the highway. "That woman is sharp. It's hard to believe she ever had dementia. I wonder if *that* was legit. Remember, I knew someone who faked it."

Edna was quiet for a minute or two. These were weighty subjects and even she hesitated to make hasty judgments.

"I saw many strange things in my nursing career," she said at last. "And yes, I heard some deathbed confessions that were either delusions, or deliberate poppycock intended to baffle those left behind. But I knew Ima quite well, and she sounded like her old self today. The last few times I saw her at events she most certainly did not." Rolling down the window, Edna battled for space with Keats to pull in the air. "This seems like a case of terminal lucidity to me. In fact, I'd stake my bunker on it."

Jilly and I sighed in tandem. Edna wouldn't put her bunker on the line even in jest. It meant that much to her.

"So we have not one murder to investigate, but two," I said. "And I haven't even done my rounds at the farm."

"Just a suggestion," Jilly said. "Since we're morally obligated to follow up on Imogen's deathbed request, how about we leave investigating Prudence's death to Kellan and crew?"

"That makes sense," Edna said. "The two cases can't be related and the clock is ticking for Ima. If she's to leave her so-called waiting room in good standing, we'll need to hustle." She muttered, "I owe her that much."

I glanced over my shoulder. "Why do you owe Imogen anything?"

"For my ill feelings toward her after she took over my school vaccination program. My pride took a hit, but it wasn't her fault and she needed the money. Teri's older sister moved home with her kids after leaving an abusive husband. There were lots of mouths to feed and Ima came out of retirement to do it."

"I hope we aren't accountable for all our thoughts," I said, "because mine haven't always been charitable."

"Mine either," Jilly said. "Especially when we were corporate sharks."

"You view things differently at my age," Edna said. "When there are more days behind than ahead." She turned away from the window and offered a genuine smile. "Both of you have paid it forward and you'll have no cause to worry when the time comes to balance your spiritual accounts."

"You have, too, Edna," Jilly said. "And you'll have plenty more opportunity."

"Particularly when the apocalypse arrives," I said. "Points for every zombie slain. Bonus points for making room in your bunker for people you don't like."

Edna grunted. "Let's see if I can't make amends without wasting space on the people who waste space on this planet. Some are better fed to zombies."

"Wrong side of the balance sheet, Edna," I said, laughing.

Keats mumbled something in the vein of agreement with Edna. She must have thought so, too, because she invited him to settle on her lap, which happened rarely enough.

We followed a twisty road away from town and I was surprised to see how upscale some of the houses in the outskirts had become. Down our way, most properties had been taken over by home-steaders or organic farmers. People here weren't working the land with a few chickens and goats out back. They probably had decent jobs in Dorset Hills or other communities and came home for the views and the solitude.

"Nouveau riche," Edna said. "It wasn't like this in my youth. People came to Bluffers Ridge to hide what they were doing. Brewing moonshine, among other things."

"Is that what Morris Tubbs did out here?"

"Not Morris, no. Like I said, he was a good man." She stuck one hand through the seats to signal a turn. "Bluffers Ridge amounted to one gas station and a general store that did everything else. It was enough to provide for people here, and they didn't come down to Clover Grove to mix much. By the time Ima and I were doing community nursing, the culture was already shifting. Crime was on the wane... or so we thought."

I took the turn onto the so-called Main Street of Bluffers Ridge, which did indeed consist of one dilapidated store and an abandoned gas station. The boarded-up windows looked like blank, vacant eyes and I had to suppress a shudder. Our trip south had made me aware of possibilities I'd never considered before. These buildings looked to be full of old ghosts, for example. Others must have agreed or the newcomers in fancy houses would have renovated the store, or at least turned it into one of the museums that dotted hill country. Small galleries were catnip to Dog Town tourists.

Jilly was less successful in suppressing her shudder but based on the circuitous discussions I'd overheard with her family, especially her cousin Janelle, ghosts might not be as foreign a concept to her as they were for me. My fingers left the gearshift and reached back between the seats to find Keats' fluffy ears waiting to receive. He offered a reassuring rumble. If there were ghosts here, they took no issue with us.

"Imogen didn't give us much to go on," Jilly said. "What exactly are we looking for?"

"A graveyard, I would think," Edna said. "Most people had their own family plot, so that would be a good place to start."

"I don't like graveyards," Jilly said.

"Does anyone?" Edna countered.

"I doubt Morris Tubbs buried someone he hated among his own people," I said. "Although it would be a smart place to hide a body."

"Good thing I have a spade in my go-kit," Edna said.

Jilly stared at me and then turned to look at Edna. "Just so you know, I won't be digging up any old bones. Secrets and clues, maybe. Actual bones, no."

"They have technology to search for human remains now," Edna said. "I doubt we'll find what Ima's after on our own. It's been far too long."

Keats poked his head right through the seats and I briefly met his eerie blue eye. I sensed we wouldn't need technology to make progress on our commitment to Ima. Even if Kellan had access to this equipment, Kellan wouldn't prioritize hunting for old bones when new ones were weighing on him. With Ima's lucidity likely to vanish at any moment, I didn't have the luxury of time. But I did have the luxury of intuitive pets and faith they might be able to put us on the right track.

The bull bar on the front of the truck came in handy as we shoved into the lane at the old Tubbs property. The overgrown path initially seemed impassable but not much stopped this truck, other than my dubious driving skills. Now, it made short work of hanging vines and bumped over rocks like an army tank. Jilly grabbed the door handle and gave a squawk of pain as Percy braced himself on her legs with a set of ten razor-sharp daggers.

"I'm surprised no one's bought the place," Edna said. "The far side of the property has a fine view, from what I recall. That's what people pay for these days and land's a pretty penny."

"Maybe Morris' descendants don't want to sell," I said. "They might dream of coming back one day."

Jilly shuddered again. "Or they've tried and buyers are too creeped out to imagine living here. Like I am."

The truck nudged the last of the brush aside and rolled into a clearing that wasn't so clear anymore. It was astounding how quickly nature reclaimed land in hill country, even on my own farm. If you blinked, the bush line crept up and got ready to ambush. The battle against nature kept Charlie, my farm manager, busy with his tractor. My sister Poppy was itching to take over that role but the tractor was an untamed bronco that responded best to Charlie's wiles.

"How big is the property, Edna?" I asked, turning off the engine. "Can we cover it before losing the light?"

It was pretty much a moot point as the sun was low enough and the foliage thick enough that little light reached us even now.

"It's one of the smaller plots up this way," she said. "I don't know the terrain well, however, and can't recollect where the Tubbs property ended and the Spratt and Guthrie properties began." Getting out of the truck, she called back, "Now, *those* were families I avoided. Once I feigned appendicitis and left Clover Grove for a month to avoid a nursing assignment with one of the Spratt women. Minerva, I think her name was. Something fancy."

She continued to mutter and whatever she said made Keats pant ha-ha-ha as he passed through the seats and across my lap to jump out. Edna was likely adding to the wrong side of her heavenly ledger again.

"Keats, wait," I said, watching the dog carefully as I got out and joined Jilly in front of the truck. The canine laughter had cut off abruptly and his ruff had risen, signaling that the place likely had secrets. His ears were still forward, suggesting he was eager to explore, so I guessed the threats were in the past. Kneeling beside him, I smoothed his ruff. "How about you boys work quickly so we can get out of here? I want to get home to the farm and do ordinary things, like kiss my pig."

"Tell me you do not kiss that pig," Edna called as she walked over to the old Tubbs house. It was as derelict as the general store in town but felt significantly less spooky. "Surely even you have limits, Ivy."

"No limits within my ark," I said. "I offer kisses to all takers. Many do not, including Drama Llama and the thugs."

Edna swept off her camouflage cap and shook it in disgust. "I need some time away from you. I'm afraid whatever you've got is contagious."

Keats went into a point and I called after her. "Wrong way, Edna. Keats wants to check out the old barn."

She marched in the other direction but the dog and cat easily got ahead of her. In fact, Edna's normally brisk boots started to drag. Meanwhile, Jilly and I linked arms to give each other moral support.

"It's felt like a lot for one day," my best friend said.

I nodded. "Coming after such a wild week at the Briars, especially. Our reserves never had a chance to rebuild. I'm in rather desperate need of rejuvenation pie at Mandy's."

Edna caught up if only to give me a scornful stare. "There will be no pie after the apocalypse, Ivy. Get used to it."

"You don't know that," I said. "There may very well be pie. We humans are a resourceful species."

"Zombie pie, maybe," she said. "Probably the only way they're palatable."

Jilly made a face. "Hard pass for me."

"Oh, come on," I said. "You never turn down a culinary challenge, Jilly. Zombie cookery would be worthy of one of those big reality show kitchen competitions."

Edna shook her head with even more scorn for me. "There won't be TV by that point. Or kitchens. Obviously."

"We'll gather in the old-fashioned way. Around the campfire, with Jilly demonstrating how to make the best from very little. It's not about celebrity but survival."

"You've convinced me," Jilly said. She even managed a sly smile for our wily neighbor. "Maybe I should start preparing early with a unit in your course, Edna."

Edna's face instantly turned into a blank mask. "Course?"

"Seminar?" I said. "Workshop? What exactly are you calling it? All I know is that Bridie Brighton paid good money to learn the ins and outs of survival from you."

"Yet our invitation hasn't arrived," Jilly added, her grin expanding. "Ivy and I expected free admission, since we're out here, well... *surviving* with you."

After chewing over her response for a minute, Edna decided to come clean about the secret course.

"It's just a basic information session for rank beginners," she said. "I've been shocked by how ill-informed people are and yet heartened by their thirst for knowledge." She lifted her chin. "It's my civic duty to help, girls. Obviously, you two are far beyond beginner level but since you've shown such interest, I invite you to make presentations. Cookery in the apocalypse is an excellent idea, Jillian, and I'll take it to my team." There was a twinkle in her eye as she turned to me. "How about you, Ivy? I'm willing to vet your proposals."

"Manure management will never go out of style," I said. "I do think that's an area of my particular expertise."

Tilting her head, Edna pretended to give it consideration. "Manure will always be with us, but I doubt we'll stay in one place long enough to make good use out of it. The post-apocalyptic life-style is nomadic. Another day, another latrine." She pretended to hit a buzzer and gave a sonorous honk. "Fail. Try again, Ivy."

I couldn't help laughing and Jilly and Edna did, too. Keats, on the other hand, was all business. He turned and my own dog withered me with his eerie blue eye.

"Right," I said. "Sorry, buddy. The levity is to keep us from getting jittery. I can tell you've got heavier news to share."

He had passed the old barn and forced his way into the bush. It was thick and aggressive, worse than the scrub on my land. In hill country, if the murderers didn't get you, the shrubbery would.

"I wish I'd brought a scythe," Edna said. "Something to add to my go-kit."

She kindly took the lead, blocking the fiercest branches with the thick fabric of her camo sleeve. Meanwhile, I flicked on my phone light and shone it into the dense foliage. It was surprisingly dim and I wondered how anything got enough sunlight to grow here. The soil must have been thoroughly fertilized with scandal and crime. A different use for the manure of society.

Finally, Percy and Keats stopped and waited for us in a small clearing. It wasn't much of an opening—just enough space for the five of us with a bit of elbow room. Keats lifted his paw and pointed but it looked like he was indicating a wall of vegetation. When we stood without moving, he gave a little whine, and Percy brushed under his chin with his tail high as if to reassure him. So often, Keats got the glory when the orange cat delivered the final answer.

That's exactly what Percy did now, with a broad sweep or two of his right front paw across hard soil that was so filled with roots and rocks that his claws barely made an impression.

The movement made quite an impression on us, however, particularly as both animals simultaneously lifted their hackles to drive their point home.

No one was laughing now.

"I'm going to guess we've located Imogen's secret," I said, crossing my arms to hug myself. It wasn't terribly chilly outside, but it certainly was in my heart.

Edna pulled camo gloves out of her pocket and slipped them on. "Hang tight, girls. I'll go get the spade."

CHAPTER EIGHT

Peace.

That's what I found in the barn after my second shower.

Technically, it wasn't peaceful in there at all. There was quite a clamor as I worked my way from stall to stall. No one was happy about being brought in early by the sheepdog they'd probably enjoyed vacationing without. Cori's border collie, Clem, had done some heavy lifting in our absence but there were evenings that Edna, Poppy and Charlie had filled the role of sheepdog. Everyone except the livestock had a greater appreciation for my hardworking assistant.

Keats gave a proud ha-ha-ha as he delivered Alvina, the alpaca, and Elaine the emu. The big bird was a wild card. She wasn't deliberately difficult, as far as I could tell, but she was... well, flighty. The bird who couldn't fly managed to get plenty of height—and even more speed—when startled. There was no predicting what would startle her. The donkey thugs lurked by the fence randomly releasing bizarre vocalizations just to get a reaction out of poor Elaine. They particularly liked putting on their little show at bedtime, when the gate would open and the possibility of dinner theater increased.

I was beginning to think I'd underestimated the intelligence and sheer guile of the donkey thugs. That's what came of housing them with Drama Llama, a wily creature indeed.

Generally I could still outthink them, at least on a good day. Today had been anything but that. Between dealing with Trelise's attempted horse thievery, and the murder at Imogen Pigeon's, it wasn't the warm homecoming I'd literally dreamed about while dozing through the long drive home from the Briars. And then came the gruesome discovery of human remains near the Tubbs homestead, and delivery of that additional bad news to Kellan. If any of the livestock pulled any tricks tonight, it could be the last straw for me. Even Keats, dog of perpetual motion, seemed weary.

The dog looked up at me and grumbled indignantly. A "speak for yourself" sort of sound.

"I am speaking for myself," I said. "Maybe *you're* not beat, but I'm ready to drop. I need to do something to stay awake and stay clean till Kellan gets here. I'd love to shift some manure right now, but that only satisfies one of my criteria. I looked forward to this reunion and I want to smell good."

Keats gave another ha-ha-ha and he certainly did seem perky. I wished I had his resilience. He'd caught a quick nap while I was showering. Now he was good to go again.

After feeding Alvina and Elaine, I went back to check on Clippers for probably the tenth time. I couldn't get enough of stroking his velvety muzzle, having come so close to losing him. He was a gorgeous little horse, with a sleek chestnut coat, a long blond mane and a white blaze. As he matured, he was filling out and had the conformation of a full-sized horse in a package that weighed less than Byron, the Caucasian shepherd and livestock guardian. Clippers was slightly taller than the average miniature horse, but in other ways a fine example of selective breeding. His personality was also on point, with a spritely, eager-to-please manner. Still, he had dark moments now and then when the early neglect at Vinnie's showed with wild-eyed flightiness that rivaled Elaine's. Rescue animals nearly always came with old wounds to heal. With time and patience, I expected to do just that with Clippers. He had youth on his side.

As usual, the small horse shared a stall with Bocelli, the singing donkey who rarely brayed these days. Bocelli "sang" when he was unhappy. With his best buddy by his side, plenty of food and a steady routine, there was little cause for complaint. Even without the vocals, I could tell he was unsettled tonight because he was restless. He paced around the pen and refused the oat biscuit I offered.

"Bocelli, don't worry," I said. "I'm on top of this abduction issue. I've left a message with a lawyer and will drop by tomorrow. Until this is sorted out, we'll all join Trelise's training class together. Clippers will not be unattended for a single moment, I promise."

The donkey stopped pacing but still refused the oatcake. Clippers happily ate what his buddy turned down. The tiny horse had a big appetite—for oatcakes and life in general. While Bocelli only wanted to cycle from barn to pasture and back, Clippers had been showing signs of boredom. He'd gnawed at the gate of his daytime pasture and then tried to crawl under it. When that didn't work, he started kicking the fence and screeching, which unsettled the rest of the animals. Cori had finally put Byron in with Bocelli and Clippers. That did the trick, but then Wilma the pig kicked up an even bigger fuss over losing *her* constant companion.

"It's a good thing we're home," I told Keats. "This crew is a constant puzzle waiting to be solved."

Alvina leaned over the wall of her pen and gave me a coquettish look. I knew full well what she wanted, but did I have the energy?

Keats answered that question by giving me a little nip on the back of my calf.

"Stop that," I said. "These are my good jeans. My *only* good jeans. My hot date jeans."

The dog mumbled something cheeky.

"Of course I can have a date in the middle of a murder investigation," I said. "Maybe not hot, exactly, but romantic." I shrugged. "At the rate people drop around here, Kellan and I need to find a bit of fun wherever and whenever we can."

I pulled out my phone, scrolled for a moment and made a selection. Then I set the phone on a ledge as a slightly tinny version of Abba's "Dancing Queen" started up. I knew from experience that while Alvina was fussy about song choice, she didn't care about sound quality. I decided to invest in decent speakers anyway. It wasn't typical barn equipment, but I aimed to please the Runaway Farm community and the alpaca wasn't the only one who enjoyed a tune.

I gave Alvina a deep bow. "May I have this dance?"

Her sweet brown eyes and big ears disappeared below the wall as she gave me a bow in return. It was a ritual and one Clippers mimicked. I'd never deliberately encouraged him to do it, so he was obviously very trainable.

Keats moved out of the way with a huff of disgust. He wasn't much for frivolities, especially when there was serious business at hand. Percy, on the other hand, enjoyed light entertainment and climbed onto a high ledge to get a better view.

As the music swelled, I gave an elaborate twirl and Alvina did the same. Clippers followed suit, accidentally shoving Bocelli into a corner. Arms raised, I spun back and forth between the two stalls, giving each of my dance partners equal billing. Alvina had all her moves down, adding a special new lunge, perhaps out of joy over my homecoming. Clippers, meanwhile, was freestyling, with pumping hooves and plenty of head tossing. Then he switched to a shuffling boogie and finally exploded into a twisting buck. My laugh brought on more of the same and I think he reached half a dozen kicks before the song ended.

Bocelli threw back his head and offered a soulful bray to say he either wasn't enjoying the hubbub or had bigger worries on his mind.

"Relax, Bocelli," I called as Abba's "Knowing Me, Knowing You" began. "We'll get this sorted out. You know we always do."

I ran a few steps from one stall to the other and did a rather awkward leap accompanied by some showy flapping. As I touched down, I noticed Kellan leaning in the barn doorway with his arms crossed and a wide grin on his face. After the expression I saw on his face at Imogen's house, that grin was like spring rain on a wilted flower.

Shoving embarrassment aside, I ran over to him. A black-and-white blur got there first, and gave Kellan's uniformed pant leg a nip that sent him into the air with arms flailing, too. Grabbing my boyfriend's hand, I led him forward and we whirled in the open space for a few moments while Alvina, Bocelli and Clippers raised their voices in a cacophony.

When the song ended, I let Kellan wrap me in his arms and hug me hard enough to leave an imprint of the police emblem on my right cheek. He kissed the top of my head a few times and then said, "I missed you."

"Me too. So much," I said. "I'm never leaving again. It was too stressful."

"Even for someone who thrives on stress?" Pushing me back a bit, he gave me a teasing smile.

"I wouldn't say I thrive on it, exactly." I tried not to smile as Kellan hopped again. The dog was determined to deflate the sweet moment from down below. "Keats certainly does."

"Well, I'm glad you were able to decompress without resorting to tossing manure," Kellan said. "Seeing you dance does my heart good."

My heart swelled knowing that this intense, serious man somehow found my clumsy antics amusing, even charming. Given what had happened today—and nearly every month since my homecoming—his fondness seemed like a miracle on par with Imogen Pigeon coming out of her coma.

"I love dancing with you and my animals," I said. "Even if it feels inappropriate right now. I was just telling Keats that we need to snatch a little fun where we can."

"Agreed." His smile told me that while I'd brought a host of new worries into his life, I'd also brought levity to lighten the load. "This was a day for the record books."

"Yeah. The rumor mill might break with two horrible and unrelated discoveries at once. I can feel gossip pulsing through the community."

"How about we counter that feeling with a walk in Clover Grove Gardens?" he asked. "I'd love to have you to myself for an hour and there are few places we can go without being watched."

"Like celebrities, only without the perks," I said, as Keats herded us both to the barn door. Orange fluff streaked past us and out to my truck. We'd attract less attention in my dime-a-dozen black pickup versus the police SUV. I left Kellan to squabble with Keats as I shut the barn up tight. There were double padlocks on each door after Trelise's blatant incursion, and additional security cameras.

"Will having you to myself always mean getting my cuffs nipped?" he asked, handing me into the passenger seat as if I were a delicate flower myself. I absolutely loved that he did that. It reminded me that I was a woman—his woman—and not just a crime-fighting farmer.

"Keats," I said. "Stop with the cuffs or spend some quality time watching Jilly sort her spice shelf. You'll probably miss a good conversation, but the choice is yours."

The dog grumbled but the descent of his jaunty tail said he got the message. Still, he parked his furry butt on my lap to maintain vigilance, while Percy climbed onto Kellan's headrest and draped himself over my boyfriend's right shoulder. "I missed you, too, Percy," he said, skillfully spinning the truck with one finger on the wheel before heading down the lane. "Never thought I'd say that, but your purr is oddly relaxing." He tried to look at me and got a face full of fur. "Deafening yet relaxing."

After gearing up on the highway, his fingers found mine, and we sat that way in silence on the short drive to the gardens. They had closed at eight but Kellan had the key and often let us in to enjoy whatever was in season. After sunset, we had to judge by shape and scent, as well as long knowledge of the layout. Nothing changed much, because the flowers were mainly perennials planted by experts who knew what flourished best where. The peonies, my particular favorites, were firing their last blast of perfume tonight, while the irises stood like stalwart soldiers. Beds of cheery lilies were preparing to launch before summer hit with full force.

My tension had gone down a few notches with the dance, a few more with the hug, and now subsided almost completely with the soothing environment, and the warmth of Kellan's arm around my shoulders.

"I love it here so much," I said, watching Keats and Percy shoot into the shadows. The garden had plenty of rodent residents that added to the allure for my pets.

"Same," he said. "I came here a lot in my first months back in town. No one wants to see the chief of police looking overwhelmed by a stack of cold cases. My predecessor didn't fully brief me on the unsolved historical crimes." He shrugged and then smiled. "Not that it would have dissuaded me from taking the job. I figured you'd come home eventually and I might as well wait for you surrounded by flora."

I hugged him hard with one arm. "Little did you know I'd surround myself with fauna."

He laughed. "There wasn't so much as a cat in my picture of our future, let alone a full complement of animals I barely knew existed. Elaine, for example. Emus weren't anywhere on my radar."

"And yet you named her and embraced her," I said.

"Only metaphorically," he said. "I hope I don't have to hug her in real life."

"You've done your part in delivering goat babies," I said. "Unfortunately, your job seems likely to keep you too busy for cuddling livestock."

He walked me around the gardens before escorting me to our favorite bench. Only then did he signal he was ready to talk business by dropping his arm.

"Are you really buying this whole terminal lucidity thing?" he asked. "I read up on it, but I can't help wondering if Imogen Pigeon is playing games."

"You know Edna's the biggest skeptic around but she swears it's true, and she's also witnessed many a deathbed confession. So yeah, I believe Imogen that her patient confessed to this murder. It seems like the bones Keats found confirm it."

"We don't know it's a murder yet," Kellan said. "It was common for people to bury family on their property, even though it wasn't technically allowed."

I glanced up at him. It was too dark to see much more than his chiseled chin. "Ima said Morris strangled the man. It's likely been sixty or seventy years. Can forensics determine that so long after the crime?"

"Probably not. And record keeping at the time was spotty. In fact, I've long suspected some files were purged by a generation of police who were no better than criminals. It won't be easy to identify this person."

"There was the rusty legion pin. That narrows it down a bit, doesn't it?"

"Most men of the day belonged to the legion," Kellan said. "The fraternity was often more of a cover for illegal activities rather than good works."

"What about the mason jar in the grave? That had to be a weird clue."

He seemed to cheer up a little at that. "Forensics can analyze the fragments inside. Looked like fabric of some kind. That could be helpful."

"I'm sure you can figure it out," I said.

"In time, yes, but it has to take a back seat to the Prudence Hoggins case," he said. "Imogen was probably right about hearing a scuffle because the back door was wide open, and there was at least one footprint in the yard. It looked like a car had left in a hurry in the rear lane, too."

"That's something," I said.

"Yeah, but it means there's a murderer at large right now who might put other citizens at risk." He took a deep breath and delivered the bad news. "The cold case will have to stay on ice a little longer."

"Kellan! We can't just leave it till after the Prudence situation is resolved. Imogen doesn't have long, and she asked me to figure out what happened before she passes. I gave her my word."

"You can't give someone your word that you'll investigate a murder without checking in with me first," he said. "Even an old one. I'm still the chief of police."

"You'd have done the same in my shoes. It's Ima's dying wish. I can't send her off with this weight on her conscience when I might be able to help."

"If she was that worried, she should have shared the information earlier," he said.

"Well, no one anticipates dementia," I said. "I'm sure she intended to say something, but time got away on her and she had plenty of other worries, according to Edna. Now the clock's ticking. I need to pull every memory she has out of her before the curtain falls again."

"You mean, *I* need to. As chief of police."

"Okay, but she told Teri she'd only speak to me and didn't even want Edna and Jilly hearing the story."

He rubbed his forehead in the darkness. "How does that

happen? My reputation here is stellar but people want to confess to my girlfriend now."

"It's really about Keats and Percy," I said. "They're getting a fan following. Teri must have talked them up."

After a long pause, he gave a heavy sigh. "If Imogen only has a few days and she'll only speak to you about this old murder, I guess my hands are tied."

I laced my fingers through his to prove that tying himself to me wasn't so bad. "The case is so old and the murderer long gone. It's more a matter of setting the record straight. Not dangerous at all, unlike Prudence's case, which I'm going to avoid."

He turned and I could feel the weight of his gaze. "You promise to stay well away from the Hoggins case?"

"Of course. I'll be busy trying to piece together the historical case before Ima drifts away. I'll share anything she tells me that might relate to the current one."

He squeezed my hand. "Okay. Just be careful, Ivy. Please. Anything you touch seems to turn to trouble."

Keats gave a ha-ha-ha from the darkness and then mumbled something sassy.

"Yeah, I know, dog," Kellan said. "It's part of the package, and I accept it. As well as you furry troublemakers."

I rested my head on his shoulder. "This case might be creepy but it won't bring trouble. I'll do some research and see what floats to the surface in the muddy swamp of the past. That's the best I can do anyway, with the Clippers situation. My animals still come first."

"All you owe Imogen Pigeon is a good faith gesture that her story will be investigated thoroughly in due course."

"Agreed. And thank you." I aimed a kiss at his cheek and hit his ear. "This will be bush-league compared to other mysteries we've faced. I'm certain of it."

Keats gave another sheepdog snicker that suggested otherwise. Luckily Kellan wasn't quite as attuned to my dog's range of snarky vocalizations, because he put his arm around my shoulder again and said, "More like investigative reporting, perhaps."

"Exactly. I'll talk to Ima again tomorrow and then track down some old-timers. Open and shut."

Keats' eerie blue eye caught a bit of light from somewhere and warned me not to get complacent. I tamped down a shiver to avoid setting off Kellan's alarm bells.

There was no getting out of this now. But at least I had help to get the job done.

CHAPTER NINE

A good night's sleep and a rigorous round of chores did wonders to restore my equanimity. All creatures great and small seemed calmer in the morning, maybe simply because I was. Earlier in my life at Runaway Farm I had underestimated the impact of my jitters on the livestock. Eventually, Cori Hogan, dog trainer extraordinaire, had enlightened me that they weren't so different from canines as I might think and keeping it cool created a positive feedback loop. Today, Bocelli's restlessness had dissipated, and he grazed contentedly beside Clippers. The little horse, however, tossed me some curious looks. Perhaps he was sensitive enough to pick up on my worry about our upcoming training class with Trelise.

There were other hills to climb first, and for that, I needed adequate fuel.

Keats herded me away from the pastures toward the truck, where Percy was waiting on the hood. We all climbed inside to set forth on what was likely to be an unusual day.

"Kellan's never given me his blessing to pursue a case before," I said, as we turned out of the lane. "How long do you think that will last?"

The dog propped both paws on the dashboard without commenting. Kellan's approval meant less to Keats than it did to me. In fact, he probably preferred going around Kellan's back to get things done. The more challenge the better for my brilliant sheepdog.

He gave me an enigmatic blue-eyed stare that suggested I may never fully understand him. That was fine with me. I was happy with the slice of Keats I knew well.

Twenty minutes later, I was also happy with the slice of pie I knew well, as I perched on my favorite stool at the counter of Mandy's Country Store.

"You have no idea how much I missed this," I mumbled around a mouthful of coconut cream perfection.

"No? Do you think your pie of choice appeared on the menu by happenstance?" Mandy said, grinning as she joined me. "I put a couple of pieces aside in case you were late."

In fact, the door was still locked when I arrived and Mandy had let me in. This was our time to catch up on gossip before the regulars arrived, and she always had plenty. The store was so well situated within the rumor mill that a debriefing with her could save me hours or even days of hard sleuthing.

"Just a couple of pieces?" I asked, closing my eyes in sheer bliss. "The sad excuse for pie down south gave me an even deeper appreciation of your gifts."

Mandy laughed. "I hoped that would be the case and allocated an entire pie to you. The rest is in a take-out container with an ice pack. Based on what I'm hearing, you'll be busy, and steady blood sugar is a must."

"What would I do without you? You're an integral part of my team now, Mandy. Both as purveyor of sweets and as a..."

My voice trailed off, wondering what to call her that wouldn't offend her.

"An informant?" she suggested. "A mole?"

"An indispensable source of intel," I said. "It's harder for me to get people to overshare these days. They used to blurt their thoughts at random but now they know I'm up to something." I looked down at the dog who was sitting beside the cat carrier. "Luckily they still underestimate Keats and Percy."

Mandy and I raised our huge mugs of coffee in tandem and took deep draughts. After swallowing, she said, "I suppose your rep works both for you and against you. That's how you got the summons to Imogen Pigeon's bedside. Her sudden and miraculous recovery was the talk of the town till yesterday. Now it's been supplanted by more salacious news."

"Everyone knows about Prudence Hoggins, I'm sure, but what about our discovery near Morris Tubbs' place?"

"I'm afraid so." She took another sip, fueling up for the day. "Hard to say which story got the most pickup. It'll take another few pies and a tray of brownies to fully loosen the town's lips. But I'm here for you, Ivy."

"I know you are, Mandy." I set down my coffee and patted her arm. That hadn't always been the case but now it was a huge help to have her highly attuned ear to the ground in this community hub. It was worth what the secrets she'd once kept from me had put me through. As I learned more about the power of family, I understood how that had happened. Her relationship with her grandmother had been fraught in ways I couldn't know at the time. That had kept her silent about things that might have prevented one of the most traumatic events of my life. However, that same event had prepared me for others to come, so it was as hard to regret it as it was to remember it.

"Don't think about it," she said, because of course she was remembering too and it may have been even more painful for her. "Eat your pie."

I considered whether to shovel in more pie or ask questions.

Normally I did both at the same time, but today I felt like I had more time for courtesy. Although I had a tight deadline with Imogen, Kellan's permission to explore the old mystery meant I didn't have to try to beat him to the punch, as was normally the case. "Does anyone know who the victim might be? It could take ages for the lab to get results, given the state of the... well, the remains."

Mandy winced and then shook her head. "Few are old enough to remember Morris Tubbs, and it seems like anyone who did is utterly shocked. He was a kind man, they say. A pillar of the community."

I finally took another bite of pie and mumbled, "Must have been a crime of passion. It's going to be tough to dig up..." I stopped and swallowed hard at the memory of Edna's skilled spadework with Keats' assistance. "I mean, *track down* clues."

She raked one hand through her fine dirty-blonde hair. "Surely, Kellan has a list of people who went missing during that era."

"He does, but it's surprisingly long and shamefully spotty. Those were lawless times in our community. Plenty of folks moved away unannounced, and he's gradually tracked down their descendants and closed cases one by one." I scraped the plate with my fork. "There's been less time for cold cases since I got home and hot ones took their place."

Mandy's face ran the gamut of expressions from guilt to amusement and landed on compassion. "It's a coincidence. These things would surely have happened anyway."

I wondered if that were true. Sometimes it felt like my poking around in the criminal cesspool broke more than it fixed. I suspected Kellan thought so, anyway.

"Where should I start?" I asked. "I suppose I'll need to talk to the oldest and best connected folks in our community. Seniors with very good memories."

She stared into her coffee mug and then raised pale blue eyes. Sadness had etched lines into her skin that were too deep for someone my age. "Myrtle," she said. "She grew up in this store, eavesdropping on conversations, and she has an encyclopedic memory."

Myrtle McCain, Mandy's grandmother, had not only murdered someone during my first weeks in Clover Grove, she'd tried to take me out, too. If not for Keats, I wouldn't be here, shivering on a warm morning with a steaming mug of coffee in my hand. I set down the mug and reached for his furry ears. Mostly I handled post-traumatic stress fairly well, but when that name dropped from Mandy's lips it triggered a wave of profound anxiety.

"I suppose Myrtle could have information," I said. "Unfortunately, she's out of touch. Permanently."

Mandy crumpled on her stool for a few moments, but then sat up straight. "Not necessarily. Just because I have no desire to visit her doesn't mean I won't. If she's the only one with information that can help, I'll drive down to the prison and see her."

I took my hand off Keats and reached for her arm. "I can't ask you to do that, Mandy. There are plenty of other ways to investigate. Someone's memory will be jogged and one thing leads to another."

"I know, but from what Teri's told me, Imogen may not have much time," she said. "That's the only reason I'm suggesting it."

Keats mumbled something from below and I hoped Mandy wouldn't understand him. Generally, only true pet lovers picked up on his tone and cadence, and she hadn't shown much evidence of that.

"Let's see how we do without resorting to such drastic measures," I said. "Ply your pie and I bet others will send me off on the right track."

She managed a wan smile as she slid off the stool. "I'll get your takeout package and a treat for the boys." Halfway to the counter she turned back. "In case you're wondering, I know full well that Keats agrees I should head off to prison for a family reunion."

This time I was the one wincing. "He should keep his opinions between us. And he's not always right."

There was an indignant rumble below, followed by a sharp nip on my leg that nature intended for obstructive livestock. He was getting far too liberal with those teeth and we were going to have a serious talk about manners.

Mandy's voice drifted back. "Yes, he is. And when Keats talks, I listen."

CHAPTER TEN

K eats and I didn't "speak" to each other during the drive to Imogen Pigeon's house. Finally, as we pulled into the lane, I said, "You could have waited to tell me privately that Myrtle was our best source of information. Do you have any idea how much it will cost Mandy to visit her grandmother in prison?"

He mumbled an affirmative... and then a little more advice.

"What? If you're saying what I think you're saying, the answer is a most emphatic no. Uh-uh. And forget you ever suggested it."

The dog directed a brown eye my way and then panted a laugh.

"Chuckle all you like, buddy. There is nothing you can do to convince me to visit Myrtle McCain in prison. With or without Mandy." I glared at him. "You *do* know the meaning of post-traumatic stress disorder? Some dogs are afflicted, too, you know. You just got lucky."

He gave a slight whine that suggested he might not be as fancy free as I'd imagined. No one knew exactly how a dog's mind worked. Certainly not me. He was my first, my only. And seemingly exceptional in every way.

"If you do suffer, I'm sorry about that," I said. "I'm at least partially responsible and I know it."

He set a paw on my hand over the stick shift, as if reminding me we were in this together and couldn't afford to let Myrtle McCain come between us.

"Fine. If it turns out we can't find a decent source outside Myrtle, I'll suck it up and face the woman who tried to kill me." A small groan slipped out. "The *first* woman. Not the only one, unfortunately."

The paw pressed harder on my hand and I felt the surge of Keats' energy. It was like champagne and sunshine and spread quickly up my arm and into my chest. My breathing eased from a rapid pant to a calmer four-count. Nothing near the yoga breathing Jilly prescribed, but it still had a good effect.

"I hope they'll let you come in there with me," I said. "Not that anything bad can happen... at least physically. If it stirs up old ghosts, I'll put them to rest like I always do, with some heavy lifting on the manure pile." Pulling up in front of the Pigeon house beside two police cruisers and another car, I added, "My PTSD is fertilizing half the gardens in Clover Grove. The first asparagus and strawberries tasted unusually good. Full of nutrients."

Keats gave a ha-ha-ha as I opened the door and released him. Percy followed at a more leisurely pace. The cat, at least, seemed untroubled by memories of murders past.

I followed the boys up the stairs and my brother met me at the door. Despite the circumstances, a wide grin spread over his face. It had barely dimmed since he went down on one knee in front of Jilly's family, along with Edna and me, to propose to Jilly a few days ago. That smile reminded me of the time he got a much-coveted souped-up bicycle for Christmas and how he'd ridden it all over town in the snow despite Mom's bleats of warning. Only now did it occur to me that she really couldn't have afforded that bike, no matter how many extra shifts she took at her job of the month. Our father had said she never once cashed his child support checks, but perhaps she accepted an infusion now and then to make sure that the items in our annual letters to Santa materialized. My requests were always small, and the one I remembered most put a smile on my face now: a toy farm set. It had arrived in all its glory with horses, cows, pigs and sheep. A harbinger of things to come.

Asher got more than the rest of us combined but that was probably because he asked, and we didn't. It wasn't really his fault he'd been favored. He had a sunny disposition, good looks and an assumption that the world would give... and it did. Now he had received the best gift of all... my best friend's hand in marriage.

"Hey sis," he said, as we reached the top step. "Sorry, but no one except the two caregivers are allowed in. It's an active crime scene, remember."

"How could I forget when I discovered the body?" I said, distracting him as Keats and Percy slipped around his boots and went inside. "That tends to make a lasting impression."

His smile diminished slightly. "Yeah, it sure does. I'm sorry Jilly had to go through that again. She might want to ease off the crazy adventures. It's too stressful."

Anger prickled in my chest. Was Edna right? Is this how it was going to go now? I understood that their deepening bond would affect my friendship with Jilly, but she was a core part of the team that helped in my crime-solving work. My hope was that things wouldn't change much until there were babies to consider.

Well, it wasn't the right time to worry about things like that. Every second I spent nursing family grudges old and new meant Imogen might slip away.

"Kellan said I could visit Ima," I said, "because she'll only speak to me. Text him and see for yourself."

My brother pulled out his phone and while he pounded small keys with big fingers, I eased around him as I had on any number of occasions growing up. As the youngest of six, I needed skillful moves and a whole lot of speed.

By the time Asher turned and shouted, "Hey! Stop! Police!" I was halfway up the staircase, laughing, and I didn't slow down until I reached Percy, who was sticking his paw under Imogen's bedroom door.

"Got it, Percy," I said, giving a quick, discreet knock. "Mrs. Pigeon? It's me. Ivy Galloway."

There was no answer, so I decided to take her at her word and just walk in before Asher caught up or the caregiver appeared. Ima had told Teri to tell me I had an open-door policy to discuss her deathbed confession about Morris Tubbs' deathbed confession.

Both pets trotted ahead of me into the room. I managed to press my back to the door and close it seconds before my brother reached it. He wouldn't presume to barge into Ima's room to evict me, I was quite sure of that. No doubt he'd already felt the rough side of her tongue, since Kellan had admitted taking a few hits himself. I had to admire her for that late-day spunk.

Mrs. Pigeon was propped up on pillows with her arms folded neatly, fingers laced together. Her bed jacket was similar to the one she wore the day before, although this one had an eye-popping fuchsia print. Her hair was precisely curled and looked lacquered with spray, and she was wearing so much makeup that she looked, well... ready for a viewing at a funeral home. In Clover Grove, an open casket was still more the rule than the exception. I couldn't help wondering, with all the historical shenanigans, if townspeople refused to believe you were actually dead unless they saw the proof with their own eyes.

I stood perfectly still, staring. Was her chest moving? Had I lost my chance to get more information about Morris Tubbs from the best source?

There was an eerie stillness in the room that convinced me she'd sailed past sleep into the great beyond. Pushing myself off the door, I took a few slow steps toward her, holding my breath. It certainly wasn't the first time I'd seen a body, but this was different. Now it was nature completing the circle of life, not a murderer. Still, it felt strange and wrong to bear witness to a private passage when we were barely acquainted.

I was standing right beside the bed when Percy took a rather dramatic leap and landed squarely on Imogen's folded hands. Her eyes popped open and she gave a little scream.

And then she laughed.

And laughed some more, as Percy curled into a ball, purring delightedly.

"Oh, Ivy, you should see your face," she said. "That was worth holding my breath until I almost expired prematurely. Could you have walked any slower?"

"You mean you faked being dead?" I stared down at Keats and shook my finger. "You could have told me. You knew full well what I was thinking."

His happy pant confirmed he was in on the joke. Percy hadn't been able to resist spoiling the punch line.

"Don't blame the dog," Imogen said. "I gave him a wink and he indulged an old lady."

"Well, I nearly had a heart attack and joined you in God's waiting room," I said. "That was a mean prank to pull on someone who's trying to help you clear your conscience within supposedly tight timelines."

She clapped a few times and gave another raucous laugh. "Very much worth it, young lady. I don't get much opportunity to laugh these days. You could at least lighten up and join me."

Shaking my head, I gave her a smile. "I suppose I'll survive the shock, but I won't fall for it twice, Mrs. Pigeon. Fool me once, shame on you. Fool me twice—"

"I'm utterly shameless at this point, so don't waste your breath." She patted the side of the bed and folded her hands again. "Don't waste your breath on principle. You never know how many you have left before darkness sweeps in on velvety paws like these." Percy kneaded her bed coat till she gave a little yelp. "It's true, my marmalade friend. There's a nasty prickle or ten when the curtain falls."

"Percy, get down please," I said. "There's no need to puncture Mrs. Pigeon, as annoying as she may be."

She cackled again. "Just call me Ima. We're past even Imogen now. I never liked either, but I hated my married name more. Pigeon. Ima Pigeon. Think about all the wisecracks about *that* combination." Her laugh faded and she sighed. "I did love Carl, though, and I must say you've chosen a fine man, too. He showed supremely good judgment in letting you take over this matter. Morris Tubbs was the nicest man I ever had the honor of seeing out of life. And there were many."

"If Mr. Tubbs was so nice, why did he strangle someone and drop him into a shallow grave? Sounds like the opposite of nice."

She shrugged. "In my view, what you see at the bitter end is the unvarnished truth. So I believe Morris was a kind man who got pushed to do something desperate. Unfortunately, the words were barely out of his mouth when he was snatched away. I've never seen a quicker demise. It was like his maker didn't want him to divulge the old secret. Yet it seems like I've been tasked with doing the job now. Obviously I was sent back for a reason and it wasn't to reminisce with Edna, interesting as that may be. She came by earlier."

"How did Edna get past Asher?" I said.

Ima pointed at the window. "Lowered herself from the roof by a rope like a superhero. She really has changed."

"She sure has. Spying on me got her out of her recliner and after that, there was no stopping her."

"Sit, Ivy. Hovering makes me nervous."

I perched on the bed and tried unsuccessfully to dislodge Percy. "I assume you heard from Chief Harper that my pets discovered the victim. It seems you were right." Ima nodded once, so I continued. "There's nothing else to go on, I'm afraid."

"There must have been something," she said, her penciled-on brows rising.

"It wasn't an elegant burial and nature took its course. There was a legion pin, which the chief tells me isn't a big help. And a mason jar."

"A mason jar? Containing what? Moonshine? There was plenty of discord over illegal booze at that time. Maybe the dead man had a distillery, and Morris objected." She shook her head even as she spoke. "Doesn't make sense, as he enjoyed a medicinal shot himself. I saw that he got it."

Reaching into my front pocket, I pulled out my phone. "I can show you if you're up to seeing photos."

"I was never squeamish, Ivy. Couldn't afford to be in my line of work."

Expanding the image, I held the phone out for her to take a look. "The police sent everything to the lab. Whatever was in the jar was little more than brown dust, but it may have been fabric."

Imogen stared at the phone. "The way the jar is situated makes it look like it was placed on his chest deliberately."

"That's what I thought, too. I was hoping you'd have an idea what may have been inside. Otherwise, I'll have to wait for the lab results while I beat the bushes for tips. The word is already circulating like wildfire."

She snorted. "Big surprise. A double dose of gossip tastes twice as sweet."

"Speaking of sweet... I brought you some coconut cream pie from Mandy's Country Store. She's a very talented baker."

She lifted one frail hand and waved. "My system can't handle that kind of thing anymore. I don't fancy food at all. I still enjoy a nice cup of tea, but that's about it."

"I'll run down and make some," I said, rising.

"Don't. Your brother likely won't let you back inside, so why risk it? He's so very much like his grandfather it startled me at first."

"His grandfather?" I asked. "You knew my grandparents? Maternal or paternal?"

"Gardenia and Albert Swingle," she said. "Dahlia's parents. They were an odd pair. Extremely reserved. Dahlia was a late life surprise I delivered into the world. I thought Gardenia would thaw a little with the baby she'd always wanted but she got more brittle than ever. It wasn't long before Albert moved them away to Dorset Hills and then beyond. There were all kinds of rumors, but I'm sure you've heard them."

"I've—I've heard nothing," I stuttered. "Never met them. Mom wasn't close to them."

Was there no end to the family secrets? Now Mom's people were coming out of the woodwork, at least in hearsay.

"That's a shame," Ima said. "Because Dahlia was very much welcomed after several miscarriages and three stillborn children. Gardenia had completely given up hope when her golden girl arrived."

I felt my mouth open in shock and stay that way. Gaping wasn't typical of me, the former grim reaper of human resources. In fact, I was known for my blank, stoic mask. But now, Keats had positioned his ears under my fingers for the second time in two hours. His energy helped my jaw move back into position and my tongue to start working.

"When did they pass, Mrs. Pigeon?" I caught myself. "I mean Ima."

"I'm not sure they did," she said. "I haven't had a chance to ask about everyone since my... recovery." Her head dropped back on the pillow as her energy flagged. "I suggest you look them up, if only because your grandfather was a particular friend of Morris Tubbs. If Morris told anyone anything, it would likely be Albert."

"All right, I'll do that," I said, getting up off the bed.

"Don't just stand there wringing your hands, girly," she said.

"Teri said you were one tough cookie. Surely grandparents can't shock you when a pile of bones didn't?"

"The pile of bones did shock me. So did Prudence's body. Just in a different way."

Ima closed her eyes and then opened them again. "Ivy, listen to me. All families lie. All families hide secrets. Yours is no better or worse."

I scooped up Percy and cradled him like a baby. "It seems worse, sometimes."

"Oh, look at poor Mandy McCain and stop whining." This time her eyes closed and stayed that way. "You'll speak to Myrtle, too, I presume? She knew everyone in her day."

I walked to the bedroom door. "You do know Myrtle tried to kill me?"

"And *failed*, Ivy. You'll have the last laugh, now, won't you?"

"Not laughing," I said, slipping out.

Her cackle followed me. "I am! Never been more amused in my life."

TERI MASON WAS WAITING by my truck when I came out. Normally, my artist friend wore full-length bright floral caftans, but she was utterly subdued in jeans and a gray sweatshirt today. Imogen's revival had apparently shocked her granddaughter into conventionality. Temporarily, I hoped, because I loved that Teri shamelessly courted gossip in a town that wanted to suppress anything unique. Sometimes, it was nice to share the burden of being quirky.

"You look like you've seen a ghost," Teri said, and then shook her head. "That doesn't sound right when Nan is practically a ghost."

"Your grandmother just pranked me by playing dead," I said.

"Which proves she's very much alive and savoring the time she has left."

"I'm sorry," Teri said, fighting a grin. "She's always had an offbeat sense of humor. I guess that's where I got it."

"And I guess that's why I like you, so I can't complain."

Keats and Percy sniffed around her pant legs in disappointment. One game they both loved was sneaking under her voluminous caftan and then exploding at passersby. It got quite a reaction either on Main Street or in her art store. I was always worried they'd break one of her fine creations—or someone's limb—but she gleefully encouraged them. The apple didn't fall far from the family tree.

"I'm sorry, guys," she said. Bending to give both animals a pat, she showed that her rainbow of hair was as vibrant as usual. "With a killer lurking around I figured I shouldn't hobble myself. Prudence was wearing scrubs and sneakers when she got knocked down the stairs. Imagine how that would work out in a caftan."

"Wise choice," I said. "Although I highly doubt the killer will come back with Prudence out of the picture."

"I hope you're right, but I can't help worrying they'll come after Nan in case she heard something incriminating."

"No one would dare, with a cop on duty round the clock," I said, dropping my eyes.

"Edna Evans rappelled into Nan's room this morning. In case she didn't mention it."

"She did, and I'll speak to Edna about it. And Kellan. Practically speaking, no one else could pull that off."

"Except Gertie Rhodes, I suppose," Teri said.

I shook my head. "Not even Gertie. She has to contend with her poncho, braid and rifle. It limits her stunts."

We both ended up laughing.

"Edna's a riot," Teri said. "And anything that makes Nan's final days brighter, I approve." She caught my arm. "Thank you for helping with her special mission."

"I'm honored she'd ask," I said. "It's going to keep us all challenged."

"What about Prudence? Are there any potential suspects?"

"A few, from the sounds of it. A deadbeat ex. A son with addictions who's been in and out of lockup. Couple of neighbors with petty squabbles." I stared up the house. "On the other hand, maybe someone just wanted to burglarize the place. Prudence would have tried to prevent that from happening."

"There's little of value there now," Teri said, "although others wouldn't know that. As soon as Nan became lucid, she called us all in to give away her jewelry and heirlooms."

"So that there would never be petty squabbles," I said, smiling. "She's a wise woman."

Teri nodded. "When she worked in palliative care, she saw too many family breakdowns over the things people left behind. She vowed that wouldn't happen to us, but the mist came down before she had a chance to disperse."

"Then she got another chance," I said. "That is a true gift."

Tears filled Teri's eyes. "Obviously I don't care about her jewels or collectibles. They're not my style anyway. The true gift has been the conversation. The connection. I always thought Nan disapproved of me and my..."

"Artistic flair?" I suggested when her voice trailed off.

"That, and my choice not to settle down early and have kids like my sisters."

"But she didn't? Disapprove, I mean?"

"Not at all. She said she respected me for going against the current." The tears cleared and her smile shone like the sun again. "Honestly, Ivy, losing her to dementia years ago was painful but I didn't really know her until now."

"She's a firecracker, that one," I said, as Keats signaled the time for chitchat was ending. "First she ropes me into clearing her record, and then she drops a truth bomb about my grandparents on me."

"Your grandparents? I thought you just learned everything there was to know about the Galloways."

I beckoned to Teri and walked to the truck. "I highly doubt I've learned everything about anyone, including the Galloways. But this revelation was about my maternal grandparents, Albert and Gardenia Swingle. Mom rarely speaks of them and always in the past tense. I thought they were long gone." Climbing behind the wheel, I rolled down the window. "They *are* long gone, but according to Google, only as far as Mt. Wilshire."

"Oh my," Teri said. "Nan always liked poking around in closets for skeletons. I'm sorry she rattled this one when she's already thrown a puzzle in your path."

"Me too. I've barely recovered from the last revelation."

She patted the crook of my arm in the truck window. "Nan believes in the power of family. She's the one who propped us all up, you know. I wouldn't be where I am today without her."

I turned the key in the ignition. "Enjoy this time with her, Teri. Kellan and I will do our very best to make sure you can."

Her fingers only released as I let the truck roll forward. "Thank you. And be careful."

Leaning out, I grinned. "I'm always careful."

It was good to hear her laughter chasing me on my way.

CHAPTER ELEVEN

Unlike my mother, I was never one for making a big entrance. On the contrary, I preferred to slip into any event unnoticed. That was true when I was a corporate shark and truer still when I became an amateur sleuth. Blending in with the crowd was a significant benefit in crime-solving, although arriving with Keats and Percy did present challenges in that regard. Without ever formalizing it, we'd worked out a routine whereby the dog and cat would slip in ahead of me to do their own legwork. Or pawwork. That meant I could often fly under the radar, at least for a little while.

My plan for arriving at Trelise Sutcliffe's academy was quite different, however. Since I wasn't there to sleuth but send a clear message to back off, I came in with guns blazing.

Not literally, of course, but I did want to make a show of strength.

My sister Poppy walked ahead through the parking lot with Clippers on a long lead and hit the button to open the double doors for the rest of us. Edna was on my right in fatigues, Gertie Rhodes was on my left in her usual battered old brown poncho, and Bocelli trailed behind wailing a mournful song. The donkey was miserable about coming but would have been more miserable staying behind.

He was inseparable from his miniature bestie, which meant making some sacrifices.

Gertie and Edna both tried to crowd through the door with me at the same time, and I felt Minnie press up against my hip in an overly familiar way.

"You brought Minnie?" I asked, as we regrouped inside the entrance. "Isn't a rifle rather provocative?"

Edna turned to her best friend. "We did agree on small arms, Gertie. Pepper spray and a discreet blade, as I recall. A long arm violates prepper partner code. I'm out-armed."

"I thought Minnie was just assumed," Gertie said, tucking the rifle further back in her poncho. "She's my constant companion. No one asks if Keats is coming along."

"Keats is a dog, not a firearm," I said. "Obviously."

"He's a weapon. So is Percy," Gertie flipped her very long gray braid over one shoulder. "Look, I was on the farm when Trelise Sutcliffe tried to abscond with Clippers. Minnie was in my van that day because I was helping Cori move livestock among pastures and even I admit a rifle can be a liability in some situations. Had Minnie been with me, as normal, do you think Trelise would have had the gall to seize that horse?"

"I suppose not," I said. "Although I don't care for firearms around the livestock, either."

Gertie brought her braid forward again and examined the end of it. "I feel terrible about what happened. I let you down, Ivy, and it won't happen again."

I patted the folds of the poncho and tried to find her arm. "It's not your fault, Gertie, and I would never have blamed you, even if Trelise had pulled off her nefarious plot. The only reason she left empty-handed is because you and Cori cuffed her into submission."

"There's a place for aversive techniques in training," Edna said. "Although the big gurus of the day say otherwise. It's all about rewarding good behavior now and simply ignoring the bad."

I patted Bocelli's nose as it rested on my shoulder. "I only endorse aversive methods for human trainers. And Trelise definitely deserved a sharp correction for trespassing on my property. We're on hers today, though, so we need to play by her rules." I glanced around and frowned. "Or at least give it our best shot."

"Oh, I'll give her my best shot if I need to," Gertie said. "And I'm a very good shot."

"Why are we even here?" Edna said. "You've put this business of Clippers in the hands of a lawyer. Doesn't showing up imply Trelise has a case?"

"She *does* have a case, in the form of a signed contract," I said, "whereas I have nothing but Bailey's statement. I do expect her word to prevail since Vinnie isn't around to say otherwise, and he was well known for treating his animals poorly."

"Then why not just hold out?" Poppy asked. My usually cocky sister seemed nervous, probably because we were outnumbered by the many students in the training ring with Trelise. I was fine with the ratio. Even without Minnie, it would take triple their cohort to rival my octogenarian ride-or-die friends.

"Optics," I said. "Jilly is teaching me, slowly but surely, about the power of diplomacy. Many a battle can be avoided by playing nice."

"Who wants to avoid battles?" Edna said, pacing across the entryway in heavy combat boots. "Life is too short for pussyfooting around people like Trelise."

Edna looked and sounded confident but I sensed she was more than a little rattled by our meeting with Imogen Pigeon. That probably had less to do with murder and more with watching her former colleague boldly staring down mortality. Reflections of that kind must be inevitable at Edna's age. She'd nearly been murdered once herself and it was familiar ground, so I didn't expect it to faze her for long.

"And why isn't your diplomat here if you're so set on soft-pedaling?" Gertie asked.

"I told Jilly to stay home and plan her engagement party," I said. "It's coming up fast and she deserves to enjoy every second of it. But she issued strict marching orders, starting with not blatantly crossing a woman whose rep is built on providing service animals for people with disabilities."

"Trelise does good work," Poppy said. "There are tons of testimonials on her website from people who have a better life because of her."

"No doubt," I said. "As the owner of a service animal, I know their power firsthand. But she doesn't get to grab my horse without my say. Or his. If Clippers takes to this work, I may consider it, but Trelise doesn't get to take away his choice. Plus I have Bocelli to worry about. I doubt her clients would want to bring on a donkey, too, and he'll pine away on his own."

Poppy nodded. "My heart will break and my eardrums explode if I have to listen to that wailing all day."

"Fine," Edna said. "What's the plan, then?"

"We blend in, of course." The words made me smirk. "Poppy will follow orders and work with Clippers. I'll keep Bocelli calm and try to dig up a little dirt on Trelise from the others, in case we need it. Edna, you and Gertie are the muscle. All you need to do is walk around and unsettle everyone."

"I like this plan," Gertie said. "It's what we do anyway, Edna. Now we get paid for it."

"Did I miss payday?" Edna said, striding toward the ring and opening the door. "Team Ivy generally works for free."

"Untrue," I called after her. "You get accolades and testimonials."

"Remind me how that's useful?" she called back. "Cash? Now that's useful."

"Testimonials will come in very handy for your survivalist course," I said. "And then again at the end of days. I mean, the *real* end in the waiting room Ima talks about. We'll all want a long list of contributions when our number is called."

Gertie laughed. "Better safe than sorry, Edna. I think I'm still in the red."

"Me too," Poppy said. "These things should work on a points system so we know exactly where we stand."

"I stand comfortably in the black now," Edna said, marching toward Trelise's pack of trainees, both human and dog. "There's no doubt in my mind."

She was bluffing. Normally the fingers of her right hand would be hovering over the pocket holding pepper spray. Instead, they were churning her tightly permed curls.

"Ladies," Trelise called out. "And Gertie. What a pleasure to host you here at my academy. Especially our guest of honor." She made a sweeping gesture toward Clippers. "This horse is going to make one of my clients very happy. He's going to liberate her from a life of dependence and despair."

"There it is," I muttered to Poppy. "Just like Jilly said. If I deny her Clippers, I'll be seen as the bad guy—the one locking someone into perpetual despair."

Poppy was the toughest of my sisters, but her smile was warm now. "Things have a way of working out for you, don't they? Jilly would say it's about going with the current and not against it."

"When did you become so philosophical?" I asked, returning the smile. In truth, Poppy's transformation had been gradual and visible. Her hair had once been dyed flamboyant colors, similar to Teri Mason's only longer and wilder. She'd favored old-style punk clothing and plenty of piercings. The more hours she spent in my barn, however, the less outrageous she became. Now it was quite common for strangers to mistake her for me. All five Galloway girls looked like knockoffs of our mom, but Pops had rebelled against that very hard until recently.

"It's something in the well water," she said. "The animals have made me question everything I used to believe."

"I know all about that," I said. "Plus we've had our share of family drama. That may get worse before it gets better."

"Why?" Poppy asked. "What's happened?"

"Ladies, are you here to chatter or do some good for humanity?" Trelise trilled.

The students surrounding her laughed. Then she raised an eyebrow and they giggled again.

Falling back, Edna whispered, "Guess they've all taken a good huff off Trelise's tailpipe. Wonder what she's off-gassing?"

Keats gave a hearty laugh-pant and I couldn't help joining him.

"What's so funny, Ms. Galloway?" Trelise said, coming toward me. "We take the training of service animals seriously here. Do you have any idea how much good we do?"

A man in a purple Sutcliffe Academy baseball cap stepped forward. "Trelise's dogs travel all over North America and demand is growing every day. We can't keep up as it is, so I suggest you ladies stop obstructing our work."

Another man in the same purple cap, with the brim turned rakishly sideways, called out, "Hear, hear. You're wasting everyone's time, including the horse's. Most importantly you're keeping the poor lady waiting for Clippers practically housebound."

A woman with gray curls nearly as tight as Edna's chimed in. "It's such a gift to be called to do this wonderful work, Ivy. You're making a mockery of it by sauntering in here with a donkey and a... a..."

"Posse?" Poppy suggested.

"Battalion," Edna said.

"Militia," Gertie finished, stroking Minnie through her poncho.

The men apparently saw the form of the rifle, because they stepped back into the student ranks.

"Trelise," I said. "I'm sorry if it seems like I'm taking service animal training lightly. Nothing could be further from the truth. My sheepdog is a certified emotional support dog and I rely on him every day."

The woman with short curls gave a derisive snort. "Fads and foolishness. That's just a scam to be able to take your dog everywhere like a posh accessory."

Poppy advanced a few steps with Clippers in tow. "How dare you dismiss my sister's PTSD like that? If not for Keats, she might be just as despairing as this woman who wants our horse. But that doesn't mean you get to just steal him. So yeah, we came with a posse."

"Pops, it's okay," I said. "I understand people are passionate about this worthy mission." I summoned a big fake HR smile and shone it around the arena. "But I assume the animals you're training showed an aptitude for the work."

"Of course," Tight Curls said. "Our dogs have all gone through rigorous and repeated testing over months, if not years, and—"

"Sylvia, that's fine," Trelise said, knowing the woman had given me an opening.

"Exactly," I said. "Clippers has had no such testing and spent his early months holed up in a dungeon in the bush. Abandoned. Neglected. Completely unsocialized. I rescued him and his donkey companion just months ago and they've been recovering at Runaway Farm ever since. It's too soon for him to do more than enjoy a quiet day in his pasture."

"That's not for you to decide," Trelise said. "Working animals need to work. Does your sheepdog want to loll on a cushion by the fire?"

I laughed at the image that conjured. "Most definitely not. But Keats was thoroughly tested before we began training and he demonstrated a strong drive to work." Bocelli pressed his head into my shoulder and let out a long groan. He hated tension, whereas Clippers was looking around the ring curiously. The little horse was quite resilient and had youth in his favor. "If Clippers shows aptitude and motivation, I won't stand in his way. But I won't allow him to be conscripted just because someone needs a horse his size."

"You don't have a choice," Trelise said, crossing her arms. "We need Clippers."

"Well-bred miniature horses are difficult to find," said the man with the rakish tilt to his cap.

"That's not Ivy's problem," Gertie said. "You'll just have to look a little harder."

"Or pay a little more," Edna added, scanning the facility. "How about spending less on fancy digs and more on good breeders? Isn't that where the money *should* go? I assume you're funded by donations."

"They are," Poppy said. "According to the website. Plenty of generous patrons kicked in to build this arena."

Gertie reached for her long braid and cracked it like a whip. "Whereas the money would have been better spent acquiring animals to place in homes where they could do some good."

"You don't know anything," Sylvia said, crossing her arms. "Trelise's work has caught the eye of competing television networks and the physical space is a big part of the appeal."

"Sylvia, never mind," Trelise said. "They don't need to know our business."

"I suppose a TV show would fill the coffers rather nicely," Edna said.

Gertie flung her braid back in disgust. "So that's what the horse-thievery was about. Clippers would be good for ratings."

"I have no comment on any of this," Trelise said. "It's idle speculation."

I shook my head. "TV offers aren't all they're cracked up to be."

"True," Edna said. "When they tried to do a show in Clover Grove, the star died."

"Are you threatening me?" Trelise said. "Us? Our work?" She pulled out her phone. "Because I am recording this."

I pulled out my phone and waved it. "Me too! Great minds think alike."

She tossed me a look of utter contempt. "Perhaps you should leave, Ivy. Until I can get a police escort to collect my horse."

"We're staying," I said. "It takes a bit of work to haul a horse and donkey around and I'm serious about wanting to know whether or not Clippers has an interest and aptitude for service. If you're done chatting, maybe we could get started."

Her glare would have peeled the skin off someone with a more delicate constitution, but not the former grim reaper of HR. She'd have to work a lot harder to intimidate me into giving up my animals.

"Form a line, everyone," she called. "Let's start with the basics for the novice."

The acolytes moved into position and my posse took up the rear, forming our own procession. I looked down at Clippers, expecting to find him wilting like Bocelli. Instead, the little horse trotted briskly at my side, and released a happy nicker. Was my sweet equine lily of the field destined to be a workhorse in spite of me?

My heart sank as we marched forward, but Keats shot me a look. His warm brown eye told me to buck up. Apparently, the games were just beginning.

CHAPTER TWELVE

We hadn't had a family meeting in at least a month, which was probably a record since my move to Clover Grove. Everything quickly fell into the usual pattern, however, with Daisy in rubber gloves scrubbing her kitchen counters with obsessive zeal, Asher leaning against the fridge and the remaining sisters and Jilly sitting around the table.

Mom perched precariously on a stool wearing a slippery red dress that threatened to pitch her to the floor. I think she liked the acrobatic challenge, because she often brought out her satins for these occasions. On the other hand, she always loved shiny things and gravitated toward slick in the secondhand stores we visited to find fodder for her sewing projects. As long as the fabric would hold a red dye, it was fair game. And she didn't save her festive outfits for parties either. There was satin for dates, satin for grocery shopping, satin for her rare trips to the barn to confront me on one matter or another. With the shock of my father Calvin's return a few weeks behind her, she had pretty much adjusted and moved back into my best guest suite. That meant I got to see more red satin than my eyes could really handle.

"Be careful," Iris said, jumping up to prevent our mother from toppling.

Mom's little smile suggested that keeping everyone off balance was her real plan. She had no idea what the family meeting was about but frequently it was her behavior that prompted these gatherings. Several times she'd been implicated in the criminal cases Asher was investigating with Kellan, and I was counter-investigating to get her off the hook.

Today she was on the hot seat for a different reason. The blasé teetering told me that she was hopeful someone else was about to get skewered. I suppose I could hardly blame her for wanting to share the scrutiny of five pairs of hazel eyes and one pair of blue. Jilly's green eyes were full of empathy, but she kept them pinned on Percy, who was cradled in her arms like an infant. Normally he loved that, but today his ears were back. My nephews' ferrets roamed the house freely and Keats was relishing the search alone.

"I'll make this fast, I promise," I whispered to my friend now.

"Don't make promises you can't keep," Jilly said. "Just do what you have to do, but remember—"

"The engagement party, yes. It'll be fine. Don't worry."

"It was your idea, remember?" She squeezed Percy anxiously and he stared at me to let me know it was all my fault. "Nothing blows up a party better than a family secret revealed. We both know that from experience."

"At some point, I'll run out of family to spring out of the closet, right?"

"I guess, if both of your parents were only children. But hill country seems like a bottomless pit of secrets, doesn't it?"

Using my index finger, I traced letters that had been etched into the wood of Daisy's kitchen table. Two sets of twin boys had left it in a rather sorry state. They'd carved not only their initials but messages in their private language intended to get around my vigilant sister. Little did they know she'd created a dictionary to keep track of their doings. It allowed her to show up just before the cops at underage parties and graffiti sprees and take her own ruffians into custody. Turned out I wasn't the only sleuth in the family.

"It's a pit, all right," I said. "If I knew any of that when I was working in Boston, I'd have—"

"Come home sooner?" she interrupted, grinning. "Small towns are boring, you said. And when I suggested visiting, you told me, 'over my dead body.'"

"Turns out there are too many other dead bodies to add mine to the pile." I grinned back at her. "I can admit when I'm wrong, Jilly Blackwood, and I seriously underestimated how fascinating small communities can be."

"Ditto, and my old community was even worse." She scratched the space between Percy's ears, hoping to get a purr out of him, but he wasn't buying it. He adored being adored but sacrificing ferret hunting was a lot to ask. "Oh, come on, Percy, you know I need you right now. These meetings are powder kegs, and it's not even my family."

"Oh, but they will be, and soon, too." I tickled Percy's dangling paw and got a low growl for my efforts. "You might want to see what else creeps out of the pit before you pick the date."

"Pick the date?" Mom leaned so far back on the stool that she was nearly horizontal. It was an impressive gymnastic feat that required great abs. As I learned from living in close quarters, she had a rigorous fitness routine that kept her limber and stealthy. She outran me whenever I let her join me in sleuthing. In heels, yet. "Is that what this meeting is about?" She pulled herself upright. "Settling on the day is a priority, girls. It could take months to choose my outfit."

"You don't want to upstage the bride," Daisy said, collecting the colorful mug she always allocated to Mom to minimize the damage done by waxy red lipstick.

Mom folded like an accordion in time to snatch the mug back, making Daisy pay for the ambush with spilt coffee to wipe up. Although, in my sister's case, work was the reward.

"Jilly wants me to be comfortable, I'm sure," Mom said. "And I'm most comfortable in red satin. That's a given. But there are so many other big questions, like long, short or in between. Strapless, halter or simple sleeveless. Sequins, glitter or rhinestones." She gave a full twirl and nearly clipped Violet's chin with a dyed red pump. "These things keep me up at night. I need a date, a theme and a setting."

"And Violet is going to need a glass eye if you gouge hers out with your stiletto," I said.

"So sorry, Violet darling," Mom said. "Especially since you have the most beautiful eyes of all my girls."

The rest of us laughed. Our eyes were practically identical with minor variations in shape and shade.

Daisy aimed her spray bottle at Jilly. "*Have* you chosen the date? I ask in my role as co-manager of the inn."

"Not quite." Jilly glanced at Asher, who was beaming, as usual. "Likely in October and definitely in the orchard."

"The orchard! What an appalling idea," Mom said. "My hem will drag in the muck."

"So that's one decision made," I said. "You'll go short, with sensible shoes and a smart cardigan."

Her eyes narrowed. "This reeks of rotten apples, Ivy Rose Galloway. Did you put her up to such foolishness?"

"I sort of saw it in my mind's eye when we were down south," I said. "Rosy apples and twinkle lights and the famous hill country fall colors... What could be more romantic than that?"

"Hardwood flooring," Mom said. "A roof over our heads. Chandeliers to glint off my sequins. That's what."

Asher pushed himself off the fridge. "I'm all for it, Mom," he said.

"Oh, you wouldn't care if Jilly said she wanted to be married on a rickety raft during high tide," Mom said.

"True. Whatever she likes is fine with me." He rested his uniformed elbows on the counter and gazed at Jilly. "Have you ruled out the rickety raft at sea? We'd need wetsuits."

Jilly laughed and then shuddered. "I had enough water adventures down south."

"Don't be so hasty," I said. "I hope to have our new pond dug out and filled by September. Calvin's taken it on as a pet project."

There was a general groan around the kitchen.

"Not another 'pet' project, Ivy," Mom said. "You're just opening another avenue for those vigilantes to dump their rescues."

"We can expect some waterfowl," I said. "Hopefully in time for the wedding photos."

Asher laughed. "With your ark parked in the background, no doubt."

"Good point," I said. "It's gotta be big. Huge."

There was another shudder, this time at my shins. Keats had returned from his ferreting mission and took Mom's side on the issue of ponds. He had an aversion to water long before our trip, and encounters with a vicious swan and a sizable alligator had only made things worse.

Daisy tried to sweep Asher's elbows off her counter but he held his ground. Then he splayed his fingers and tore his eyes away from his bride. "You called this meeting, Ivy, and in the middle of a criminal investigation. My boss didn't free me to sort out mother-of-the-groom problems."

"True." I was a little surprised at how distracting a wedding could be when it was months away and not my own. A little heat rose in my cheeks as I realized I was enjoying the planning vicariously. "I guess I'm just avoiding delivering my update."

"On the cold case?" Asher asked, pushing himself upright. The perma-grin contracted into something more appropriate for a discussion of murder. "Does Kellan know?"

"He does know what I'm about to tell you, but at the moment it's more of a family matter than a police matter."

"How are the Galloways involved in this cold case?" Mom asked. "I wasn't born or even thought of at that point."

"Born, no," I said. "Thought of, definitely."

Now she spun and stared at me. "What are you talking about?"

"It's not a Galloway thing this time," I said, observing her closely. "It's a Swingle thing."

Mom's lips pressed into a thin red line. As much as she despised my father for abandoning us, she'd never abandoned her married name. Swingle was common, she'd said. Pedestrian. Completely lacking in style. It was a symptom of her need to distance herself from her family.

Asher spoke first. "Mom's parents? I thought they were dead."

Daisy cast a surreptitious look at Iris and Violet before spritzing the counter rather violently. Were Asher and I the only ones who didn't know? A prickle of anger started in my midriff over the deception but Keats reminded me with a deep rumble to let it go—at least for the moment. I couldn't afford to let things like that derail me anymore.

"They are," Mom muttered. "Dead to me, anyway."

"Mom certainly led us to believe that," I said. "At least *some* of us. But it turns out Albert and Gardenia Swingle are alive and well and living up the range in Mt. Wilshire."

"Wilshire?" Mom blurted. "The tackiest town in hill country. It figures."

"It looks very pretty on the website." I tried to catch her eye and failed. "Kellan did some checking and says they're living quiet lives off the grid."

"That figures, too." Mom nearly lost her balance on the stool and no one tried to help this time. "Those two couldn't be duller if they tried. And they do try."

All eyes were glued to Mom, including those belonging to Keats and Percy and even the ferret who popped up on Asher's shoulder. If she found her parents that dull, it was no wonder she was drawn to shiny things, like a magpie. But dull didn't make them bad people. Kellan said neither had ever had so much as a speeding ticket.

Daisy put the spray bottle down and had a brief tussle with Mom over the coffee cup that ended in a brown puddle that dripped onto red satin. Sliding off the stool with a shrill squeal, Mom pulled Iris' scarf right off her neck and started patting down the spreading stain. "Daisy Galloway, how dare you? Do you realize how rare this fabric is? I barely salvaged enough and it's irreplaceable."

"Whereas parents are?" I asked. "Replaceable, that is?"

"I didn't replace them. I chose to become an orphan. That's all."

"Mom!" Many voices overlapped, including Asher's deep bass. Of all of us, he was probably the most sentimental about family and this shock was enough to banish his grin to the depths where Mom had tried to bury her parents.

"How could you just abandon your parents?" he asked.

"I didn't. At least initially." She was patting her dress with one hand and fending off Iris with the other. "They disapproved of your father, and no wonder. But we didn't lose touch for years after that. It was only when Calvin got sucked into the criminal underworld that they drew the line."

"Drew the line?" I asked. "What exactly does that mean?"

She finally relinquished the scarf to Iris and tried to smooth out the wrinkles left behind. "It means they offered to take us all in."

"How is that so bad?" Poppy asked.

"It sounds generous, actually," I said.

"There are worse things than dull," Daisy said, at last. "And we lived through them. Mom, we barely survived on your pay checks. It was a life of—"

"Genteel poverty. I know." Mom awkwardly tried to climb back on the stool and failed. News of her parents had robbed her of strength and agility. "They offered their ultimatum before your father left us and I wouldn't desert him. Sadly, he had fewer scruples."

"But afterward?" Poppy said. "Why not later, when we were on our own?"

Mom sealed her lips and took another go at the stool. Again, she failed.

"Pride," I said. "She wouldn't go crawling back to her folks when they'd been right all along. Just like she wouldn't cash the support checks Calvin sent."

Finally, Mom managed to hoist herself onto the stool, wobbling perilously. Violet raised her hands, more to protect her eyes than save Mom from a tumble.

"There's nothing wrong with keeping some dignity in difficult circumstances," Mom said. "It was a different time. I salvaged what I could and carried on." She stared around the kitchen and her chin tilted up. "We survived. Without Calvin and without your sanctimonious grandparents."

"Survive and thrive are two different things," Daisy said. "As the eldest, let me say it was hard work squeezing a penny till it squeaked." She picked up her spray bottle again and then paused with it dangling. "Hey. Is that why I'm the only one without a middle name? Was it Gardenia? Did you erase that from the family record, too?"

"No big loss," Poppy said, with a smirk. "Imagine going through life as Daisy Gardenia."

Mom reached for her purse and pulled out a compact. Only after she'd reapplied her lipstick did she speak again. "I did the best I could with what I had at the time. We weren't hiding under a rock and they could have driven their boring sedan down here any old time and apologized."

"For what? Offering to take us all in?"

"Trying to break up the family when your father was still trying to do the right thing," she said. "Believe it or not, I loved Calvin and wanted to make it work. And after he left, perhaps I'll be excused for falling apart for a little while."

"Decades," Poppy muttered.

"Pops," I said. "Leave it. We have the rest of our lives to pry the details out of Mom. But I have a better idea."

Everyone brightened. At least, everyone except Mom.

"Road trip," I said. "When's the last time we did one of those?"

"Half past never," Poppy said. "Mom couldn't keep her license long enough."

"There were buses," Asher said. "We could have visited."

There was a clamor of voices and I stood and conducted them into silence. "I'll set something up and let everyone know. Imagine their faces when we all pile out. I bet it won't be dull at all."

"I won't be there to see it," Mom said. "Knock yourselves out."

Asher caught Jilly's eye and then mine. "Why now, Ivy? Curious as I am, it's hardly the time for a Swingle family reunion."

Mom winced at the sound of her maiden name. "Yes, Ivy. Why now?"

"Imogen Pigeon suggested I contact them," I said. "Albert and Morris knew each other, and she thought our grandparents might know something helpful."

"They won't know anything helpful," Mom said. "They never mixed much. Holier-than-thou types."

"It can't hurt to try, Dahlia," Jilly said, finally speaking up. "Maybe on the way back we could stop at a few new consignment stores and look for your mother-of-the-groom dress."

Mom slid off the stool with a deliberate clatter of heels. "I see what you're doing, Jillian, and I'm disappointed. Very disappointed. You're on their side."

"I am not on your parents' side, if that's what you mean," Jilly said, glancing at me helplessly. "My first priority is making sure Ivy and her ark are safe. That's what best friends do."

"You may need to switch up your priorities before long," Mom said. "Husbands always demand to be the first in line or they make your life miserable."

Asher's grin reappeared. "I want Ivy and her ark to be safe, too," he said. "Besides, I'd never presume to tell Jilly what she can and can't do."

All five Galloway girls gave a spontaneous round of applause, with Daisy's gloved hands making squelching noises. "I raised him well," she said, pretending to wipe a tear from her eye.

"Enjoy that feeling while it lasts," Mom said, strutting to the front door. "You'll find out soon enough what it's like to have a thankless child. Or six."

"Oh, come on, Mom," I called after her. "When have you ever shied away from a new adventure?"

"I'll catch my own ride home," she called back as she stepped outside. "Thank goodness I can count on the many fine men in my dating rotation to treat me with the respect I deserve."

"Fishing's been that good lately?" Asher called.

She poked her head in to deliver the last shot. "It has, darling. One of your colleagues is utterly charming. I'll leave you to decipher whom."

He started after her. "Hey, my work is strictly off limits."

As she closed the door in his face she managed to land the last word. "A young officer would make a delightful date for an orchard wedding. No more bad apples for me."

CHAPTER THIRTEEN

I expected The Morgenstern Institution to look like the penitentiary it was, instead of a retirement home. It was a reasonable expectation, given that a woman who tried to murder me was confined here for the rest of her days. If the magnificent gardens outside the gates reflected the environment inside, Myrtle McCain wouldn't be suffering for her crimes nearly enough to suit me.

Normally, my repression machine worked beautifully. I was able to lock away memories of those I'd helped "put away." There were quite a few people in those ranks, now, starting with Skint, the criminal who'd brought Keats into my life. For months, that creepy little man had lurked on the sidelines of my subconscious, popping out to wave when my defenses were down. Then Myrtle joined him, and several others after that. It's not like I'd forgotten, and I certainly hadn't forgiven, but I had found a way to move forward.

The way forward was the dog who got me through the first episode and all the others. Both white paws rested on my leg now, as I pulled up to the security station.

"I'll be okay, buddy," I said. "Mainly because you can come in. I guess that's the upside of a lower security prison. Therapy animals allowed. Even cats without the official paperwork."

Keats' back end rested on Jilly's lap, while Percy had retired to the back seat to offer his emotional support services to Mandy McCain. It was hard to say who was more traumatized by the prospect of this meeting, but at least we had backup, in both human and animal form.

Jilly squeezed my arm before I rolled down my window. "Remind me why we're doing this again? There's got to be a better way to get information on this case, Ivy. Yoga breathing is no match for the stress of meeting a former attacker."

My friend had obviously taken note of my shallow panting during the latter part of our early-morning drive. Morgenstern was nearly two hours from Clover Grove and housed "lower risk" female convicts. Kellan told me Myrtle resided there because of her age and the presumption that her declining mental state had driven her to homicide after eighty-plus years as an upstanding citizen. There were better supports here, including counseling and recreation programs.

"It's not about coming to terms with what happened, if that's what you're wondering," I said. "That would be a full-time job, unfortunately. We're here only because Imogen thinks Myrtle would be the best person to identify our victim and possible motives. Or at least the quickest. The forensics report could take a while because of the age of the remains and the lower priority of the case. But Ima doesn't have that kind of time and I promised her I'd figure this out."

"Imogen's holding on so far," Jilly said. "I'm sure she'd understand if you found other sources. Or let someone else question Myrtle."

"The only one I'd trust is Kellan and he's too busy dealing with Prudence Hoggins' murder." I pressed the button and rolled down the window. "Myrtle is wily. It will take all three of us to manage her, Jilly, because I won't be fully on my game."

"She is wily," Mandy said. "And I sure won't be on my game." She gave a humorless chuckle. "I have no game at the best of times."

I glanced back and saw Mandy was paler than ever. It looked like she might faint at any second. "Mandy, you don't need to come in. Jilly and I have handled worse than this, alongside Keats and Percy."

Jilly turned, too. "Strangely enough, we have. This killer is locked up, so any threat is purely emotional." Summoning a smile, she added, "Not to discount emotional threats. Sometimes they're worse than the real thing."

"Definitely," I said. "I'd far rather face a killer for real with fists raised than see them on parade in my dreams like a freak show."

Squeezing harder, Jilly said, "Is that what it's like for you, Ivy? How horrible."

Keats whined an affirmative before I had a chance to backpedal. At least twice a week he woke me from horrible nightmares with a reassuring poke from a wet nose. Sometimes he jumped on my chest and Percy added some claws for good measure. It was a harsh way to awaken, but they had my best interests at heart.

"This might help," I said, "although that's not the main goal. I'm confident the five of us can get through this together."

I reached out and pressed the button for the speaker. Any more reflection and I'd back out. We'd come too far for that, both literally and figuratively.

"How come it looks so nice here?" Jilly said. "Decorating prison grounds seems like a poor use of tax dollars." She glanced through the seats again. "Sorry if that sounds callous, Mandy."

"Don't be sorry." Mandy's hands flew over Percy, sending up clouds of orange fluff. "My grandmother shouldn't have the pleasure of looking out at these gorgeous lilies. In fact, she shouldn't have a window at all. She murdered Lloyd Boyce, and while that may have been a crime of passion, trying to kill Ivy was very much premeditated. The courts were too kind, in my opinion. The longer we've been apart, the more I realize Myrtle was a sociopath. All it took was the right circumstances to bring that out. Or the wrong ones."

"You know her best," I said. "Jilly and I will take the lead in questioning her. You can either say nothing or jump in when you feel she's leading us off track."

"She'll try, trust me," Mandy said, as we parked. "The very best advice I can give you is to keep this short and ignore the red herrings she tosses into your path." She didn't seem to notice that she was fanning her face. "Our life was full of red herrings and now any time I smell fish it triggers my memories. I moved apartments before realizing the stench was all in my head."

Keats was first out of the truck, probably sensing he needed to take the lead for all of us. Percy was right behind him. Jilly insisted on preceding Mandy and me, and I felt better knowing she was wearing her sky blue "lucky suit." To my knowledge, that suit hadn't seen an outing since the move from Boston, where it had wooed and won many executive clients. She used to joke that it contained a metaphorical girdle that gave her a strong backbone. It spoke volumes that she needed that support today.

I, on the other hand, had dressed down more than usual in ripped and frayed overalls. My hair was in pigtails, which was rare and deliberate. I'd also worked on the manure pile before getting into the truck, as much to fill the treads of my boots as to build up courage. I wanted to look and smell the part of the simple farmer today, in hopes that Myrtle might underestimate me.

One look at her waiting at a table in the visitor's room blew that hope out the barred window. Myrtle McCain's blue eyes were as sharp as ever. Perhaps even sharper because the emotions fueling her crimes had faded. They scanned Jilly and me briefly and then landed on Mandy and stayed there. Her lips pressed together and her hands, folded on the tabled, parted and then came together again and clenched. Mandy was wrong, I realized. Myrtle wasn't a complete sociopath because she was capable of strong feelings for her granddaughter. Her mental wiring was more complicated than someone like Skint's, I suspected. That's probably how she convinced the court she was a feeble old woman who should age out peacefully here at the Morgenstern resort.

It was far from a retirement villa, of course. Aside from barred windows, there were multiple locks on the doors and the metal tables and chairs were nailed down. Myrtle wasn't wearing a prison uniform but stretchy pants and a floral tunic, however, and her long white hair was twisted into a ladylike knot. She didn't look like the down-to-earth storekeeper she'd once been, but she didn't look like a prisoner either. If her posture and gaze were to be trusted, she was unbowed and unrepentant.

My fingers dropped and Keats' ears were waiting. He might wander out of range on the farm or during an investigation, but he knew when he was needed in his original role as my emotional support dog. That said, I sensed he was fighting emotions of his own. His ears flattened and when I moved my hand back, his ruff rose, too.

"She can't get to us, buddy," I murmured under my breath, as Jilly strutted ahead of us to the table. "Not unless we let her get under our skin. So we won't."

He murmured something back that sounded vaguely threatening, like, "just let her try."

Percy rode into the room in Mandy's arms, flopped fetchingly over the crook of her arm. She was wearing a tan shirt and pants that looked more like the prison uniform I'd expected to see on Myrtle. Maybe Mandy felt more trapped than her grandmother, and I hoped our visit could show her the way out of this mess. I'd do what I could to help once I got the information I needed.

After Jilly and I reached the table, Myrtle rose from her metal seat and opened her arms. Mandy stopped dead, and I turned to see her hugging the cat harder than ever.

"You've never liked cats, Mandy," Myrtle said. "This is new."

"I always loved cats," Mandy said. "I just never said so."

"Well, give your grandmother a hug," Myrtle said. "Hand over that bit of fluff to Ivy, the zookeeper."

And there it was, the first dig. It proved she had no regrets at all about what she'd done to me, and the growl deep in Keats' throat confirmed it.

"I like holding Percy," Mandy said, coming forward. "He belongs to Ivy but she'll find me the cat of my dreams some day."

"The McCains are dog people," Myrtle said. "Sheepdog people, to be precise."

"Some genes skip a generation," I said. "Mandy's her own person."

Myrtle turned a blue-eyed stare on me that chilled me to the bone. "I know my granddaughter."

"Let's all sit down and chat," Jilly said. Her voice was assertively cheerful and I looked quickly around the room to reassure myself that no one was here except the guard. It was his job to eavesdrop without showing it, I presumed, and his expression was appropriately bland. "There's so much to catch up on."

"Let me save you the time," Myrtle said. She sat down and then did her best to lounge in her uncomfortable seat. "I'm up to speed on pretty much everything that's happened in Clover Grove since I left. And there's little to tell on my end, other than that I've taken up gardening and crafts. I'd offer to knit you all sweaters, but no sharp objects allowed."

"How about yoga?" Jilly suggested. "Good for both body and soul."

Myrtle turned her gaze on Jilly and my friend's imaginary girdle kept her back straight. "Don't you worry about my body or soul, young lady. You're marrying that Galloway buffoon, so you've got plenty of worries of your own."

"I agree with you there, Myrtle," I said, sitting down across from her. "Asher's always been a handful, but he's still my favorite sibling." I rested one arm on the table and let the other dangle to keep in constant contact with Keats. "And you've proven the town's rumor mill has even more reach than I thought."

"I'm surprised anyone keeps in touch with you," Mandy said. Her voice was faint and her face drawn, but her back was straight too. "After what happened."

"No one liked Lloyd Boyce," Myrtle said. "I did the entire county a service." She jabbed an index finger in my direction. "This one was collateral damage. An accident. Now, sit down Amanda."

"I'll stand, but thank you, Ms. McCain."

Surprise flickered across Myrtle's face. "I'm still your grandmother."

"I know. I can't forget that," Mandy said. "No one would ever let me."

"How is my store?" Myrtle asked, dropping the nonchalance, and leaning forward. "You renamed it but it's still my store."

Mandy nodded. "It's still the family store. And it's doing fine, all things considered."

There was a greedy look in Myrtle's eyes. She had killed Lloyd and tried to kill me to protect that store. She said it was to protect Mandy but I sensed it had more to do with how entwined her identity had become with the family legacy.

I understood that feeling because of my very strong attachment to the farm, and more specifically, to my animals. There was no way I'd kill to protect Runaway Farm. But was it within the realm of possibility if my beloved critters were directly threatened? It didn't feel as impossible as it would have a year ago. Back then, I was known by my boss as "Killer." Only by leaving the city and big business behind for the simple life could I begin to fathom all the nuances of that word.

Today, I needed to turn that killer instinct on Myrtle. She had put my animals in peril and if she was still so connected with Clover Grove, she might find a way to do so again. It was time to take control of the conversation.

"Myrtle," I said. "Thanks for seeing us. I'm sure Mandy will relax after we get an important matter out of the way. We're here at the suggestion of Imogen Pigeon."

"I heard Ima came out of her coma," Myrtle said. "I always wondered if she was faking it, to be honest. If my granddaughter dressed in caftans with rainbow hair, I'd probably fake a coma, too."

Mandy backed up a step, hugging Percy. "I hope you'll help Ivy out if you can. It's the least you can do."

Waving a languid hand toward the guard, Myrtle said, "I'm in here for life. That's what I can do for Ivy."

I recognized the red herrings Myrtle was tossing out like chum to sharks. My best strategy was to just stick to my script. "Imogen asked me to help her solve a mystery that a patient divulged decades ago."

"The pile of bones at the Tubbs place," Myrtle said. "I know about that and you don't need my help sniffing around, Ivy Galloway. Your record is available even to common criminals like me." She examined her fingernails, which had crescents of soil underneath. "Not *that* common."

"If you know all that, perhaps you know whose bones they are," I said. "Ima's patient died without divulging that."

"Well, who went missing that year?" Myrtle asked. "Did you think to check the town archives?"

The way I figured out Myrtle was behind Lloyd's murder was by doing legwork just like that. I didn't need her help with Sleuthing 101.

Keats mumbled a reminder not to let her get under my skin and shoved his ears into my hand again.

"Right," I said. "Chief Harper gave me a list of men who supposedly moved during that approximate period. There are gaps in the record and we don't have a date, either."

"How do you know it was a man?" Myrtle asked.

"Legion pin. And every man who moved away was in the legion."

She shrugged impatiently. "Every man was in the legion back then, period. That's no help."

"Exactly. Imogen thought you'd know Morris Tubbs and what feuds he may have had."

"Morris didn't have feuds. He was low key, even timid. I wouldn't have thought him capable of doing something like that." She kept her eyes on her dirty nails. "You never know what drives a person."

"Eventually we do," Jilly said. "People reveal themselves if they live long enough."

I slid down in my chair. "I guess this was a wasted visit. I'm sorry, Mandy."

"Don't be," Mandy said, stroking Percy with hypnotic repetition. "I'm sure my grandmother knows more."

Myrtle's eyes lifted at the words Mandy tossed out. Turned out two could dish chum in this family.

"I don't, actually," Myrtle said, but she glanced at me. "Show me the photos. I'm quite sure you and your so-called team took some. Edna Evans? Gertie Rhodes? Even you could do better, Ivy."

"Ms. McCain, I'm part of that team so I'll thank you to be civil," Jilly said. Her girdle suit was working wonders today. "Ivy, show her the remains."

I looked down and found Keats holding me steady in his brown-eyed beam. As much as I hated the thought of showing a killer someone else's bones, I had to give it a try.

Fishing my phone out of the pocket of my overalls, I cued up the images of the open gravesite. When I passed the phone to Myrtle, my fingers touched hers and I flinched. She must have felt that because her lips tipped into a smirk.

Enlarging the photo, she said, "What's in the mason jar?"

"We don't know yet. It had disintegrated, I'm afraid."

"Moonshine, most likely," Myrtle said. "Men of that day did terrible things for hooch."

"More likely fabric of some sort," I said. "Or so the chief thought. It'll be weeks till we get the lab results, which may not reveal much anyway."

"They'll reveal something in that bottle, if Morris decided it was important enough to toss into the grave." She slid the phone over to me across the table. "Come back when you get the results. I'd love to see you again. Or at least Mandy. And the dog."

Keats mumbled something but his muzzle was directed at Mandy. It sounded like he was urging her on. To do something. Anything.

Mandy looked down at him and blinked a few times. Then she did something entirely unexpected: she walked around the table and offered Percy to Myrtle. "Would you like to hold him? He's a wonderful cat."

"Wait," I said. "That's *my* wonderful cat."

Myrtle opened her arms and accepted Percy. I figured the cat would squirm away but he accepted the transfer with grace. He even dangled his paws over Myrtle's arm alluringly. He was playing the old lady, probably confident he could gouge her eyes out if the prison guard didn't reach us in time.

"I wouldn't hurt an animal, Ivy," Myrtle said. "I made you that promise the day I—"

"Gran," Mandy interrupted. Her voice sounded strained but determined. "Take another look at the photos. Think harder. It's very likely the victim came into the store, too. That you sold him groceries and delivered his mail." She paused and then threw out another tasty fish. "Our store gives us a unique opportunity to know the community, doesn't it?"

Myrtle nodded. "You can learn so much just by keeping quiet. You were always a quiet girl. Like me when I was your age."

Mandy didn't even wince at being compared to a murderer. Instead she nodded and gave a little smile. She was giving this all she had and it was an admirable performance. Myrtle was slick, but her Achilles heel was her beloved store and the power it had given her.

Cradling Percy in her left arm, Myrtle accepted the phone with her free hand. She set it on the table and stretched the image between her fingers. "Huh," she said. "Look at that hair. How come it didn't decay?"

"It all depends on the properties of the soil, I've heard. Bits of fabric survived, too."

She held the phone up to her nose and I reminded myself to douse it in disinfectant later. Keats gave a little ha-ha-ha beside me and I silenced him with a tap.

"That's not regular hair," Myrtle said. "It's a toupee."

"Really? That's interesting," I said.

"Only one man I knew wore a rug like that, and my father mocked him ruthlessly behind his back. It was made of horsehair, you see. It fooled no one and made him ridiculous."

"Who was it?" Mandy asked, hands clasped to her chin.

"Earl Spratt," Myrtle said. "He was a town councillor for a time but left to make money as a rumrunner and purveyor of other illegal goods." She slid the phone over to me again. "He still bought groceries like anyone else. And then one day his mail started piling up. He didn't leave a forwarding address, but he wasn't the first or the last criminal to disappear, voluntarily or otherwise."

"So Morris Tubbs was a criminal, too?"

Myrtle stroked Percy and pondered. "Not that I knew of. There must have been bad blood between them for a meek man to drop Earl Spratt and his toupee in a shallow grave. I'm guessing your answer is in that mason jar." The cat unleashed a loud purr, proving Mandy wasn't the only skilled actor here. "Ivy, tell your handsome boyfriend to speed up the analysis and we'll talk again. Bring your service horse next time. He'd be a huge hit among the residents."

I noticed she didn't say prisoners. Or inmates. They were just residents of this reasonably nice villa.

"Clippers just started his training," I said. "He's smart but I doubt he'd be welcome."

"You'd be surprised," Myrtle said. "They actually want us to be happy here. Can you believe it?"

"Well, he's a fun little horse. Full of spirit. You'd like him, Myrtle," I said, just to keep her talking. I had the feeling she knew even more than she was letting on. "He's no sheepdog, of course."

Keats mumbled his agreement from my knees.

"You know I'm a sheepdog fan," Myrtle said. "And honestly, I've never seen anything like your Keats. He was my primary reason for hacking into the town archives. I wanted to read about his exploits."

"Gran!" Mandy said. "You hacked into—?"

"Amanda, don't sound so shocked. It's the least of my exploits, isn't it? If it makes you feel any better, some of the amateur historians in town share information freely."

There was a twinkle of genuine humor in Myrtle's eyes and for a moment I caught a glimpse of the ordinary storekeeper I'd known from my childhood. It was hard to believe she had tried to drag me to death behind my own tractor. But it was true, nonetheless.

"Is there anything more you can tell us about Earl Spratt?" I asked. "Any tip could help."

She stared at the cat and then gave me a Cheshire smile. "I'm sure more will come to mind. Come back next week and we'll see."

"Imogen could be gone by then, unfortunately."

"Yes, most likely," Myrtle said. "Unfortunately, there are no rush orders in the clink."

I got to my feet and said, "Thank you for your help. I've got a training session with Trelise Sutcliffe later, but perhaps you know that, too."

"I know she tried to steal him and you've got a fight on your hands," Myrtle said, reluctantly surrendering Percy to Mandy. She tried to move in for a hug but Mandy eluded her, and I threw out more chum to help.

"Training is good for both of us. Clippers will turn into an amazing service animal down the road if he's motivated. There's some reverse engineering to do. For example, he takes a little love nip now and then. I doubt that's a highly desirable trait in a service animal."

"Well, do give him a fair chance," Myrtle said. She looked smaller and I realized we were all gradually receding across the room to the security guard while she sagged in her seat. "Any animal deserves that. Don't they?"

I suspected she meant herself, but I wasn't fooled. It had been close to a year since she'd killed Lloyd and attacked me. If the flower of remorse was going to take root in the fertilizer she'd dumped, it would have done so already.

The whole situation stank, and for once, I had nothing to do with the foul air.

CHAPTER FOURTEEN

I didn't expect Jilly to join me on my training jaunt through town with Clippers, but she said she needed the fresh air and exercise to shake off the effects of our visit to the Morgenstern resort, as we'd taken to calling it.

"Definitely one of the more awkward things we've done," Jilly said, as we unloaded Clippers and Bocelli from the trailer. She didn't hesitate to take the donkey's lead rope, proving she'd come a long way in her confidence around large animals. Watching her head down the road in her power suit and heels blew some of Myrtle's bad vibes out of my heart.

"Very awkward," I said, following with Clippers. "But it would be much harder to desensitize the horse without his big docile buddy."

Jilly turned onto Main Street and smiled over her shoulder. "I meant visiting Myrtle. Facing an unrepentant killer unsettled me far more than parading around in my best suit with a donkey."

"You could have changed first," I said. "We had time."

"I know, but I need my sartorial girdle for this, too. Even if it makes people stare more."

We were impossible to miss. Mom had stitched together

makeshift "service vests" for both animals out of an orange neon tarp with lettering that said, "I'm in Training."

"Not only stare but video," I said. "We'll be the talk of every dinner table tonight."

"Like most nights," she said. "Life in Clover Grove would be so bland without us."

"That must be why fewer people are telling me to leave town," I said. "They either want the comic relief or actually feel safer having me around to take the hits for them."

"A little of both, I'm sure." Jilly dropped back and we let the animals trail behind us as we walked side by side. It was fun watching other pedestrians scramble to avoid us. "What's our plan, other than feeding the rumor mill?"

"I've been reading up on how to train miniature horses for service," I said. "Unfortunately the best window to socialize Clippers was when he was abandoned by Vinnie Swenson. Those were key months in his development and there may be no making up for it." I led the horse around a series of planters and a sidewalk patio and he didn't hesitate at all. "On the other hand, he's more resilient than I expected, so he'll get a fair chance to see if this is his calling."

"You're a good farm mama," Jilly said. "But I'm glad we have a lawyer on board to make sure it's your choice. And Clippers' choice."

I scanned the street for potential hazards. The key to desensitizing any animal was slow and gradual exposure to stimuli, accompanied by rewards. Today there was just the regular afternoon bustle. Delivery trucks and buses weren't permitted on the main drag during business hours and it wasn't even that busy.

Keats trotted ahead to continue the environmental scan. At the first corner, he stopped and woofed a warning. We slowed until the "threat" came into view. Heddy and Kaye Langman were coming toward us, each pushing a wheelbarrow full of what looked like thrift store rubbish. Some of those finds would end up on the shelves of their antiques store, The Langman Legacy.

"Hey ladies, can you slow down a little, please?" I called. "I have a service horse in training."

Contempt and amusement competed on their faces and amusement won. They stopped walking, probably to keep their loads steady rather than out of compassion for the animals.

"What now, Ivy Galloway?" Kaye asked. "Is there no end to your ridiculous hijinks?"

I shrugged. "Ultimately, yes. But I hope to cram in lots more hijinks before the apocalypse Edna and Gertie predict arrives."

The mention of my prepper friends had the desired effect of making the sisters cringe. A few months ago, the Langmans had crossed Gertie and ended up on ice, literally, as punishment. They bounced back with the resilience of the cockroaches to which Edna likened them. She meant it as a compliment. The sisters Langman were survivors, and that meant something to Edna, even if they were constant thorns in our side. They hadn't committed a murder I could pin on them, but I was confident it was just a matter of time.

"We heard you visited Myrtle McCain in prison this morning," Heddy said. "Are you a masochist, Ivy? The woman tried to kill you."

"Everyone deserves a second chance, Heddy," I said. "Sometimes even a third. You know that better than anyone, right?"

Her face had already been flushed from the exertion of pushing the wheelbarrow and the color deepened. "I didn't try to drag you behind your own tractor."

"No, but you've put me and my animals in danger. Since you're keeping in touch with Myrtle, we'll need to keep a closer eye on you."

"Who said we keep in touch?" Kaye asked. "The grapevine works fine long distance, Ivy. You should know that by now."

I nodded. "Sadly, I do. The military should try to clone our system. Nothing is more efficient."

Heddy set down her wheelbarrow so she could cross her arms.

"Did you find out anything more about the old bones you dug up? I assume that's the only reason you'd put poor Mandy through a visit like that."

I wasn't sure if the grapevine had missed a beat or they were playing us like fish on a line. Either way, I'd grab the hook and dive.

"It was Mandy's idea, for the record," I said. "But Myrtle was as evasive as ever."

"It was so unnerving," Jilly added, playing along. "Much harder than we expected, and only to come up empty."

Heddy and Kaye exchanged another glance and shook their heads. "I'm sure Myrtle knows something. No one's better connected in Clover Grove than she was."

I scratched Clippers' forelock and then offered him a small square of Jilly's irresistible oatcake. He deserved a treat for enduring this discussion, but encounters with human cockroaches were very much part of a service animal's job description.

Keats made a subtle bid for my attention with a whine so high-pitched I thought it was in my head. The sisters were wise to Keats and his ways, however, so I pretended to adjust Clippers' halter while dropping my eyes to the dog. He lifted a paw in a point at Heddy and Kaye to signal they knew more than they were letting on. Or knew more than they thought they did. Either way, Keats wanted me to do a little more digging.

"Ladies," I said, "you're every bit as informed as Myrtle, if not more so. Dealing with the region's antiques has taken you into homes throughout hill country, often at emotional times for families. I bet you even joined your father on scouting missions to the Tubbs place when you were kids."

"Dad didn't like going up that way," Kaye said. "He said some things aren't worth the money."

His daughters hadn't embraced that philosophy. I'd known them to crawl through dumpsters and worse in search of potential treasure.

Percy decided he was needed and waltzed over to weave a figure eight between Heddy's feet. Many times, the cat had lowered their defenses and exposed their ruses, yet they couldn't resist his charms. That meant they had a glimmer of goodness somewhere, I figured.

"Then Bluffers Ridge must have been pretty dangerous," I said. "Or Morris Tubbs himself. Because I heard your dad was fearless in pursuit of quality artifacts."

Heddy and Kaye swelled with pride, as always when their father came up. He truly was a legend in these parts, and had died too soon —at least before passing on his scruples and horse sense, along with his passion. His daughters took over the business in their twenties and it had become a shared obsession. Without families of their own to offer perspective and balance, they'd become quirky, jaded and even warped.

"Dad didn't have a bad word to say about Morris," Heddy said. "And the Tubbs family sold us some nice pieces before moving away. It was more about Bluffers Ridge generally, I would say. The men's legion held retreats up there and Dad hated going. Right, Kaye?"

Kaye nodded reluctantly. She didn't want to give us a scrap to go on, but perhaps the feeling of fluff against her pant legs as Percy transferred his moves to her eased her resistance. "It was hard for Dad to say no to anyone. Relationships are everything in our line of work."

Jilly faked a sneeze into her sleeve to cover a snicker. Keats was less discreet with his ha-ha-ha, but the sisters didn't notice. Percy's swish from one set of legs to the other had the Langmans mesmerized.

"Every so often, he said he had to show up," Heddy said. "That it was a 'command performance.'"

"A command from the brotherhood?" I asked. "Is that how it works with legions?"

Their shoulders rose and fell in unison and Kaye took over. "Dad was quiet for days after those events. He didn't like mixing with them. At least not up there."

"Bluffers Ridge was bootlegger country," Heddy said. "So maybe it was a drunken party. Dad wouldn't like that. He was a gentleman."

"A teetotaler," Kaye said. "Or at least as far as we knew. Mom would have nothing less, even for the sake of fine collectibles."

"It didn't take that much to upset Dad though," Heddy said. "He was a shrewd businessman but a softie underneath. An animal lover, who was never without a dog and a cat. It was Mom who was the tough negotiator. The one who collected when people didn't pay."

"I'd like to know more about those legion parties," I said. "There must have been something worse than moonshine to upset your dad for days."

Percy gave Heddy another elaborate swish, twisting his tail right around her calf and then unfurling it slowly. "One time I heard him arguing with Mom about it," she said.

"Oh?" I said, as Percy stood on his hind legs to give her dangling fingers a head butt.

She scooped him up and he fell back in the crook of her arm, kneading the air and teasing the memories right out of her.

"Dad wanted to go to the police because of something that happened that night," Heddy continued. "He was yelling and that was so rare. Right, Kaye?"

Kaye mustered a smile. "Very. Mom had the temper."

"Did he do it?" I asked. "Go to the police?"

Heddy rocked Percy like a cat baby and shook her head. "She talked him out of it. Said it would be bad for business. Bad for us."

A chill ran down my back. In the same moment, Keats' ears flattened and his tail stiffened. On top of that, Clippers showed the whites of his eyes and Bocelli released a long, low bray.

"What could be *that* bad?" I asked. So bad that all my animals were upset except Percy, who was fully focused on his job. "So bad that it threatened your family?"

"I never found out," Heddy said. "But after that Dad came up with elaborate excuses not to go to those events."

"Like leaving town on scouting missions," Kaye said. "Mom would lock the door when he was gone. No one locked their doors back then."

"But nothing ever happened?" I asked.

Kaye looked at her sister and shook off the spell. "Put that cat down, Heddy. We have things to unload and can't be strolling down memory lane with Ivy Galloway."

Setting Percy on the pavement, Heddy flushed again. "I suppose everyone will be speculating about this discussion. Since we're not exactly friends."

"We're more than friends," Jilly said. "You two are part of our community. That's why we want you to give a seminar on antiques at the inn."

I turned to catch her eye and then said, "Yes, we sure do. As part of the Culture Revival Project. We can hold the session outside since the weather is good."

No way were they getting into the house. The last time they invited themselves inside they poked around like they owned the place.

"You could get people to bring along an old treasure and then tell them its worth," Jilly suggested. "Like that reality show."

Kaye laughed. "We're not stupid, girls. It's better for us if everyone thinks their stuff is worthless junk."

"Like the old guy who just let us clean out his back shed," Heddy said. "He thought we were doing him a favor."

"You didn't just pilfer his stuff," I said.

"Of course not. We're good people, Ivy," Heddy said. "We gave him exactly what he thought it was worth."

She turned to her sister and they both laughed over their scam. In the moment of distraction, Clippers reached out and yanked an old leather belt from the wheelbarrow.

I tried to get it back but he was rather pleased with his find, and did a little sideways shuffle that dragged me along with him. The horse wasn't big but he was solid and could tow a good load.

"Give that back right now," Kaye said. "It's a valuable piece."

"It's an old belt. How valuable can it be?" I offered Clippers a piece of oatcake in exchange, but he spurned it. The belt was obviously quite valuable to the horse. He had a better eye for antiques than I did.

"It's a schoolmaster's strap," Kaye said. "Probably eighty years old."

"Eighty? I had no idea leather could last that long." I tried to pry open Clippers' jaws. That had always worked with Keats, but the horse came with a different operating manual. One I didn't own yet.

"If it's properly tanned. Otherwise it becomes brittle and breaks down sooner." Kaye eyed the horse anxiously. "Obviously this strap won't be whipping anyone again."

"Just as well," Jilly said. "Corporal punishment doesn't work with children."

Kaye rolled her eyes. "You won't find many of my generation who agree with you, Jilly, and look how we all turned out."

Keats gave a snuffle-pant of laughter, either over her comment or my increasingly frantic attempts to free the strap from Clippers' jaws. The dog mumbled a question and I answered, "No, buddy, you can't help. It's all about positive reinforcement."

Now Kaye gave a derisive snort. "I see you're still talking to your imaginary friends, Ivy. Poor thing."

"They're real friends," I said. "More reliable than some humans."

"Enough mollycoddling," Heddy said. She came forward with her fist raised. "Sometimes a shot in the kisser is exactly what's needed to make a point. The point here being that this horse is making short work of a priceless antique."

"Don't you dare hit Clippers, Heddy Langman." Jilly stepped

into her path and crossed her arms. "I've never slapped a woman, but I'm prepared to make today a first."

"Wait, wait, I've got it," I said. "There's a rewards hierarchy, just like with dogs." Since oatcakes weren't sufficient incentive for Clippers, I needed to upgrade the offering. Reaching into my pocket, I pulled out a peppermint. The horse eyed the bribe for a second and then released the strap. "Good boy," I said, in a perky voice, letting him nuzzle the mint out of my palm.

Heddy started to jerk the strap away from me and Kaye said, "Careful." She meant with the old leather, not my hand, but I was glad to let it go. The idea of holding something once used to hurt children made me squirm. The good old days weren't always good.

"You're too soft, Ivy," Heddy said, as they hoisted their wheelbarrows.

"Like your father?" I said.

Kaye gave me a malevolent squint. "Don't ever compare yourself to our father. He was an extraordinary man."

"And Ivy's an extraordinary woman," Jilly said. "Your invitation to the farm just expired."

"Technically, it expired months ago," I said.

"It expired all over," Jilly said, picking up Percy. "It's a shame but threats to animals mean we need to go old school and expel people."

"Starting after your engagement party, you mean," Heddy said, grinning. "Dahlia invited us."

"Excuse me? That is a small, private affair," Jilly said.

Both sisters laughed as they trundled off. "Tell that to Dahlia," Kaye said. "She hands out an invite with every haircut."

"We wouldn't miss it for the world," Heddy called back. "That's true community, Jilly. You're one of us, now."

My friend's cheeks lost their color and I quickly exchanged Clippers' lead rope for Bocelli's. "Just lean on the horse if you need to, my friend. That's in his job description."

Clippers had other ideas and set off at a rather brisk trot, pulling Jilly behind him. Someone was going to have to sit down with this horse and review performance expectations. Luckily, I still had enough HR chops to get this runaway train back on the tracks.

But first, I'd have to catch up with him.

CHAPTER FIFTEEN

I was feeling pretty good about myself when I arrived at the Sutcliffe Academy the next morning. Our socialization outing may not have gone quite as planned but overall I'd been very impressed with Clippers' poise and response to positive reinforcement. Trelise's materials said it took at least a year to turn a horse into a reliable service animal. I had to remind myself that Clippers wasn't Keats, and Keats himself wasn't a normal dog. Looking back, I realized he had practically trained himself. I was a complete novice and yet he'd leave every class with a new repertoire. Skilled dog trainers like Cori Hogan said it took about 50 repetitions to instill a habit. With Keats it was more like two, and the second time he was indulging me. I always assumed his first owner—the one before the dirtbag murderer—had spent time training Keats. These days, I was more inclined to think his aptitude was about our connection. This dog knew what I wanted before I did. What's more, he was inspired to offer that behavior freely. The term "obey" didn't really come into the equation because of our mutual respect. We were an incomparable team.

It wasn't fair to measure Clippers by anything other than his own performance. Time and again, I'd seen that once I understood what motivated an animal, what they *really* wanted, we could find an effective way to work together. Where I'd failed, I'd usually failed to put in the time or let my emotions cloud my observation. In short, as skilled as Trelise Sutcliffe unquestionably was with service animals in general, I was in a better position to know my particular horse. If Clippers and I could connect on the right level, we'd get on like gangbusters.

"Ivy," Edna said, opening the door to the training ring, "get out of your head or you'll find Trelise in there with you."

"There's no room at the inn for her," I said. Percy rode into the ring on Clippers' back, then leapt lightly onto Bocelli's, while Keats just hustled everyone along. "I'm working out my strategy."

"Let your lawyer work out your strategy," Edna said. "Though I have little patience for people of the law, I admit."

"Me either," Gertie said, giving Minnie a pat through her poncho. "They certainly let me down when I was trying to keep treasure hunters off my land, and I spent a bomb on them. Minnie was much more reliable."

"So far the lawyer's dragging his heels," I said. "Keats didn't like him, so Trelise may have gotten to him first."

"Or Vinnie before that," Edna said. "You'd do better to hire outside Clover Grove."

I sighed. "But where? Corruption runs all the way down to Wyldwood Falls in the foothills, from what Janelle said. And probably to the peaks, too."

"Don't worry," Gertie said, taking Bocelli's lead rope from me. "We'll just keep playing along for now. Aren't you the one who says things work themselves out?"

"Yeah, although that usually happens the hard way." I scratched the rakish tuft of blond hair between Clippers' ears. "These boys have been through enough without ending on a shootout. It does seem like we're living in the wild west, complete with horse thieves."

An arm lifted across the ring. "Ladies. My time is precious. Have your tea party after class."

Gertie marched across the ring ahead of me. "Don't call me lady, Trelise." She popped her hip and the rifle peeked out of the poncho. "Although my good friend Minnie doesn't mind that at all."

The groupies flinched back as one, making Gertie and Edna grin.

"You can't have guns in here," said Sylvia Vesper, the woman with tight curls. "There are innocent animals on the premises."

"Minnie's mission is to protect innocent animals," Gertie said. "Don't worry."

"Of course we're worried," the man with the sideways Sutcliffe Academy cap said. "People are dropping like flies in hill country lately. Poor Prudence. That one hit too close to home for all of us."

"Barkley," Trelise said. "Let's not get sidetracked even more. This ring exists outside of the cares of the day. I don't need to tell you that animals—particularly animals as smart as these—pick up on our emotions. And a horse is a flight animal. Calm is utterly essential."

"I'm utterly calm," I said. "Although I'm a little surprised to hear Barkley knew Prudence Hoggins."

"We all did," Sylvia said. "Everyone knows everyone in hill country. Besides, she came out to all our fundraisers. One of her caregiver clients had a service dog trained by our very own Hawk Bustard."

The only other man in the group gave a proud smile. "Ollie was one of my best. I did a lot of home visits at the beginning and I saw Prudence often. She wasn't exactly—"

"A charmer," said Barkley, "although she did like to talk. In the end, she had her patients' best interests at heart. A true professional."

"A professional who pretended she was a registered nurse," Edna muttered.

I silenced her with a look. "I met Prudence the day she died," I said. "I got the distinct impression she didn't like animals."

"You can't tell much on one meeting," Hawk said. "Maybe she just didn't like *your* animals."

"Or you," someone else muttered. I couldn't pinpoint the voice, but Keats raised a paw helpfully to point out another woman who was also wearing the purple academy cap.

Barkley gave a shrug. "Prudence was probably protecting her patient. I heard Imogen Pigeon was fresh out of a coma, and Ivy's pets aren't service animals."

I looked down at Keats and found his mouth hanging open, not in the least offended. Meanwhile, Percy leapt from Bocelli's back to my shoulder and took his parrot position. He did that less now, but in the presence of half a dozen unknown dogs, it made sense.

"As I've mentioned before, Keats is a trained emotional support dog from a recognized school in Boston," I said. "My cat... well, you're correct about that. Percy marches to his own drummer."

Trelise stepped forward and her acolytes automatically fell back. "No disrespect to your Boston program, Ivy, but I'm sure you'll agree that working with one border collie doesn't make you an expert in training. Especially with a very different species."

"I do agree," I said. "That's why I'm glad to be learning under a true expert like you. And I'm sure *you'll* agree that the cornerstone of training any animal is a trusting connection. That's where I do have a bit of expertise. Clippers wants to please me, and that's half the battle, right?"

Pulling out her phone, Trelise tapped a button and then gestured to a large screen overhead. Clover Grove's Main Street came into focus. She hit play and the video zoomed in on Jilly and me chatting with the Langman sisters. All heads tipped back to watch, and there was a collective gasp as Clippers seized the leather strap out of the wheelbarrow. The gasp turned into a snicker as they watched me try to bribe the horse into releasing it, and then finally to horrified gasps as Heddy came at Clippers with fist raised.

"Those Langmans," Sylvia said. "When is someone going to stop their antics? This should be enough to put them behind bars. Has anyone called Clover Grove animal services? Tess Blade is a force of nature."

"Tess would only make things worse," Edna said. "She's a bull in a china shop and even Trelise can't train an animal like that."

"Don't underestimate me," Trelise said. "I've worked with a bull or two in my time. You just need to speak their language." She pointed to the screen again. "Let's identify the issues of concern in this video so that we can all learn."

I raised my hand and waved. "A big issue of concern is that you were following me and filming without my consent. How about that for starters?"

"It's my responsibility to keep tabs on the animals I own. I paid Vinnie Swenson a fair price for Clippers, remember. You're holding my horse hostage and now we see you're bungling his socialization. Here, he's being overstimulated on Main Street, with pedestrians and traffic all around. You run into two of your many enemies and they threaten him. Remember, he's a flight animal. Gradual exposure is key. You probably flooded him, Ivy, and I'll have a heck of a time reversing the damage you're causing." She paused the video and crossed her arms. "I can only guess that you're trying to ruin his temperament so that I won't want him."

Now I was the one gasping in horror. "How dare you? I would never deliberately ruin an animal's temperament."

"Ivy," Gertie said. "I believe Trelise wants a private word with my best friend. Let me see if Minnie will take her call."

If she meant to make me laugh, it worked. "It's okay, Gertie. She's just trying to get under my skin and sadly, I let her. She hit me where it hurts most."

Trelise came over and her unlined face was impassive. "That's where you're wrong, Ivy. I always have the animal's best interests at heart. Your delicate feelings aren't my concern at all."

I looked down at Keats and saw his ears flattening. Trelise had received poor ratings on first meeting and they were declining fast. It was time for me to show some backbone.

"If you really cared about Clippers' delicate feelings, you wouldn't stress me out with false accusations." I gestured to the screen. "Not to mention spying and exposing me to public ridicule. If you upset me and thereby upset Clippers, he could be worse off. Don't you trainers have some sort of ethical code to do no harm?"

Her face didn't twitch but the fingers on her right hand balled into a fist. That told me her weak point was her pride, her reputation, which gave me something to go on. I had underestimated that because she seemed unfazed by the video of her stealing my horse. In that case, she must have seen herself as a hero working on the side of the animal. Now I'd threatened that notion.

"Let me worry about my ethics," she said. "You're the one dragging a horse and donkey around like a circus act. That's not in the lessons I provided to you. I suppose you think owning a farm for a few months trumps my decades of experience."

"She needs to enroll in your animal handling program before getting into this ring," Barkley said.

"I wouldn't accept her," Trelise said. "To train a service animal you need humility. A willingness to learn from the best." She turned and hit play again, so that everyone could watch Clippers pull Jilly down the street. As ever, I was impressed by my friend's agility in heels. She kept up a pretty brisk pace as she got hauled around the corner and out of sight.

Edna snickered and said, "That girl needs to lose the stilettos. She's shortening her calf muscles and won't be able to run from... well, you know."

"I'd have to agree," Gertie said. "There are no heels in a bunker."

"Ladies, you're babbling," Trelise said. "I suppose it's understandable at your age, but my time is at a premium."

A silence fell over the arena. Everyone seemed to know that Trelise had made a dreadful misstep in disparaging two seniors who could, quite simply, kick her butt into the grasping hands of zombies.

I raised my hand again before matters could escalate. "You owe my friends an apology, Trelise. You owe me one, too, but I'm willing to forfeit to keep the peace for my critters."

She stared me down with amber eyes that reminded me now of a feral cat. A big one. "The only person I owe an apology is my client." She waved toward the spectator seating area, where two women sat. The seats had been empty when I arrived. I always made a point of scanning the place thoroughly.

"Client?" I asked. "What kind of client?"

Trelise beckoned and the women came down the stairs slowly and then entered the ring. Both had auburn hair, and the younger one, who was about my age, walked very slowly using a cane.

"Meet Monica," Trelise said. "The future owner of Clippers. If I can reverse engineer your mishandling, that is."

I didn't wait for the women to reach us, because Keats, my ambassador, was already making his way over. Percy jumped down, too, and they pranced happily around the women, taking great care to avoid the cane. Keats circled back and drew me into the loop, cutting Edna and Gertie out. Then he paced back and forth to dissuade Trelise and her groupies from joining us. Clearly, he wanted me to have a word with these strangers alone.

"I'm so sorry you had to witness that," I said, offering my hand. "I'm Ivy Galloway, and I can assure you that I do my very best to give my animals a good life."

The woman with the cane gave me a smile that spread over her face and up to her eyes, which were the same shade of warm brown as Keats'. "I'm Monica Branham, and this is my sister Macey," she said. "We've been following you since you came home. Following your story, I mean. In fact, I was following Runaway Farm even before you owned it. When there was that show, The Princess and the Pig."

I smiled, too. "Hannah is a wonderful person, and I'm trying to continue her good work as best I can."

"What you've done is amazing," Monica said. "Considering all the obstacles you've faced. So when Trelise said you were offering Clippers for training I was beyond excited. I've been on the waiting list for a service horse for nearly five years. Ever since my first hip replacement. It was Prudence who hooked me up with Trelise, after caring for me."

"Prudence?" I said. "It seems she was well known in these parts."

Macey squeezed her sister's arm and gave me a frosty look. "We didn't know her well. But she saw what a difference a horse would make to Monica, with her degenerative condition."

"If you don't mind my asking, Monica," I said. "Why a horse when dogs are easier to come by?"

"A few reasons," she said. " A horse is just sturdier, even in comparison to a dog of the same weight. Plus I'm allergic to dogs and it's harder to find a trained hypoallergenic breed. I did have a wonderful goldendoodle who helped me for four years, until..."

"He retired?" I said, to help her avoid the difficult words.

She nodded and stared down at Keats, perhaps wondering whether to continue.

"It's okay, you can be honest," I prompted.

"After my dog... retired, I couldn't bear the thought of starting over with another who'd only be with me a few years. Miniature horses can live to thirty-five. Three decades before my heart needs to break again."

"I know that fear," I said. In fact, I worried about losing Keats every day. I tried hard to focus on the present moment, but sometimes the threat of impending loss swept over me. With one glance, Monica and I connected on a fundamental level I couldn't have imagined earlier, under siege from Trelise. Come to think of it, appealing to my emotions was likely exactly what she had in mind. It was a good tactic, and very effective. Putting a face on this situation —and a heart inside it—made me think differently.

Macey Branham caught my eye. "Maybe you can imagine what this means for someone who's been in pain most of her life. This horse represents freedom for Monica. She can't run around hill country trailing animals like you do."

Keats stopped pacing long enough to nudge my fingers and I shook off the cloud that had fallen over me like a drop cloth.

"I *can* imagine what it's like," I said. "I was in a different kind of pain after saving Keats. Both physical and emotional. I wouldn't presume to compare it with Monica's but I do know how a connection to an animal can liberate you."

"It's okay, Ivy," Monica said. "I hoped Clippers would be that horse for me, but if it doesn't work out, another will come along."

Keats circled to draw the two of us together and I took that as permission to squeeze her arm. "I'm giving him the chance to be that horse for you, but he needs to decide if service is right for him."

Macey made an impatient gesture. "Trelise said training is the critical factor. That any animal can be taught."

"Possibly, but to me, it's about passion and drive," I said. "Keats is driven to work." I looked down at Percy and smiled. "Even my cat chooses to work. Revels in it, actually. If Clippers proves that's what he wants, you can have him under two conditions: that you also give a good home to his donkey best friend, and that they both come back to me if circumstances change."

Monica smiled and squeezed my arm back. "I've got a barn big enough for two," she said. "And I would only want a horse that wanted me, too."

"If it doesn't work out with Clippers," I said, "I'll use my network to see if we can't find the right horse. They're rescue matchmakers."

Now she laughed. "I know. I watched the show, remember."

"Come visit the farm, Monica," I said, reaching into the front pocket of my overalls to find a business card.

"Don't tempt her," Macey said, smiling at last. "She'll leave with an emu instead."

I laughed. "Big birds live a good long life but Elaine definitely doesn't meet anyone's specs for a service animal."

Walking back to the group I said, "Let's get started, Trelise. Unless you have more distractions up your sleeve."

It was nice to see that when push came to Botox, she was still able to scowl.

CHAPTER SIXTEEN

A fter the training session, Gertie followed my truck and trailer to an abandoned gas station on the main highway, where the rest of my family had agreed to convene before our road trip to Mt. Wilshire.

Edna was riding beside me, musing aloud about Trelise's chances of survival after the apocalypse. "I don't give her a week, Ivy. The bigger the ego, the harder and faster they fall. Yet she had the audacity to challenge you about humility."

I laughed. "I think that's what therapists call projection, Edna."

"Well, I don't have patience for psychobabble, as you know, but it sounds about right."

"I expect to see plenty of projection during our visit to my grand-parents today," I said. "How is it that you've never mentioned Albert and Gardenia, Edna? I assume you knew them."

"Knew *of* them," Edna said. "They moved while I was working down the range—long before I came back to Clover Grove. They wanted to disappear and they did a very good job. I guess part of me respected that and I put them out of my mind." She tapped her permed curls. "There's a lot going on in here, Ivy, and I can't keep up with all your family dealings. They weren't relevant, before. Now they are."

"Okay. Makes sense." I wasn't sure I fully bought her story, but Edna wasn't a collector of information like Myrtle McCain. She had her own obsessions, and Gertie did, too. The latter was a relative latecomer to Clover Grove who'd spent years fighting crazy treasure hunters. I doubted they'd deliberately kept this information from me, or if they had, perhaps they were waiting for the right time. And there was never a right time.

"I'm hardly in a position to advise on family issues," Edna said. "So I'll just stick to what I know, which is tactical warfare. Go in with an open mind and you might add more bodies and knowledge to the side of good."

"That means less room in the bunker," I said, smiling.

"There's always room for smart, capable people who contribute. If they don't contribute, just delete them again. That's what I do."

At the gas station, Jilly and Asher waved from his truck. Daisy's van sat behind them holding everyone else.

Mom hopped out and called, "I'm riding with Ivy. Edna, you'll need to ride home with Gertie. Be a love and drop Keats and Percy at the farm? My parents are animal haters. It's one of their many flaws."

"I'm taking orders from Dahlia, now?" Edna grumbled.

"Hang tight," I said. "I'll get this sorted out."

Mom clicked toward my truck on her favorite heels. Those red alligator pumps had taken a beating and still looked brand new. Some evenings, I found her polishing them lovingly, the way I decompressed by patting Keats and Percy. Today, she'd paired them with her power suit, also red, which probably had an imaginary girdle just like Jilly's.

Despite the polished outfit, it was obvious she was completely flustered. Her eyeliner and red lipstick were not only excessive but uneven, which meant her hand had trembled as she applied them.

It was tough to feel compassion for her when she'd gotten us into this situation, but I'd dig deep and try. This road trip was going to be stressful for everyone and worse if our mother fell apart.

"Mom, there's no way I'm sending Keats and Percy home," I said, getting out of the truck. "You've got your lucky shoes, I've got my lucky animals."

"Those animals don't bring you luck," she said. "How many times have the three of you nearly died?"

"Yet we're still kicking, and ready to meet another skeleton from our family closet."

"Couldn't you have pulled something a little nicer from *your* closet?" she said. "Overalls? My parents will be appalled."

"If they're so easily put off, there are four other Galloway girls they can eyeball who are nearly identical."

She fluffed her hair with a huffy sniff. "They'll probably only notice Asher anyway. They always wanted a boy, you know. I was a disappointment from birth."

Yanking open the passenger door, Mom gestured for Edna to leave.

I expected Edna to resist but she seemed happy to go. She met me at the front of the truck, grinning. "How about I haul Clippers and Bocelli back to the farm and you ride on from here with Daisy or Asher?"

"I want to do this under my own steam," I said.

"You cannot take a donkey and a horse to visit those people," Mom insisted. "They'll dismiss you immediately as being your father's daughter. And they hate your father."

I shrugged. "I look like you, only taller, so maybe they'll give me the benefit of the doubt."

Mom started pacing back and forth, her circuit getting longer each time. "There's no benefit of the doubt with these people. Disabuse yourself of that notion right now."

Glancing over at Asher, I found him trying hard to smother a grin and more or less succeeding. No doubt Jilly was helping with her silencing pinch. He'd better get used to seeing tiny bruises on his arm.

Daisy didn't roll down the driver's window, but Poppy hung out the back seat of the van, grinning. "The more you talk, the more excited I get, Mom," she called. "Albert and Gardenia are going to love me."

My rebel sister hadn't colored her hair for months, but there was a streak of vibrant teal in it today that she'd likely paired with her favorite punk mini kilt. Hopefully that would divert some attention from Farmer Ivy.

"Don't call them that," Mom said. "I doubt they've used their given names since they exchanged wedding vows. It's Mr. and Mrs. Swingle."

Edna's boots started moving. "Sorry to miss the fun, Ivy. I'll ride home with Gertie."

"Please come, Edna," I said. "I want someone casing their property. You can take Clippers and Bocelli on a stroll."

"Ivy Rose Galloway," Mom started. "You can't—"

"Mom, I have a lot of plates spinning and one of them is getting this horse socialized to his lead and new situations. There aren't many safe opportunities, so yeah, they're coming."

"Safe is not how I'd describe this excursion," Mom said.

"All the more reason I should come," Edna said. "I'm fully armed, Dahlia. If you want these folks detonated, I'm at your service."

Mom stopped pacing and her eyes lit up. A clown-like smile spread over her face and the runaway lipstick collided with her nose, leaving a scarlet splotch.

"No explosives," I said. "It's a family reunion that they agreed to readily." I gestured to Keats and he jumped down from the truck. "Take care of Mom from here on in, buddy."

"Don't you dare nip my hose," Mom said, hopping ahead of the dog as he dove at her feet. "I will not see my parents for the first time in decades with a run."

"You've got five substitutes in your kit bag, as well as two changes of clothes," Poppy called. "After poking around in there, I'm thinking you should have popped one of the tranquilizers. It's a little late now, but I'll pass them around the van."

"I decided to keep my wits about me," Mom said, getting into the truck before feeling the nick of Keats' teeth. "My parents are wily."

I sent Keats back into the truck and slid behind the wheel. "You said they were painfully dull. They can't be wily *and* dull."

"Oh, but they can," Mom said, shoving Keats into the back seat with Percy. Normally she was gentle with them but the fear of arriving covered with pet hair made her abrupt. "It's a still-waters-run-deep situation. Don't be fooled."

I waited till Edna was in the back of Asher's truck and let him pull out first. Daisy followed and I took the rear, waving goodbye to Gertie.

For the first hour or so, we drove in silence. There was no reasoning with Mom in this state, and yet I had to do something. Otherwise the meeting would turn into the Dahlia drama show, and this was more than just a family reunion to me.

Keats let me know when her nerves were settling by creeping back into her lap. He hated being relegated to the back seat on important missions. Using all his senses meant we went in fully informed. Knowing this, I cracked the window open to make sure he could pull in the scents of upper hill country as we headed to Mt. Wilshire, a tiny town near the highest peaks. It could barely be called a town, from my exploratory search. There was no website, no local paper, and the library, post office and civic services all operated out of one general store.

"Do you think they're really off the grid?" I finally asked. "That's a hard way to live for people way up in their nineties."

"They're tough old nuts, I'm sure," she said. "But no, my mother wouldn't sacrifice electricity and plumbing. As antisocial as she is, living remotely had to be my father's idea."

She'd started to stroke Keats' sleek sides without realizing it. He forfeited paws on the dash to make sure she had full access, giving me a baleful look to show it was a sacrifice for the greater good.

"Mom, this will be stressful for everyone, most of all you," I said. "But remember, I have a good reason for coming and it isn't about climbing my family tree. Imogen Pigeon thinks your parents have information that might help solve the Morris Tubbs case."

"A case that has nothing to do with you. A case that could have stayed cold forever, just like my parents," Mom said. "Why did you have to stir everything up for a stranger? You could try putting your family first for a change."

My hackles rose at this but I took a few deep breaths and imagined Jilly's pinch on my arm. I had put my family first countless times since I got home. Mom herself had been accused of murder twice and I'd made the problem go away. I didn't expect much in return except for her to dial down her theatrics now and then.

"Imogen came out of a coma to make this request," I reminded her. "She believes this situation is blocking a happy hereafter, so of course I'm going to help. Besides, it's the right thing to do. Kellan agrees, or he wouldn't have let me investigate."

"Ima had decades to do something if she cared so much. Why leave it so late?" After a beat she added, "Most of us don't get a last chance to fix our mistakes."

"True, which is a great reason to do our best today... in case that's all we have." I glanced over at her and smiled. "As you say, I'm always pushing my luck. If things stop going my way, I might be glad I met my grandparents."

"Don't get your hopes up," she said. "They cut us out of their lives. Moved so many times I lost track. Saying yes to a meeting means nothing and a last-ditch change of heart shouldn't change much in the hereafter." Her hands moved faster over Keats. "At least in my view."

"Leave some hair on my dog, Mom. As for your parents, if all I get is the information Imogen wants, that's fine with me. But I can't deny I'm curious about the people who produced you. And so late in life, too. Imogen said your mom had a lot of miscarriages."

"Five, at least. And three stillborn babies, all boys." She continued her assault on Keats' gleaming pelt. "They said I was a miracle and practically kept me prisoner through childhood. Over-protective doesn't begin to describe it. I was a vibrant girl, of course, and nearly suffocated under their watch."

"But you went to the dances at the Palais Royale, as I recall."

"After escaping from a second floor window." She couldn't help smiling at the memory. "I climbed down an oak tree in a party dress and heels and came back the same way. The third time I wasn't so lucky. Your grandfather caught your father dropping me off and fired on him with a rifle."

"Seriously?"

"Very much so. Deflated his tire." She was still smiling. "Good thing Calvin was athletic because my dad could move well for a man of his age."

I laughed. "So Dad ran?"

"Like the wind. Collected his truck the next day and there was a dent in the fender to remind him not to come back." She sighed. "Calvin wasn't easily deterred and eventually persuaded me to elope. That's when I really came to life."

"And had all the children your mother wanted," I said.

Mom nodded. "Without the devoted husband to support them, unfortunately. And when Calvin left us high and dry, as my parents had predicted, they let me know I'd made my own bed."

There was a quaver in her voice and I quickly switched conversational gears. "Mom, you did amazingly well on your own. You should be proud of raising six good kids without Calvin. And whether you like it or not, you inherited something from your parents, which is perseverance. They clearly went through a lot and you did, too."

"Close the window," she said. "The dampness is frizzing my hair."

She wasn't wrong, and the frizz added to her clownlike appearance. I flipped down her visor and said, "Why don't you use the mirror to touch up a little? I know you'll want to go in looking like a million bucks."

Checking her reflection, she gave a small scream. "Oh my goodness, what happened?"

In the flurry of wipes and reapplication that followed, I cracked the window again. Keats had his muzzle up and his ears forward as we passed the sign welcoming us to Mt. Wilshire. There was information for us here, I was sure of it.

The country store on the main drag—the only drag—was as quaint as Mandy McCain's, and I would have loved to pop in to check out the pie offerings. Asher turned right soon after, however, so I carried on.

Our convoy traveled a long gravel side road before turning onto a twisty dirt road and finally, a pair of deep ruts in a lane. Albert and Gardenia might not be fully off the grid but they sure liked their privacy.

Mom's breathing became a shallow pant and I was relieved when we rolled into the wide area in front of the house. It was an old yellow brick farmhouse like so many others in hill country, but perhaps the best maintained I'd ever seen. The roof looked freshly shingled, the painted trim was blindingly white, and the gardens were full of pastel blooms.

"Not a trace of red," Mom said, snapping up the visor. "Mom hates garish colors."

"Well, that explains your fondness for scarlet," I said. "But I don't understand why you'd carry on the family tradition of naming us all after flora."

That gave her a moment's pause. "It was a sad failure of imagination, wasn't it, darling? I was running out of options by the time you came along, so you got a creeping vine."

Following the tradition told me Mom had missed her parents more than she cared to let on. But now she slumped in her seat as I parked. We both watched Asher leap out of his truck and run up the porch stairs. My brother pumped the arm of the tall, stiff-looking old man who came out of the house wearing a denim sports jacket that probably hailed from the 70s but still fit nicely. Charging back down, Asher collected Jilly and escorted her up the stairs as if she were a princess. By now my grandmother had emerged. Her white hair was coiled in a tight bun and her simple navy blue dress almost matched Albert's denim. Jilly reached out with both hands to greet the tiny woman. Gardenia evaded Jilly's hands and gave her a curt nod.

"See?" Mom said. "That says everything you need to know."

Keats mumbled something motivational and when Mom didn't move, his tone became assertive. We both reached for the door handles at the same time.

"Let me get what I came for, Mom, and I promise to extract you as soon as I can."

"Fine," she said. "Can't be worse than that double root canal I had last year. It was dreadful, but it did increase my threshold for pain."

I laughed as I got out. "You've got your humor back and you look great."

"If the drilling goes on more than an hour I'll open the flask in my purse," she warned. "I'm not a drinker, but there's a time and place for mandarin vodka. Neat."

"Maybe Poppy left you a tranquilizer," I said. "If you pass out, I'll toss you into the back on the way home."

"Don't bother," she said, as we met in front of the truck. "If it gets that bad, just shoot me. It's the humane thing to do, Ivy."

Then she straightened her shoulders and strutted up the walk like it was a red carpet.

CHAPTER SEVENTEEN

After Asher broke the ice, Daisy lined the rest of us up according to age, like we were heading into elementary school, except Mom insisted on coming last. My big sister introduced each of us to Albert and then Gardenia, and we moved off to allow for the next. I observed carefully from the rear and there was no mistaking the deepening frown when my turn came around. Maybe my bibbed overalls or pets caused the reaction, but I couldn't help suspecting they knew more about me than I did about them. There may not be a newspaper or even wifi, but gossip would bubble up at their country store just like it did everywhere else.

"Hello there," I said, offering my best corporate smile. Their chilly demeanor didn't faze me much, and I was glad the grim reaper of HR still lurked in my shadows for occasions like this. "It's a pleasure to meet you both. This is my dog, Keats, and—"

Gardenia jumped back with a little squeal as Percy did a tight figure eight around her sensible oxfords and thick support hose.

"My cat, Percy," I finished.

"I don't like house pets," Gardenia said. Her tone was clipped and it seemed like her bun twisted just a little bit tighter on its own.

"Mom said so but I didn't believe it," I said. "We're a family of pet lovers, even if she wouldn't let us have any growing up."

"I'm not," Daisy said. "I only tolerate the ferrets because of the boys."

Gardenia turned icy blue eyes on my sister. Clearly we girls inherited our hazel eyes from Albert, although his weren't much warmer. "I've heard about your boys, Daisy. One of them has already been arrested."

"Two," Daisy said, as if compelled by a truth serum. "Not technically arrested but the police did bring in the younger twins after a graffiti incident."

"They're fine boys," Mom said, although she was usually the first to dump on Daisy's rambunctious offspring. "I'm proud of my grandchildren and I try to cut them some slack."

Gardenia stepped backward into the closed door as Mom's first shot hit home. A tendril of white hair escaped the bun and drifted on the breeze. It was very long and as fine as gossamer. The fairy tale of Rapunzel came to mind and I wondered if she wanted to be rescued from her remote turret. Keats seemed to think so, because he was prancing on the spot in front of her like a dressage horse, with his ears forward. The dog had chosen to focus on her, which told me that despite Albert's height and presence, Gardenia ruled the roost here. Nonetheless, Albert was the one to gesture to the door and invite us inside. After Gardenia went in, we once again lined up according to age, except Mom got swept into the middle this time. When she passed, Albert stepped back, as if to avoid any accidental contact.

The dining room table was set for a tea party, with a dozen china cups and saucers, a silver tea set, and a plate of lemon squares, each about the size of my thumbnail.

There weren't enough seats, so Asher and I leaned on opposite sides of the doorway while everyone else perched on old-fashioned hard-backed chairs. It looked like Mom and Gardenia had no choice but to perch as their feet barely reached the floor. My grandfather stood up and offered me his seat but I declined with a smile. I felt trapped as it was. Perhaps he did, too, because he stayed on his feet and then leaned against the wall across from me.

"Ivy, animals don't belong in the house," Gardenia said. "Can you please send them outside to your, uh, bodyguard? The one in camouflage?"

"That's my friend Edna," I said. "She's going to walk the horse and the donkey while we catch up in here."

"You came with a donkey and a horse?" Gardenia sounded incredulous.

"Just a miniature horse." Keats mumbled to let me know there was no reason to diminish either Clippers or myself. "As a hobby farmer, I do have my hands full sometimes. Keats and Percy the cat are my constant companions."

The latter jumped onto the sideboard and then took a bold leap onto the plate rail that was, regrettably, adorned with china plates. Gardenia screamed and Mom didn't hold back a grin. I called for Percy to come down but he ignored me. He was probably trying to help by deflating some of the tension in the room.

"What is it you find so amusing, Dahlia?" her mother asked. "Did you come all this way just to mock us?"

Mom raised her perfectly groomed eyebrows. "This trip wasn't my idea but I couldn't let Ivy come alone."

Gardenia's lips puckered as she poured the tea and then passed the dessert plate. My brother had his work cut out for him trying to balance a teacup and saucer in his big mitt while trying to pinch just one tiny lemon square. Finally he grabbed three, popped them into his mouth and swallowed seemingly without chewing.

"Delicious," he said, puckering himself. "Very tangy."

It was all I could do not to laugh but Gardenia's icy stare froze the sound in my throat.

"And why is it you wanted to visit after all these years, Ivy?" she asked.

"Well, for starters, we couldn't come earlier," I said. "Because we didn't know you existed. At least some of us. Right, Asher?"

"I sure didn't," he said, reaching for another lemon bar. "Otherwise I'd have been up here years ago. You're the best kept secret in hill country. I just want—"

Gardenia raised one hand as he started to babble. Then her eyes drilled into me like the dental instruments Mom had mentioned. "You didn't know we existed? How could that be? What about the gifts we sent? The fancy bicycle for Asher, the hair styling set for Iris, the little oven for Daisy, and the farm set for you? Among many others. We filled every order in your letters from Santa."

A gasp went around the overcrowded dining room but I spoke first. "You sent the farm set? I loved that! One horse came with plastic poop that dropped out of a little hatch in its stomach. Not anatomically correct, but so fun."

"That explains your obsession with manure, Ivy," Jilly said, grinning.

"It does. I know it's belated, but thank you so much, Mrs. Swingle."

"Mrs. Swingle? What kind of a way is that to address your grandmother?" Gardenia said.

"Mom said you'd prefer that. I'm trying to be respectful."

"If you were trying to be respectful, your cat wouldn't be jeopardizing my grandmother's heirlooms," Gardenia said. "One of you might like to claim them when I'm gone."

"I would." The voice came from the least likely source: my brother. "Jilly, my fiancée, is a brilliant chef and one day we might have a daughter to inherit those beauties." He flashed his trademark grin. "If Percy leaves anything in his wake."

"Percy, come down," I said. "You might be Jilly's baby now, but one day there will be another who collects china."

Gardenia stared at me again. "You're a very strange child."

Keats gave a hearty ha-ha-ha and I laughed, too. "I *was* a strange child and I suppose I'm a strange adult, uh... Grandmother Swingle. I never pressed Mom for details about you two and while some of my siblings may have known about you, they chose not to say." Daisy, Iris and Violet stared into the depths of their teacups, so I added, "This probably feels like quite an invasion today."

Fanning herself with a napkin, Gardenia nodded. "Rather, yes. When you called, Ivy, we thought you finally wanted to thank us for the money we sent to help with your education. You're the first Swingle to go to college."

I turned to my mother and found her eyes on Percy, who conveniently offered an orange focal point for everyone. Even my grandfather kept glancing up at the cat.

"I didn't know about that either," I said. "Mom said she picked up a second job to help out. Of course, I repaid her."

"Then I suppose we'll collect that back, Dahlia," Gardenia said. "It seems like you were playing fast and loose with the truth. I confess I'm a little surprised. You weren't an easy child but you were honest."

Mom's red lips opened and I could tell from the glint in her hazel eyes that the past was going to erupt with volcanic force if I didn't intervene. Keats mumbled encouragement to get to the point. Fast.

I looked down at him and nodded. "You're right, buddy. The sooner the better." Raising my eyes to Albert, I said, "Let's consider this the first of many visits. And while we got off on the wrong foot, I still need to be honest about why we came."

"Did you just speak to your dog?" Albert asked. I was pretty sure I detected bemusement in his eyes that were so much like Mom's... and mine.

I decided to own it. "Yes. I talk to Keats and Percy all the time. And many of my other animals. Some of them talk back, in their way."

"That's what you get for giving her a farm set," Mom said. "Complete with manure."

My grandfather actually laughed. "Interesting. Do go on, Ivy."

"*Don't* go on about manure," Gardenia said.

"About your reason for coming," Albert said. "When you apparently didn't know we existed."

Keats nudged my leg and I moved into the center of the doorway. "I heard about you first just a couple of days ago from Imogen Pigeon. Does that name ring a bell?"

Gardenia's eyes fell to the plate that now only held one lemon square. "Yes. Imogen delivered your mother. And other children who didn't survive."

"I was sorry to hear that had happened," I said. "But glad Imogen summoned me in time to learn about you. She's about to pass on, I'm afraid."

"She called you to her deathbed to tell you about us?" Gardenia looked confused. "That was kind of her, if somewhat odd."

"That was an aside, actually. I had never met Ima but she thought I might be able to help her solve an old murder."

"An old murder?" Albert said. "That's even odder."

"Not when you know Ivy," Mom said. "She gets embroiled in the strangest messes."

"Don't mention the manure again, Dahlia," Gardenia said. "It was plastic. And apparently she loved our gift."

"I really did, and ultimately it turned into my dream come true," I said. "But back to the murder. So, Imogen Pigeon was in a coma and came out of it determined to share a confession from one of her patients long ago. His name was Morris Tubbs, and he told her he'd killed someone and buried the body at Bluffers Ridge."

Albert straightened and buttoned his blazer, but as he said nothing, I continued.

"Morris Tubbs died before sharing the name of the victim or

why he did it. Ima and others said it was out of character for him. Morris was known as a good man."

"He was a good man," Albert said. "An honorable man. I'm surprised to hear about this." He unbuttoned the jacket again as if feeling constrained. "He was a mentor of mine in the construction trades. I worked alongside him for years creating some of the public buildings you still see today."

"Imogen said you might know why Morris would do such a thing," I said.

My grandfather shook his head. "I only know what I've said… that I worked with Morris and he seemed like an honorable man. I have no idea why he'd… he'd do something like that."

There was a brilliant flash of orange as Percy staged a dramatic descent from the plate rail onto my grandfather's shoulder. The old man didn't even jump. It seemed like he'd sunk into reflection, and Percy settled into his parrot pose, swishing his tail. The cat was used to making more of a splash.

"Percy doesn't believe you," I said. Keats piped up with an assertive grumble and I added, "Keats doesn't either."

My grandfather's eyes swam into focus and he turned to get a face full of fur, and then sneezed. "Would you mind?" he said, either to the cat or to me. "I'm ninety-seven, and my skin isn't as tough as it used to be."

"Percy, dismount," I said. "Let my grandfather tell us what he's avoiding."

The cat jumped onto the table, swished deliberately under Gardenia's chin and batted at the last lemon square. Asher reached over hastily to grab it, nearly knocking the plate off the table. Jilly steadied the plate as my brother popped the treat into his mouth, choking a bit as he swallowed. "Sorry," he said, in a raspy voice. "My bad."

"I have nothing more to say." Albert's voice was nearly as dry as

Asher's. "Imogen Pigeon sent you on a wild goose chase. I have half a mind to—"

"You won't confront a dying woman who delivered our children, Albert," Gardenia said, crisply. "But I do think we've had enough for one day. It was good of you to visit, Ivy, no matter what your motivation. As your grandfather said, however, we aren't as resilient as we used to be. I really need to lie down."

"You do that, while I see everyone out," Albert said, gesturing for us to get moving.

"Don't you want to know who Morris killed?" I asked.

"No," he said, shooing us from the dining room. "The last thing you want at my age is more bad news."

My mother refused to take the telling. "We drove for hours to—"

"Dahlia," Albert said, "you lost the right to be indignant decades ago. Probably the first time you left your bedroom window in a ball dress and heels. I still don't know how you survived climbing down that oak tree."

"And back up," Mom said, letting Daisy pull her to her feet. "Not so much as a mark on the dress. I'm an elegant dancer to this day and still like going to the Palais Royale with—"

"That's enough, Mom," I said, to keep her from introducing her parents to the concept of rotational dating. There was no need for them to know about her stable of boyfriends. "Maybe on our way out, your father could tell us—"

"I've told you everything I know." Albert lurched ahead of me out the door. "Ow! Did your dog just nip me? I am not a sheep to be bent to his will."

Keats' happy pant said otherwise.

Gardenia followed, perhaps worried her husband would indeed fall for the sheepdog's incentive.

"Just take your circus and go, Ivy," she said. "I already regret that farm set."

"Good thing you didn't give her a circus set," Mom said. "Can you imagine?"

"I wish I'd thought to ask Santa for that, too," I said. "Thanks again for helping to make me what I am today. Would you like to come outside and meet my mini horse? The poop does not fall out of his stomach, I'm afraid."

"No," Gardenia said, scanning the big yard for Edna. "We would not like to meet this horse."

My grandfather's eyes said otherwise but he dutifully shook his head.

"Don't push it, Ivy," Daisy said. "Let's give everyone some breathing room and maybe we can meet again sometime."

"Let sleeping dogs lie," Albert said. "It's for the best."

I wouldn't have let this chance go so easily, but someone else unexpectedly picked up the baton.

"Come to our engagement party," Asher said, dropping his arm over Jilly's shoulders. "I've been lucky enough to find the love of my life, like you two obviously did. Please help us celebrate. It would mean a lot."

The two seniors looked at each other and visibly softened under the influence of romance. "Well, perhaps," Gardenia said. "If we've recovered by then."

"Plenty of time," Asher said, as Jilly tugged him away. "It's not till tomorrow night," he called back. "And I wouldn't say no to some of those lemon bars. Whew! Those beauties bite back."

The kerfuffle that followed Asher's invitation gave me a chance to wander around the property looking for Edna.

"You know what, buddy?" I said to Keats. "I think those two are okay under the starch. We can probably win them over eventually."

He gave a mumble of agreement. His tail was up and I had the feeling he liked my grandfather, at least.

"He's a pet lover, I'm sure of it," I continued. "Some of those toy farm animals were hand-carved and I noticed wood wildlife sculptures around the house. He's got skills."

The dog wasn't particularly interested in this line of thinking but the way I saw it, the more I learned about my background, the better prepared I'd be for what life had to throw at me. And it tossed plenty of curveballs.

Another mumble from below sounded happier. Bring on the curveballs.

"Easy for you to say," I told him, as we found Edna marching along the fence of a large empty pasture with the horse and the donkey. Her hand gestures suggested she was teaching them army maneuvers.

Bocelli stopped suddenly and offloaded a sizable pile of manure. Edna looked over at me questioningly and I shrugged, grinning.

"We'll leave them an appropriate souvenir," I told Keats. "After all, they started it."

CHAPTER EIGHTEEN

E ach time I followed Keats and Percy up the stairs to Imogen
Pigeon's bedroom, my heart raced. Would she still be with us?
Would she pretend she wasn't and scare the life out of me instead?
Would she send me on another mission that rocked my world, like
meeting grandparents I didn't know existed?

The black tail and orange tail were jaunty today, which told me
that Imogen was not only alive but awake and ready for action.
Ready for *me* to take action, anyway.

"Are there any secrets left in hill country?" I asked Keats. "We've
been up to its peaks and down into the bowels of its bunkers. Is there
anything more to explore?"

Keats mumbled something that sounded disapproving.

"The new pond, yes. Calvin and Charlie are in discussions, but
don't worry, it'll be shallow. I lost some of my enthusiasm after what
happened on vacation."

Now Keats' commentary turned into a decided complaint, likely
about the prospect of swimming reptiles.

"There are no gators or crocs in these parts. Just a snake or two."
I shook my head. "I'm not big on those, either, but I do feel like we

owe it to waterfowl to provide safe haven. That's what we're all about at Runaway Farm."

A shot of cool blue eye told me there were limits to our hospitality. Or should be.

"Let's discuss it later," I said, as we paused at the door. "Imogen has more pressing concerns than your hydrophobia."

I knocked twice and she told us to come in. The new caregiver—a brave woman, given what had happened to Prudence—fluffed pillows and propped Imogen up before giving me a curt nod and leaving. Even with a police officer on duty 24/7, most would be nervous with a killer at large.

"I owe the recommendation to Edna Evans," Imogen said as the door closed behind the caregiver. "It's someone she knows from the gun range in Dorset Hills. Ready for anything, Edna said. Apparently that's what you need in a modern caregiver."

Her laugh was hearty but there was a rattle deep in her chest that hadn't been there two days ago. It reinforced the fact that time was short.

"I'm glad you and Edna are healing the rift," I said.

Imogen raised her eyebrows, which had been penciled on with a steady hand. "I appreciate her help, and it's been good to chat about old times. But I didn't wake from a living death to smooth over petty grievances, Ivy. Those don't amount to much on the other side, I reckon, no matter what people say. But undisclosed murder? That probably does."

I took the seat beside the bed. "I guess I think of it as one of those old-fashioned scales... where the pile of good deeds needs to outweigh the pile of bad."

She patted the bed for Percy to join her and he didn't wait to be asked twice before curling up on her lap. "It's not at all what you imagine, at least based on my visits to God's waiting room. But a big pile of good deeds can't go amiss, and you've got that."

I reached for Keats and his ears were already exactly where they needed to be to offer comfort. "There's plenty on the wrong side of the scale, too, Imogen. When I worked in HR, they called me the grim reaper because I circled the globe firing people. Uprooting families and ruining a few lives. I don't know that I can ever put enough on the good side of the scale to make up for that."

"You already have," she said, running a gaunt hand over Percy's fur. "It's not one for one. You didn't make those decisions when you worked for a company—you were a corporate stooge. Now you put killers away and save lives."

Keats filled my heart with his best energy, a constantly renewable source. "I told myself those criminals had killed in haste and were repenting at leisure. But Myrtle McCain wasn't repentant at all. She said she did us a favor in removing Lloyd Boyce from the world."

"She wasn't sorry about the impact on her granddaughter?" Imogen asked, scratching Percy under the chin, exactly as he liked it.

"Myrtle seemed annoyed that Mandy didn't see it as... well, a gift. Meanwhile, Mandy has to live with this blight on her name forever. She feels like the person who got a man killed. It's a terrible weight to carry when all she did was fall for the wrong guy."

"Something we've all done, no doubt," Imogen said. "Before my husband Carl came along I had my share of wrong guys."

The warmth Keats offered turned into sunlight in my heart. "I never did, actually. Kellan is my one and only, although there was a long hiatus."

"Where you both matured and learned to appreciate each other," she said. "There's no denying you chose well with the chief. He's a good man, although it seems like you're making more headway with your case than he is with his. Why is it taking him so long to figure out who killed Prudence? I feel like this may not have happened if I hadn't come back, and worry that it tipped the scales more to the wrong side."

"That wasn't your fault," I said. "It sounded like she had plenty of enemies of her own."

"I know she did," Imogen said. "And we all have a story. But I can't help worrying that I brought her bad luck. She was a good care-giver, even if she couldn't take down a zombie, at least according to Edna."

Keats gave a happy pant and I smiled, too. "Let's not venture too far down the apocalyptic path, Imogen. Save your strength to hear about my grandparents."

She folded her hands over her chest, already tiring from the effort of scratching Percy. "I bet they didn't cough up a single detail."

"Not about the case, although there were a few truth bombs that rattled our world. Turns out Mom kept more than a few secrets from us."

"Dahlia," Imogen said. "She was the prettiest girl I ushered into the world. Then she let out the loudest wail I'd ever heard from an infant. Felt like unnecessary drama even then. Gardenia seemed quite taken aback. I don't think she'd so much as whimpered during a very difficult labor. They're night and day, those two."

I laughed. "Sounds about right. There was so much tension in that dining room I was afraid the house would explode. The moment I asked about Morris, Albert shut up even tighter. I didn't even get the chance to tell him about Earl Spratt before he tossed us out. But he knew something. Keats and Percy told me so."

"You'll try again?" Imogen asked. "I don't need to tell you the clock is ticking."

"Yes, tomorrow, thanks to my brother," I said. "He invited our grandparents to the engagement party. I half-expected them to cancel but they're driving down and staying at the inn. What I forfeit in comfort I'll gain in access. If I can get Albert alone, I think we can pry something out of him."

"They're inseparable," Imogen said. "Married for love in a time that was uncommon, yet disapproved of your mom for doing the same."

I sighed. "True, but at the time my dad's roots in hill country crime ran deep. I'm not sure how much to believe of her story of parental abandonment, though."

"More wailing and railing at the world," Imogen said. "I wasn't sure you'd get much out of Albert, but a girl should know her grand-parents, for better or worse." Keats added a mumble of endorsement and she added, "In my view, there's more on the good side of their scale, Ivy. Glad you're keeping an open mind."

"My mind doesn't close properly anymore," I said. "After I got thumped in the head rescuing Keats, there's so much gray area."

"Nursing did that too," she said. "Seeing people sick and in pain, I realized how much we're all alike at the core. Things could go either way and it takes a conscious decision every single day for some folks to stay on the right path. Maybe especially in hill country. An unfortunate collision of nature and nurture."

She closed her eyes for a moment, and I said, "We should go. You're tired."

Lifting her lids with what seemed like an effort, she muttered, "Tired of living, to be honest. I'm ready to depart for good, Ivy, so you and your brilliant pets had better push the pedal down."

Percy took his cue and slipped off the bed to follow Keats to the door. When I pulled on the knob, I found the caregiver standing just outside the door. She had very likely been eavesdropping because she bustled away with a guilty expression. I mentally ran over the discussion to see if we'd revealed anything important.

Looking back at Imogen, I found her with one eyebrow raised. "Let her feed the rumor mill. It's always hungry."

"But are you safe with someone who'd shamelessly eavesdrop?" I asked.

"Safe enough. What's she going to do? Kill a dying woman?"

"Maybe. It's your choice when you go and you've decided to wait till this mystery is solved."

"It's my hope but not my decision," she said. "So get a move on before the decision is made for me."

––––––––

KELLAN WAS WAITING for me at the farm when I got home, leaning against the police SUV and looking about as tired as I felt. Jumping out of the truck, I walked straight over and into his arms. It was a good few minutes before I had the energy to move or speak, and I might have dropped right off if Kellan hadn't jumped and startled me. Keats and Percy had apparently sided with Imogen in wanting to lash us on to the finish line. The dog was working his sheepdog magic on Kellan's uniform cuff and the cat was raking claws through Kellan's perfect hair from the roof of the SUV.

"Can't a guy get a single moment with his gal without being mugged?" he asked.

I grinned up at him and shook my head. "Imogen just impressed upon them how short life can be and urged us to keep digging on our cases." I tried to snuggle up to him again but the moment had passed. "There's so much dirt in the dirt of this region. Did you know that before you came back?"

Kellan nodded, leaving one arm over my shoulders as he turned me around and walked us to my truck. "I did my research and thought long and hard about taking the job. The pile of cold cases was staggering in Clover Grove, let alone the region, and plenty more are missing."

He hopped again as we circled the truck. If he were a cursing man, he'd have dropped a blue word at Keats. Instead he clenched his free hand into a fist and shook it. Keats just laugh-panted. He lived for this stuff.

"Where are we going?" I asked. "I just got home."

"It's going to be a lovely sunset and we deserve to smell the roses."

"Sold," I said. "I was planning on smelling manure, but my idea stinks."

He helped me into the passenger seat and then walked around the back of the truck to the driver's side. If he chose the longer route to avoid my seeing his hopping, the move failed. Worse, his man squeal reached me through the closed doors and windows. Keats had a strange way of showing how happy he was to see Kellan, but I knew those nips came from a good place. And every hop made me love Kellan more for putting up with us.

"Can you tell him to stop?" Kellan asked, as he got behind the wheel. "The chief of police deserves some dignity, especially when he's driving in the community."

"Agreed. Keats, leave the chief and our boyfriend alone. That's not a request, it's an order."

The dog offered a string of cheeky mumble-talk that made us both laugh, and Percy added a drawling meow for good measure.

"It really is good to have you home," Kellan said, squeezing my knee and sending a shower of fireflies straight to my heart. "All of you. I never had a moment's peace while you were gone."

I rested my hand on his. "You have peace now? With all that's going on?"

He laughed. "Not exactly, but at least I can see you and hug you."

"I missed you, too," I said. "Being down south without you was unnerving, especially given all the odd quirks of the situation. Chief Gillock seemed like a decent cop, though, and I think he'll help Janelle get the Briars back on track."

"Good, because I can't deal with long-distance crime when there's enough at home." He sighed as he pulled out of the farm's lane and geared up smoothly. I was always impressed and somewhat chagrined by how easily he handled my truck when it still threw hissy fits on me quite often.

"Have you made any inroads with Prudence's case?" I asked. "What did the autopsy report say?"

"There was no sign of her being struck, so we have to assume she was pushed," he said. "And pushed hard, judging by the extent of her injuries. There were some marks on her arms consistent with fingertips but nothing more." Glancing over at me, he said, "We still can't entirely rule out Imogen. People in an altered state can show great strength."

I knew that, because I had seen it and felt it firsthand. But my head was shaking even before I formed the words. "Maybe she was capable of the push, but not of setting up the signs of the getaway out back. Anyway, I know she didn't do it. Keats wouldn't let me sit beside Ima's bed day after day if she were a killer. You know he senses that."

"I believe that, yes," he said, as the truck picked up speed. Normally he stuck to the speed limit to set an example but tonight he gunned it. "I'm just frustrated. This case shouldn't be so hard."

"What about her supposed enemies?" I asked. "The deadbeat ex and drug addict son?"

"Alibis," he said. "Neighbors, too. She did raise some feathers as an animal rights activist back in Chicago and I wondered if that spilled over here. The older generation in this farming community doesn't take kindly to the notion of treating livestock like children."

"She was in a radical group? That sounds promising."

"It seems like she came home to escape all that. Although she rubbed some people the wrong way, I haven't found anyone truly motivated to want her gone. Many found her a gentle, reliable caregiver."

"Are you sure these two cases aren't linked in some way?" I said. "Is it possible the real target that day was Imogen? Or both?"

"It occurred to me, yes. What if Prudence overheard Imogen talking about the case with someone else? Like Teri?"

"Ima said she only told Teri one day when the house was empty. She's still ashamed for not revealing all this sooner." I rolled down the window and sucked in a deep breath. "But Morris Tubbs' case is so old. Who would really care now? His family is long gone from the area, and Earl Spratt was the last of his line."

Kellan glanced over at me and frowned. "She was so set on having you and your crime-fighting squad deal with this. Even before Prudence's death. Why?"

"I don't think Ima trusts many people and I guess Teri spoke highly of me. Or the crime-solving dog may have intrigued her. She's so curious about life even now."

"With every case, I worry it's not just an old crime but a new-again crime," he said. "That's how things go around here. In the rest of the country, most cold cases stay cold until DNA advances close them long after the killer has died and escaped punishment. But in Clover Grove, they bubble up like geysers."

"Well, we know Morris has long since passed, so there's no hope of punishing him anyway," I said. "I can't imagine how it would link to current times."

Keat gave a short, teasing mumble that sounded like, "Yet."

The hand on my knee was distracting enough that it took me a good while to notice we'd passed the turnoff to Clover Grove Gardens. By that time, Kellan was already signaling to turn down a side road and then into a lane I'd never seen before. The opening was nearly grown over with vibrant vines.

"Is this a back way into the gardens?" I asked.

"No, although there's a back way into anything around here. It's the house where Prudence grew up. I just wanted to take a look around. See if it prompted any ideas."

"Who owns it now?" I said. "It's a wreck."

"The family left town. This place has changed hands many

times. Most properties sell like hotcakes to homesteaders. I've never understood why a few don't stick."

"Like the Galloway homestead that couldn't stay sold?" I said. "Must be old ghosts." I thought about how that might sound and added, "Not real ghosts. Just bad vibes."

"In the case of the Galloway property, people likely worried your dad would come back one day, which is exactly what happened. That's the specter that scared everyone off."

"Maybe he'll buy it back and renovate it," I said. The treasure we'd uncovered on the property would be caught up in red tape for some time, I figured, and I didn't like to ask questions. Calvin and I were on the way to healing our old wounds but that wasn't an overnight thing. Not for me, anyway. Asher and Violet had put the past behind them quite quickly, and were spending a lot of time with Calvin. The golden boy had lost some luster in Mom's eyes and been further tarnished now by his rash invitation to Gardenia and Albert.

The engagement party was going to be tense. Mom really wanted to work the mother of the groom angle but now she had to contend not only with her ex being there but her estranged parents. When we got home from Mt. Wilshire, she withdrew to her room—make that the best suite in the inn—to recalibrate. I heard the incessant whir of the sewing machine whenever I passed. The right outfit was no longer a pleasure but a necessity and I wondered if she would fan the flames by bringing a date. Charlie would be the safe choice from her rotation, since he was invited to the party anyway, but he was drifting down her list after spending too much time with Calvin. The two old cowhands spent much of the day working in silence together as if they'd always known each other. At any rate, it was probably awkward for Charlie to squire Mom about too much now.

After a long pause, Kellan said, "I think Calvin's reluctant to make that sort of commitment too soon. You're not the only one scrutinizing him."

"You too?" I asked, sitting up straighter. "Why? Don't tell me he's still tied to the hill country crime syndicate?"

"No, I'm quite sure he's put them well behind him. The question is whether they've put him behind them."

I stared at him in surprise. That thought hadn't really occurred to me and I didn't like it. "Are you worried?" I asked.

Kellan shook his head as he turned the truck into what used to be a parking area but was now pretty much a meadow. "Not really, but it's crossed Calvin's mind that some old threats might surface. He certainly doesn't want to put any of you in danger. He's ready to exit suddenly if necessary."

He turned off the engine and winced as Keats and Percy jumped into his lap in the never-ending competition to be first out of the truck. They achieved a tie and trotted through the grass and up the rotting front stairs side by side.

"I hope Calvin can stay for the wedding, at least," I said. "Family is so important to Asher. I really had no idea how much until lately. Poor Jilly just wants a quiet, tasteful celebration and that's nearly impossible now."

Kellan laughed as he got out. "Jilly knew what she was getting into." We met at the front of the truck and he slung his arm around me and kissed my forehead. "As do I."

"Thank you for that," I said, as the fireflies he always awoke buzzed from my forehead down through my limbs. "The engagement party will be torture. Mom is beside herself and her parents are, well… forbidding is a good word." He led me around the house and I added, "If they confront Calvin it won't go well. But Calvin can't skip the party or Asher will be devastated. And Mom, well…"

"Seeing red, of course," Kellan said, and we both laughed. "Honestly, I shouldn't be taking time off work right now but I can't miss this event."

"Wear your uniform," I said. "We need a cop on duty."

He laughed but his attention was already shifting. After

watching Keats and Percy explore the place, he called, "Come on back, boys. This is a bust."

"How can you know that? We've only been here five minutes."

He gestured to the pets. "I won't admit this anywhere else, but I trust their intuition. Look at them."

The cat began openly baiting the dog with flutters of his fluffy tail and they took off around the corner of the house. There couldn't be any clues around here. Where there was play, there was no work for my sheepdog.

"You're right," I said. "But it was worth a look. And you never know where a hunch will lead."

When the furred frivolity stopped, we all got in the truck and headed back out to the road.

Kellan slowed a couple of times and then adjusted the rearview and side mirrors. Meanwhile, Keats sat up on my knee and stared over my shoulder between the seats. He was still panting hard from the horseplay.

Too hard? Was there more to it?

Just before we turned onto the highway, Kellan said, "Hold on tight, everyone. We're being tailed."

CHAPTER NINETEEN

"Tailed! Who'd have the audacity to tail the chief of police?" I asked.

"Someone who doesn't know I'm behind the wheel of your truck," he said. "People like to tail you. It's become the most popular sport in Clover Grove."

"And far beyond," I said. "Never was I tailed more than during my vacation." I craned over my shoulder to see what Kellan saw but there wasn't a vehicle in sight. "That said, I did a bit of tailing, too. What goes around comes around."

"Well, we're going to go around and then come around. Maybe they think we don't know our way through the trail system, but few boys of my generation came of age in this region without learning that map inside and out. In my case, even before I had a license."

I stared at him. "Really?"

"Don't sound so shocked. I broke a few laws before I got trained to enforce them, Ivy."

"But you didn't have a car in high school. You rode your bike everywhere."

"I borrowed my dad's Oldsmobile sometimes. That car had great clearance, which few did in those days."

He turned my truck quickly and plunged into one of the many secret access points to the trail system. Secret to me, at least.

"And you never got caught?"

After a couple of quick pivots that I could never have pulled off, he gave me a grim smile. "My dad was usually drunk and passed out by eight, so getting away wasn't hard. The challenge was making sure the Olds was exactly as he left it when he came out sober in the morning. Clean, but not too clean. Asher and I spent a lot of time and effort making sure that car sparkled and then applied just the right amount of dust afterward."

"Asher! You and my brother went joyriding underage?"

"Along with a few others. Asher's handling was superb, and his eye for detailing impeccable. I knew he'd make a good cop, which is why I strongly recommended him to the local chief when your brother was finally ready to believe in himself." Kellan picked up speed on the straightaway, bumping over such rocky terrain that both pets retreated to the rear footwell. "Asher was wasted as a personal trainer, although his brawn comes in handy on occasion."

"That's all very... surprising," I said, trying to focus on everything at once. I'd been on car chases back here before. Once Edna was at the wheel, and she was probably as skilled a driver as Kellan, although I'd never say so. I gave her equal credit because she was piloting this truck in a terrible blizzard on Christmas Eve. The other chase was even more notable because Mom was driving—the person voted by the police department as most likely to kill a road sign. She had done just that at the end of our wild drive.

Neither woman currently had a license, or my full confidence, but with Kellan driving, I could almost relax. The most worrisome part was that the light was going and dusk was a tricky time for a perilous adventure. I trusted that he not only knew the way around the trails but also the way around my truck. What's more, if things didn't end in our favor, he was armed and legally so. For once, I was in good hands back here.

Kellan was so calm and composed that I figured he could continue to take questions.

"What did you guys do back here?" I asked. "Just tool around all night?"

He shot me a quick glance. "Do you really want to know?"

"Uh... if you were giving girls thrill rides, then no."

"You and I weren't dating yet, remember. I couldn't, until Asher gave me permission."

"You really asked his permission?" I'd always taken pride in the fact that Kellan and I had managed to creep into a relationship under Asher's very nose.

"Do you really want to know?" he repeated, and this time I saw a glint of teeth.

"Yeah, I think I do."

"Well, if you insist on hearing the story... I have a few minutes to chat while I elude these goons." He crested a hill, ran the truck along the ridge and then rolled down the other side and into a creek. "So, I must have asked your brother a dozen times if I could date you and he kept saying no. We were best pals, and it was a direct violation of the friend code."

"But you finally wore him down? Or what, got him drunk?"

Kellan charged through a swampy area, sending up a spray of water on either side of the truck. I could see why car detailing was a big part of their teenage larks.

"Neither," he said, clearing the windshield. "I raced him for you."

"You *raced* Asher? We didn't even have a car."

"That's what took so long," he said, maneuvering through thickets of trees, constantly checking the mirrors. "We had to liberate one."

"You stole a car?" The story got better at every turn.

"Borrowed. Just for a few hours. Gave it a great wash, of course.

We hid in the bushes the next morning, laughing our butts off when the owner came out and circled it like a brand new car."

"And this car belonged to whom exactly?"

"Rod Preacher," he said, without missing a beat.

"Mr. Preacher? Our high school principal?" My voice was a shrill squeak. "You stole the principal's car to drag race… over *me*?"

"His car was the only option," he said. "The cars had to be equal, you see. It took us ages to find another Oldsmobile of the same caliber and then figure out how to pull things off. During those months, I wasn't even allowed to look at you, although of course I did. Asher had spies everywhere, but I still managed."

My face flushed. "That is insane."

"Maybe. But it was also the best summer of my life. We had a mission that took our complete focus. Choosing the course. Finding the right car. Developing the plan and liberating said car on a night when the conditions were optimal. Completing the race and cleaning and returning both cars by sunrise, without being caught. We pulled it off together. And I won." His smile was wide and bright at the memory. "I won the girl fair and square. Or at least my chance to go to bat. You made the final decision, of course." After a pause, he added, "In full disclosure, I wasn't the only contender."

That shocked me even more. "You stole the principal's car again? And you call *me* reckless!"

"How do you think I know reckless when I see it? We have more in common than you know."

"Who else ran these drag races for my hand, as it were?"

"That I will *never* tell you. Two of those guys are still in Clover Grove and one challenged me to a rematch after you came home. Don't underestimate your charms, Miss Galloway."

My face had pretty much exploded into flames by that point. Keats gave a mumble of reproof from the back seat. I had a feeling it wasn't the first one because he sounded annoyed. "Okay, Keats," I said. "I'll focus on Kellan's moves and try to learn something."

Kellan simmered down, too, weaving in and out of tall pines that seemed too evenly spaced to be pure coincidence. It was like Keats working an agility course, back when he indulged me in activities like that. Now he wanted to work for a purpose, rather than sport.

"Did you plant these trees, Kellan?" I asked.

"Ah, see? What a great investigative mind you have. A bunch of us did exactly that one summer. There's sort of an unspoken rule in the area that trail users need to give back. To not only maintain but also enhance. That row of pines was one of our contributions."

"Pretty cool. I'll have to do something like that myself, because these trails have had my back a few times."

"If I weren't the chief, and there was no such thing as cell phones and social media, I'd help you," he said. "But the fun is just about over for tonight. I've got our pursuers exactly where I want them."

"Who do you think it is?" I asked. "What are they driving?"

"A white van," he said. "Souped up, unless I'm much mistaken. Whoever it is, I'm hauling them in on principle."

"You could have evaded or trapped them ages ago," I said. "You enjoyed this."

"Not at all," he said with a smirk. "That would be irresponsible."

"This could be an armed murderer," I reminded him. "The same person who killed Prudence."

"It isn't, though," he said.

"You know that *how*?"

"The same way I knew there was nothing going on at the Hoggins homestead."

"My pets?" I turned and saw Keats with his paws up on the back seat. The white tuft of his tail was high, even as he struggled to keep his balance.

"You'd have noticed that yourself if you hadn't gotten so caught up in your own love story." He gave a full-on laugh now. "Keats showed me some time back that he knows and maybe even likes our pursuer. That's when he got up on the seat and started enjoying the ride."

"Is it Asher? Playing some sort of bachelor party game?"

"Not Asher," he said. "I'd fire him for a prank during an investigation and he knows it."

Finally, Kellan drove the truck into a small clearing, turned on a dime and raced back at the white van in what felt like a death-defying game of chicken. For the first time, terror rose in my throat and I screamed.

Both drivers had complete control of their vehicles, however. They braked sharply, pulled a short skid and then stopped, mere yards apart.

"Stay here," Kellan said, flinging open his door. "Keats has been known to like people who are hazards to the public."

"Who is it?" I said, still craning to see in the dazzling collision of headlights.

Ignoring me, he shouted, "Raise your hands and step in front of that van immediately."

With one hand, he reached for his gun, and with the other, the switch for the high beams.

"Dagnabit," the shout rang out. "There's no need to blind an old woman, Chief."

CHAPTER TWENTY

I jumped out of the truck with Keats and Percy. "Edna, are you crazy?"

"You have to ask?" Kellan said, without taking his eyes off my neighbor, whose usual fatigues were topped by a pith helmet. "Mrs. Rhodes, get out of the van. And turn off that camera."

I wished he'd told them to turn out their lights because the glare was indeed blinding.

Keats frolicked over to my friends, tail fanning. What had begun as a boring trip to the gardens had turned into a thrilling adventure and he was well pleased.

I followed, shaking my head. "You've done plenty of risky things before, Edna, but tailing the chief of police and forcing him into a car chase might be the worst."

"Nobody forced anybody," she said. "The chief was in the lead the whole time in case you didn't notice." She muttered another "dagnabit" under her breath. "I didn't get anywhere close, and it wasn't for lack of trying."

"You did a terrific job," Gertie said, joining us. Her pith helmet was a bit lopsided, probably due to the volume of hair. "I almost lost my dinner a few times and my stomach is normally sound."

"I might have lost mine, too, if I'd had time to eat before this escapade," I said. "Would you two care to explain before Kellan has to ask? It might mitigate his ire."

"Ire?" Edna hooted with laughter. "He's fighting a grin. That was the most fun he's had since he stole Rodney Preacher's car twenty years ago."

"He stole the principal's car?" Gertie asked. "Why, Chief, you've got even more guts than I gave you credit for. I always admired you, but I didn't realize you'd bend the laws like that."

Kellan walked over and held out his hand, palm up. "Give me the phone, Mrs. Rhodes. I know you're still recording this."

"I will not." Gertie backed away. "I promised Edna."

Both women crossed their arms and I crossed mine, too. They'd put my boyfriend in a compromising position by filming, and it was more than a prank now.

"Let's start from the beginning," I said. "Did you know Kellan was driving? Please say you thought it was me behind the wheel."

"Don't be silly," Edna said. "I'd never put you in danger like that, Ivy. You can't handle the truck or these trails. You should take me up on my offer. You'll need to know this eventually."

"So that means you've been following us since we left the farm," I said.

"Thereabouts. Actually, we followed the chief from the station," she said.

I closed my eyes for a second. "You're not helping your own case. Why don't you just spill the story?"

She cackled again. "And miss your interrogation? Not a chance. This is the fun part."

Kellan stepped closer to me and cleared his throat. "It won't be fun when—"

I caught his arm. "Would you let me handle this, Chief? Please? Gertie and Edna are normally my allies and I owe them a lot. I'm sure they'll give you enough rope to hang them."

"Fine," he said. "This had better be good."

"All right," I said. "Going back to the beginning, Edna. You decided to follow the chief to Runaway Farm, despite all we have going on. There are two murders to solve and you have time to play games?"

She gave me a smirk. "There are two murders to solve and you have time to go on a date?"

"The chief and I were investigating the Hoggins homestead, as you apparently know, having tailed us."

"That was just a pit stop on your way to canoodle in Clover Grove Gardens, where you've been canoodling since high school. More recently the canoodling happens at the strangest hours."

A gasp escaped me. "You follow us all the time?"

"Not all the time. I'm a busy woman, Ivy," she said. "I do routine surveillance with the worthy goal of keeping you alive. It's difficult to predict what you might get up to and when."

"She's not wrong about that," Kellan muttered.

"Ivy follows the whims of the animals, Chief," Edna said, gesturing to Keats and Percy, who were playing tag around the two vehicles. "These two have her chasing her tail, and theirs."

"I'm aware of Ivy's peccadilloes," he said. "It's yours I'm concerned about this evening. There appears to be no rhyme or reason for your reckless pursuit of the chief of police."

"It only became a pursuit when you ran," Edna said. "You could have turned as soon as you saw us."

"I make the best decision I can in a given situation," he said. "I liked my chances better on the trails. I didn't anticipate your knowing them as well as I do."

"Better, no doubt," she said, "although you boys spent plenty of time out here in your dad's car, learning the ropes. I used to watch you from one of the hills."

Gertie piped up again. "You actually stole the principal's car. For a race?"

"He did," Edna said. "Rodney told me himself on a school vaccination day. He asked me to give you a booster you really noticed."

Kellan shifted uncomfortably. "Mr. Preacher never said a word to me about this."

"Rod's a good man," she said, "and no stranger to these trails himself. He figured you and Officer Smiley needed to blow off some steam. Things weren't easy at home for either of you."

"Edna, that's none of your business," I said.

"Rod brought it up," she said. "But he learned his lesson and stopped leaving the key on the wheel after the second time."

Kellan opened his mouth but I grabbed his arm. "Confirm nothing. Edna probably has her phone on too."

She grinned and shook her head. "I got what I needed."

"You'd better not be planning to blackmail the chief, Edna," I said. "Because I won't stand for that."

"Not at all," she said. "No one will know from the footage that Chief McSnobalot was at the wheel. I'll blur out your plates in editing, Ivy."

"Give me the phones," Kellan said. "You cannot post this footage in any capacity, Miss Evans. It will encourage boys to come back here and eventually a race won't end so well."

"Plenty of them ended badly," Edna admitted, "although no one's died yet. This is a Clover Grove rite of passage for a certain kind of youth. I was one of them. Ivy was not. She showed every sign of being a dud, but she was just a late bloomer."

"A very late bloomer," Gertie said.

I ignored the red herring and got to the point. "I assume car chases are part of the curriculum in your survival course and you wanted some how-to footage."

"Exactly," she said. "Gertie and I are demonstrating how to cope after the end of times. It's noble work."

Kellan's expression was incredulous. "Don't encourage people to take chances like this. Not even likeminded seniors."

"You can't stop me from educating people about what's coming, Chief." Edna lifted her chin defiantly. "That's beyond your purview."

"Protecting people in this region is squarely within my purview and I can't have you supporting stunts like this."

"The type of stunt your girlfriend pulls all the time," Edna said. "Is there one rule for her and another for helpless seniors?"

"Don't fall for that, Kellan," I said. "As for you, Edna, you get the chance to break plenty of rules with me to solve crimes in present times. Training others to prepare for the zombie apocalypse is different and you know it. Some of the people you're recruiting won't be capable of making good decisions."

"I have a very strict admissions process," she said. "Few are welcome in my army."

Kellan rubbed his forehead, muttering, "Her army... What next?"

"Seminars, that's what," Edna said. "Live drills. Online work can only take you so far. People are willing to pay good money for this, Chief, but I only want to cover my costs. With the state of the world today, people are scared. They're looking for ways to feel empowered."

"No one trusts cops anymore," Gertie added.

I glared at her. "That's a terrible thing to say after the way Kellan's supported and protected you."

She gave her braid a saucy flip. "Clover Grove cops are an exception to the rule, thanks to him. Even so, everyone needs to be able to fend for themselves."

"That's even before the end of times," Edna said. "After that, lawlessness reigns."

I sighed. "We're not there yet. Despite all I've faced—that we've faced together—I still believe most people are good. If the apocalypse ever comes, there will be a big crowd of smart people behind us." I signaled to Keats to bring my friends closer. "And that's when you should hold your seminars. Not now. Not online. It's too hard to control the fallout."

"You can't stop me," Edna repeated, jumping as Keats delivered a different message through her camo pant leg.

"I can," Kellan said. "Try me."

"You've already seized my driver's license," she said, trying to swerve out of Keats' way and failing. "What more do you have?"

Kellan crossed his arms. "Oh, let me see. I could get a warrant to search your home."

"Do your worst. It's clean," she said.

"Okay, then," he said. "How about I empty out your bunker and fill it with concrete?"

Edna flinched. "Only if you can find it."

"I've already mapped it *and* your fallbacks, Miss Evans," he said. "Just because I ignore some of your antics doesn't mean I don't keep track. You're not the only one who values routine surveillance."

The light was too bright to see if Edna paled, but her mouth worked and then pressed into a grim line as Keats brought both women in the rest of the way.

"Edna will find another way to fulfill her noble cause," Gertie said.

"Then she'll have to do it without internet access," Kellan said. "Because I'll cut that off. And use some newfangled spyware to monitor every breath she takes."

"My spyware's better," Edna said, buckling her pith helmet a little tighter. "Off market."

"Phones," Kellan said. "Hand them over. You can have them back when I've done my due diligence."

They exchanged glances and stalled long enough to get toothy pressure from below.

"I'm sorry," I said. "I know you meant well."

"You don't think this is over, do you, Ivy?" Edna said. "We've got another card to play."

"Oh yeah?" Kellan asked. "Now's the time, ladies."

"Maybe you'll be a little more lenient when you hear what you missed back at the Hoggins homestead," Gertie said.

Their grins returned and it made me nervous. "He didn't miss anything. Keats and Percy said the site was clear."

"Then I guess Keats was asleep at the wheel," Edna said. The white tuft on the dog's tail drifted down and he mumbled a sharp retort. "Look, dog, you took the chief's side and that means we're done. For now, anyway."

Keats crouched to take another lunge at her calf and I called him off. "Don't, buddy. We need to know what she has to say."

Both women straightened and in the harsh clash of headlights, they looked like another kind of apocalyptic hero. The undead kind.

"If I have your word you'll forget about my bunker, I'll point out a photo on Gertie's phone you'll want to examine more closely," Edna said. "It may help your case."

"Depends on the value of the intel," Kellan said. "I give you my word that if it moves my case along, I'll pretend your bunker vanished." He glanced at me. "Mainly because you keep Ivy safe. I can solve this case without your help, though."

"Probably," Gertie said, as her helmet slid over her eyes. "But you can solve it faster *with* our help and perhaps save someone else from Prudence's fate."

He sighed, knowing he'd lost the battle. "Tell me."

"Over to you, my friend," Gertie said. "We wouldn't have been there if not for you."

Edna waggled her phone tauntingly. "So while you two were romping around the Hoggins homestead blinded by love, someone was coming in off the trails. They caught sight of your truck and lurked in the bushes until you were gone."

Keats' tail drifted further until it tucked right under him. It seemed that he blamed himself for missing it.

"It's not your fault, buddy," I said. "We called you off duty early, and I'm sure it was nothing."

"Did you get a plate?" Kellan asked.

Edna found her cackle again. "Did we get a plate? What do you take us for, Chief?"

"We got a plate and a face," Gertie said, shoving her helmet back up. "Can we keep our phones now?"

"That's not enough anymore," Edna said. "I want my license back."

Kellan snorted. "Ain't gonna happen, Miss Evans, no matter how good a driver you are."

"If this evidence exposes the murderer, then I formally challenge you to a proper back country race, Chief," she said. "I'm sure you've impounded some good vehicles. Or we could see what Rod Preacher drives these days."

Kellan shook his head. "What I will do for you is delete only the footage you took tonight and send myself the evidence you've got. Offer the phones freely, ladies, or I'll toss you in the bed of the pickup and take you in for all to see."

"You wouldn't," I said. "That's totally unsafe."

"I'll cuff them and go real slow," he said. "Just inch along Main Street to the station."

The idea of being exposed like that finally broke the warriors down and they surrendered their phones.

"I really can't forgive you," I said, glaring at them.

"For what? Embarrassing your boyfriend?" Edna said.

"He won the race over a very seasoned driver," Gertie said. "Edna, you should have let me drive like I asked. I know my van's nuances better than you."

"Get a helmet that fits over that braid and we'll talk," Edna said.

"Kellan came out of this looking great," I said. "But you hurt my dog's feelings, and that's totally unacceptable." Keats was slinking around the side of the truck with his tail still tucked. "Look at him. He's crushed."

"That'll teach him to nip me," Edna said, although I could hear a hint of regret in her voice.

"After all that dog's done for you," I said. "You may not have survived the attacks on your life without him."

"If this turns out to be a bum lead I'll apologize," she said. "You know that doesn't come easily."

"And if you've ruined his confidence, you'll do more than that," I said, turning to follow him. "Because that dog keeps me on the right side of the grass every day."

"I can see where your allegiance lies," she called after me.

"There was never any question," I said, climbing into the passenger seat and hugging my dog hard. The fact that he collapsed into my chest showed his spirit was gone.

"Now you've done it, ladies," Kellan said. "You're on the wrong side of this particular apocalypse."

CHAPTER TWENTY-ONE

"Keats, I'm quite sure that clue will turn out to be a dead end," I said, as we drove down to Wyattville the next day. It was the only town in hill country with the right terrain for an airstrip. Smaller planes flew in and out of some of the bigger communities, including Dorset Hills, but the landing conditions were so tricky that it cost a bomb. Those with deep pockets hired a helicopter, but that was rare, too. With Dog Town's popularity, however, it would become more common, and our quiet part of the world would crack right open. While part of me resisted that idea, shedding more light into hill country crevices might reduce crime.

Keats mumbled his disagreement, but his voice was less assertive than usual. He was still quite down over Edna's mockery the previous night, and that wouldn't change until Kellan confirmed who had been at the Hoggins place after us... and why.

"I guess you're right about the crime situation," I said. "It's baked in too deep. Some day, when we have more time, I'd like to interview those amateur historians Myrtle mentioned. I bet they're not young anymore and it would be a shame to lose that information. Especially if they're afraid to share it with the police for fear of repercussions."

The dog turned from the passenger seat with a blue-eyed

endorsement of the idea, but it was half-hearted at best. His paws weren't on the dash, which showed the state of his spirits. Percy, on the other hand, roamed the cab with his tail high.

"Look at Percy, buddy," I said. "He's good at picking up trouble, too, isn't he? And yet he didn't issue a red alert last night. My instincts are good and Kellan's even better. None of us saw this coming. So please cut yourself some slack."

Keats moaned, letting me know that his standards were higher for himself than the rest of us. There was no slack allowed in Keats' world.

"Here's the thing," I continued. "If you let yourself fall into a funk, you could end up missing something very important. The next couple of days are critical. You must sense that."

Percy lashed his tail, but Keats collapsed into a heap. If he refused to be cheered up, it was time for tough love—just as he had given me countless times.

"Look, I get it. You're a perfectionist and I respect that. But I will not let you lie around feeling sorry for yourself today. If you missed something crucial—and I highly doubt you did—then you need to roll on, like I do when I hit a dead end. It's part of this crime-solving game we play. When I get discouraged I dig deep and bounce back and you're always there for me. You had better believe I'm there for you, too."

He rested his muzzle on his paws, the image of dejection.

"Fine, I'm calling Kellan again in case he's found something to heal your pain. The engagement party tonight is going to take all our reserves, especially with my grandparents coming. I'm quite sure Albert knows something of value and you boys are going to help me pick it out of him."

Keats tucked his nose under the tuft of his tail and opted out completely.

Shaking my head, I hit Kellan's number and his voice came over the speaker. "Where are you?"

"On the way down to collect our surprise guest," I said. "Happily it got me out of decorating and food prep. Not to mention away from Mom."

He laughed. "Good call. I won't be able to stay long tonight, unfortunately. That photo of Gertie's opened a new line of investigation."

The white tuft moved enough for Keats to target me with a baleful expression.

"Who was it?" I asked.

"Hawk Bustard," he said. "I believe you've met."

"Hawk? Yeah, at the Sutcliffe Academy. Why on earth would he be at the Hoggins place?"

"That's what I'm going to find out. My preliminary chat with Prudence's agency shows his deceased father was a client last year. By all accounts, the family was satisfied with her service, but perhaps he harbored some resentment over her care."

"Or maybe Prudence stole something, like a family heirloom, and he thought she hid it there."

I glanced at Keats again and got nothing. The blue eye had disappeared under the tail once more.

"It would have to be a big grudge for him to attack Prudence in the home of another patient in broad daylight," Kellan said.

"Maybe it wasn't an attack but a confrontation, and she fell," I said. "Maybe the fingerprints were from Hawk trying to catch her."

"What does Keats think?" he asked.

It meant a lot to me that Kellan was consulting with my dog openly now, especially with said dog being in the pit of despair.

"Keats is on strike," I said, earning another baleful look. "He took what Edna said very much to heart."

"Keats, buddy," Kellan said. "I want you to listen to me."

Black ears came forward just a little. "You have his grudging attention."

"Bear with me," he said. "It's not my first pep talk to one of my esteemed officers, but it is my first to a dog."

The white tuft shifted and nostrils flared. "Keep going. You're speaking his language."

"So I wouldn't admit this to just anyone," Kellan said, "but I make mistakes all the time. Last night, for example, I didn't realize we were being tailed soon enough. I didn't recognize Gertie's van, although I've seen it countless times. It didn't even occur to me I was being played. And why? Because I was distracted by your winsome owner. I let myself go half off-duty for an hour. I'm human."

Keats offered a mumble at that.

"He's saying he's not human," I said. "Border collies are supposedly infallible."

"You're human enough for this truth to apply," Kellan said. "I wanted you to look around for me and you did. And when you were done, I told you to stand down and enjoy yourself. You deferred to your senior officer and if anyone's to blame it's me."

The muzzle lifted off the seat and Keats offered a sassy rejoinder along the lines of, "I don't report to you."

"Kellan, do you feel bad over what happened?" I prompted. "Or are you cutting yourself some slack?"

There was a long pause before he answered. "I feel embarrassed over getting played by Edna and Gertie, yeah. If that hadn't happened, Keats would have sensed something was amiss. I recall he was staring out the back window as we left but there was no time for him to get a read on what it was before we took off." He waited and then asked, "Is that correct, Officer Keats?"

The dog sat up and unleashed a long grumble.

"I'll take that as a yes," Kellan said. "And as your superior officer, it's on me that I let two octogenarians lure me into indulging my boyhood passion of back country racing. All along I sensed something bogus about the situation and you said as much. I let the thrill of it overtake me. And you know why? The same winsome lass I mentioned earlier. I was trying to impress her, like that hormone-addled teen who won her hand fair and square. After our breakup, maybe I still feel like I have something to prove."

"You have nothing to prove," I said, and I couldn't help laughing. "As if driving like a maniac would prove anything anyway. Honestly."

"Boys will be boys," he said. "I want you to know I'm capable of protecting you and thank goodness I squeaked through over those crazy preppers. But if my poor judgment undermined your canine security detail, then I've proven myself unworthy instead. Is that the case, Officer Keats?"

The dog put his paws on the dash where they belonged and directed me with a curt mumble to crack open the window.

"He's back on duty," I said. "And there's something I want to add here. Keats, you're not even assigned to Prudence's case."

"Correct," Kellan said. "I slipped up on my own case, and I'm correcting it now. You two are supposed to focus on the cold case."

"Exactly, and on my even colder grandfather. We'll be pumping him tonight."

"Good luck with that," Kellan said. "I confess I'm nervous about meeting him. Especially with the shame of last night clinging to me like a bad smell."

Finally Keats' mouth fell open with a ha-ha-ha.

"You smell great to me," I said.

"Why thank you," Kellan said, "although your nose isn't exactly discriminating."

"That's why I have Keats," I said. "My private security detail, as you say. He's my eyes, ears, nose and more." There was a meow from the back seat. "Officer Percy has fine skills, too."

"I leave you in good paws, then," Kellan said. "I'll be there in uniform tonight to thaw the old gentleman's heart."

"It's Gardenia you need to worry about," I said. "She's the exact opposite of my mother, just remember that. Anything you'd say to Mom, reverse it for my grandmother."

"Got it," he said. "Good luck today, Ivy."

"Back at you," I said. "And thanks for the thrill ride. You really know you're alive when you survive the back country trails."

"Now you're playing my song," he said.

Keats didn't waste another laugh. His muzzle was up and his tail wagging like crazy as we pulled into the parking lot at the airstrip. A helicopter whirled overhead and he obviously had a good idea who was in it.

My hair whipped in my face as I got out. I tucked Keats under my arm despite his protests and left Percy behind in safety. Choppers were new territory for me and I didn't intend to lose a pet to whirlwinds and blades.

Once the propellers stopped, I walked forward in time to see a pink snakeskin stiletto emerge and touch down. It was followed by another, and a streamlined dress in muted cranberry. The visitor released a cascade of dark curls from a silk scarf, pushed up her shades and flashed a smile as the pilot fell all over himself to collect her garment bag and small suitcase. He insisted on carrying them to the truck, which left her arms free to embrace me. Keats, who never liked being squished, not only embraced being embraced, but reveled in it. He let out a shrill whine that suggested we'd parted from Janelle Brighton years ago instead of last week.

Laughing, she handed the pilot her purse, too, and accepted the dog into her arms and hugged him again. Janelle was the type of woman who dressed to the nines yet didn't mind a designer dress getting covered in pet hair.

I took the three bags from the pilot and let Janelle carry Keats the rest of the way to the truck, where the canine abasement was augmented by the feline equivalent. She was sneezing before we left the airstrip, and I rolled down the windows to blow some of the allergens away.

"It's so good to see you," she said. "Almost good enough to offset the creepy hill country vibe. As long as no one figures out I'm here, your party should go off as planned."

"Is that what the helicopter's about?" I asked. "While I pegged you as the Janelle Bond type, I underestimated your expense account."

She laughed again. "There's barely a cent in my piggybank but Gran splurged for the ride. Since she couldn't be here, she desperately wanted me to represent the family. But with our enemies down in Wyldwood Springs, the goal is to get me in and out in under a day before the rumor mill does its thing and someone arrives to shoot up the party."

I stared at her and then put the truck in gear. "Is it really that bad?"

"It isn't that good," she said. "We can't be sure, but with those black cars chasing you and Jilly, and what happened at the Strathmore Hotel, better safe than sorry. In a couple of months, when things are straightened out at the Briars, I'll head home and see for myself." She stuck her nose out the window and let the wind blow back her hair. "It smells wonderful. Like home, without the reek of murder."

Now I laughed. "Sadly, there's been a murder since we got home."

She turned back with green eyes wide. "Not again! It's only been a week."

"What's more, there's a very old case that Kellan is letting me run lead on. More or less."

Keats curled up in Janelle's lap, grumbling, and she rubbed his ears. "You're doing your absolute best, my friend. Over and above. I don't know what you're fussing about."

"See?" I gave him a pointed look. "Janelle thinks you're doing your best and she's got a little something extra in the intuition department."

"I do. But we don't talk about that in front of Jilly, remember?" She twisted her hair up and clipped it before rolling down the window all the way. "This is a big day for her and I want my arrival to be a pleasant surprise—not a reminder of our zany family."

"Your family is no zanier than mine," I said. "A couple of grandparents I hadn't met came out of the woodwork this week. My mom spoke of them in the past tense and some of us believed they were dead. Turns out they're very much alive and oozing disapproval of us."

Janelle turned to stare at me. "How could you possibly not hear about them given the power of the rumor mill?"

"I wonder about that myself. They went about as far away as they could go, so maybe people respected their desire for privacy."

She kept staring at me till I laughed. "It's hill country, Ivy. There's no respect for privacy. So, what does that leave you?"

"Threats," I said. "Maybe my grandparents have information that silences people. That's how it usually works around here. The only way to keep a secret is to have a bigger secret."

"Yeah, that's *exactly* how it works. I bet they had scuttlebutt on enough key players to disappear themselves successfully."

I geared up carefully, hoping not to stall out and embarrass myself in front of Janelle. She could drive anything, possibly even the copter she rode in on. Her years working first as a carnie and then in nearly every role at swanky resorts left her with skills this former corporate suit could not help but envy.

"Well, you'll meet them tonight. Let me know if you pick up anything suspicious with your intuitive powers."

She gave a noncommittal shrug. "My goal is to leave here with an invitation to the wedding, Ivy. And to get that, I need to be... normal. Ordinary. So don't expect any strange stunts from me on this visit."

I grinned at her. "No snake hunting?"

"If you've got a snake problem, I'll cover you, as long as Edna has the right weapons. I'm bound to protect all animals with the full force of my skills. Otherwise, I'm just plain old cousin Janelle."

There was nothing plain about Janelle and she couldn't be ordinary no matter how hard she tried. But I would do my very best to keep her from getting into trouble with Jilly before she flew out again. With the overwhelming Galloway and Swingle presence, my best friend needed her people, too. One day, I hoped Bridie, their grandmother, could come for a good long visit. But this quick injection of family would warm Jilly's heart.

"Tell me all about these cases," Janelle said, as she stuck most of her head out the window. Her hair got loose and whipped around. Keats joined her, muzzle close to her ear, mumbling his own version of events.

I had the feeling she didn't hear much that I said. She was immersed in a hill country homecoming of sorts.

Finally she pulled her head back in as we turned into my lane. "Remember, I'm being ordinary today. Otherwise, I'd tell you the story is more convoluted than you think. But I know you and Keats will handle this perfectly." She grabbed the dog's muzzle and stared at him. Normally he hated that above all else, but apparently it was fine coming from Janelle. "You shake off that sulk, hear me? Just keep doing what you do and all will be fine."

His tail rose in a full-on jaunty wag and his mumble assured her he would do just that.

"Thanks for the vote of confidence," I said. "I guess we've both been feeling a little overwhelmed."

"Family. Weddings. The big stuff of life," she said. "But you've got the best dog in the world. I can't wait to find the second-best dog. I hope my sweet girl is just like Keats."

We drove under the arch that read "Runaway Far" because the last "m" had rusted out, and Janelle laughed at the sight of it.

"I had this sense that your dream dog would be longer and lower, remember?" I said. "And unless I am much mistaken—and it does happen—your dog will have plenty to say."

"Sounds good to me," she said, staring around raptly. "I've spent too much time alone and that'll get worse when I leave the Briars. It would be great to have a chatty, intuitive dog like Keats."

"Be careful what you wish for," I said. "You'll never have a thought to call your own again."

CHAPTER TWENTY-TWO

A few hours later, Jilly, Janelle and I gathered in the door of the dining room to discuss strategy. We'd been working with a large team to get the party set up and now everything was in full flow. Most of the guests had arrived, including everyone we liked in town and a few people we didn't, including the Langman sisters, who were being diligently shadowed—and subtly menaced—by Gertie Rhodes, who had shocked us by wearing a nice dress under her poncho. Minnie had come along without an invitation.

Teri Mason and I had grabbed a few minutes on the patio to chat about Ima and the case, but there were too many spies around for privacy. It was enough to see her smiling and wearing her blue "dress" caftan. My pets poked around at her hem but returned to my side. They knew this wasn't a night for pranks, although the Langmans, at least, deserved a jack-in-the-caftan surprise.

Jilly's small, private affair had turned into a full house. When you ran an inn that suffered from setbacks of the murderous kind, sometimes you had to sacrifice comfort for community goodwill. Besides, once Asher had invited my grandparents, it totally changed the dynamic. It wasn't about fun anymore, but survival. It would take a concerted effort from everyone to keep Mom from turning it into an unforgettable spectacle.

Since my sisters were focused on keeping the affair running smoothly and Asher was utterly clueless about family management, we'd asked Evie Springdale, Remi Malone and Sasha Wildwood to handle that crucial job. They were the most diplomatic and charming of the Dog Town Rescue Mafia and they dressed well, which was essential to credibility in Mom's view. That trio should have been plenty, but Mom was elusive, fluttering around like a confused butterfly.

What she needed more than skilled female handlers was a hand-some gentleman on her arm, but she'd decided to attend solo. Perhaps she worried about losing a valuable member of her rotation by tossing him into the family cauldron before he was ready for the heat. Charlie was of little use to her because he stayed outside on the patio with Calvin. Meanwhile, Cori Hogan, Bridget Linsmore and other Mafia joined Edna in supervising the property. We knew this was exactly the type of event Trelise Sutcliffe might exploit to seize Clippers. That also gave Edna an excuse to avoid Kellan, who was still miffed at her. He assigned himself to watch over Calvin, which allowed them both to stay as far from my grandparents as they could.

I wished I had the luxury of avoiding them, too, but I needed to seize my chance to grill Albert about Morris Tubbs. The first chal-lenge was parting him from Gardenia. They had arrived in a spiffy new pickup truck with only two small bags that apparently contained nothing but black. Their casual travel outfits had been replaced by a severe black dress in Gardenia's case, and a suit in Albert's. They looked ready for a funeral rather than an engagement celebration.

"Oh my, this room is swimming in family drama," Janelle said now. "You can taste it."

"What does family drama taste like, exactly?" I asked her, grinning.

"Lemon," she said. "Tangy with a big bite."

Instantly my tongue tingled with zingy citrus and I puckered. "You're right," I said. "Sour."

"Yet invigorating," she said. "Like your grandmother's lemon squares. Lemon keeps you on your toes."

My toes were complaining about the heels I'd worn for Jilly's sake as well as Kellan's. It was a point of honor to look nice tonight, and Janelle had popped into my room to help, likely at Jilly's suggestion. She used a flatiron to turn my long hair into a shiny sheet, and a tube of eyeliner to transform me into Cleopatra. I had resisted borrowing a dress but it turned out she'd packed five to have choices. They all looked too small coming out of her bag but the one I chose fit me like magic.

Jilly gave me an approving look that turned lemony when she glanced at her cousin. "No weirdness, okay? Let's keep things real tonight."

"As real as freshly squeezed lemonade," Janelle said, lifting her hands. "I reek of it."

Indeed, she'd spent two hours mixing batches of a cocktail so irresistible that Kellan eventually left Calvin and Charlie to station himself by the open bar to monitor public consumption.

"Notice my grandparents won't try your cocktail," I said. "Tap water, room temperature. No silly bubbles for them."

"What did you put in that drink, Janelle?" Jilly asked. "It's like a—"

"Magic potion?" Janelle asked, unable to resist baiting her cousin. "Just a little something I learned as a bartender during my many years of resort experience."

After the initial surprise and delight over Janelle's arrival, there had been a tug-of-war over party setup. Jilly was essentially the creative director of Runaway Inn and ran the place with taste and grace. Janelle had held senior hospitality roles and was eager to show off her chops to her cousin. Jilly, the elder by nearly two years, didn't want to be impressed.

Anyone else might have been dismayed by their bickering over everything from table layout to the arrangement of twinkle lights, but as the last of five sisters, I knew this was par for the course. The fact that they were never far apart and moved almost in synchronicity told me I'd made the right move in springing Janelle on Jilly. Their relationship would mellow over time. The clashes I used to have with my sisters had dwindled away, even though I was disappointed that Daisy was so good at keeping secrets. I knew she'd carried the heaviest weight in the family, and gave her some grace.

Keats poked my shin to make me focus. "You're right, buddy. We'd better get moving. My grandparents will likely repair to their room early."

Their room had been Mom's until today and she was more indignant about that than anything else. It took most of the afternoon to move her things, which proved how entrenched she'd become at the inn and in my life. Still, she knew the deal. If I needed the suite, she had to vacate, and I wanted to turn things around with my grandparents.

"I'm ready to deploy," Jilly said. "I'll lure Gardenia upstairs and keep her there, while you two cut Albert from the crowd and question him."

"Are you sure about this?" I said. "Gardenia's the tougher nut to crack."

"I'm sure," Jilly said. "Janelle can turn the Brighton charm on Albert."

"You have loads of that yourself," I said. "I've seen you tame the most terrifying corporate sharks."

Jilly shook her blonde curls and frowned. "I'm losing my edge. Maybe that's what engagement does to you."

"Regrets?" I asked, as Percy announced his availability to be coddled by Jilly. The cat always knew when she needed support.

She lifted him into the crook of her arm. "Nope. It's an adjustment, that's all. I need to draw on new skills and I'm going to practice tonight with your grandmother."

"What's your strategy?" I said, as Percy kneaded the air and purred.

"Working the perfect daughter-in-law angle," she said. "I might be next in line to give Gardenia great-grandchildren. That could grab her interest."

"Maybe, but she's hardly the doting type," I said. "None of us are brave enough to talk to them. Even Asher."

The dour duo had taken a position near the vegetable tray, as if carrots and celery were the only things to be trusted in the vast and varied spread. Gardenia's perpetual frown didn't stop her from being an attractive woman, however, and Albert was handsome, too. The Mt. Wilshire water was serving them well.

"Gardenia doted on Dahlia too much," Jilly said. "Albert, too. That's understandable, given their losses, but it turned into a clash of wills that everyone lost. Now they have another chance with a new generation. I bet she'll seize it once she gets over the shock."

"Well, good luck working your 'bride of golden boy' angle," I said. "As always, I'm playing the barn card. That's where I do my best work."

"The barn? Really?" Janelle said. "These shoes cost me a month's wages, Ivy."

"You can borrow some boots," I said.

"The charm is in my shoes," she said, and for a scant moment, this beautiful, confident woman showed doubt.

"The charm is in your genes," Jilly said, firmly. "So use it as if lives depend on it."

"Because they do," Janelle said, lifting her chin. "Don't ask me how I know."

"Oh, I won't," Jilly said. "I'll leave you in Ivy's capable hands."

Jilly wove through the crowd, and Janelle and I followed to make our move once she extracted Gardenia.

"Mrs. Swingle—Gardenia—could I take you on the full tour of the inn?" Jilly asked. "So far you've only seen your suite, which I hope you've found comfortable."

"It's a little extravagant for the likes of us," Gardenia said. "Albert and I are simple folk."

My mother materialized out of the crowd, bristling. "That room has the best view of the property and the lighting is perfect for sewing."

"Who sews anymore?" Gardenia said. "We get alterations done at the dry cleaners."

Mom pressed her lips together. "I sew, Mother. Just like you taught me. It's my... my—"

"Art," Jilly said, since Mom's stutter gave away her nerves. "Dahlia makes stunningly original creations, like the dress she's wearing now."

Gardenia looked Mom up and down with a lemony pucker. Mom had many red dresses that would have suited this occasion nicely, but she'd designed a new one with a plunging neckline framed by what looked like a feather boa. The satin skirt had boning at the bottom that made the hem undulate as she walked. It was impossible to miss and that was no doubt the point. When my grandmother finally tore her eyes away, she said, "What an interesting frock, Dahlia. You certainly didn't learn that from me."

Jilly's cheeks flushed as she realized there were piranhas in the waters where she expected only sharks. "I'm counting on Dahlia to help me choose an interesting wedding dress. She knows all the best stores in hill country."

"I could *make* a gown for you, Jilly darling," Mom said. "It would be an honor."

I wondered how far Jilly would take her sacrifice, but she danced back from the edge before committing to a Dahlia Galloway original bridal production. "Let's talk about it upstairs," she said. "I have some ideas and I don't want the rumor mill to get hold of them early."

Mom stepped right in front of Gardenia to follow Jilly. "I have something to show you, too. A beautiful christening gown I hand-stitched for Asher. It'll be perfect for your own child."

Jilly turned so quickly that Percy meowed a complaint. She took the glass Janelle offered, and swallowed the cocktail in a single gulp. Then she forged upstairs with the warring women she'd soon call family.

"Our turn to deploy," I told Janelle. "Did you recover your siren skills?"

"Doubt is the enemy of the spy," she said, setting down her own glass. "And booze makes for a slow getaway."

Albert initially resisted our offer to tour the grounds. "It's already dark," he said.

"It's the golden hour before dusk," I countered. "The farm is at its most beautiful then. Plus you can see to sidestep the manure."

"Gardenia wouldn't like it. I'll just wait for her here and we can— Ow!"

"Keats, don't nip your great-grandfather," I said, as the dog herded Albert to the front door.

"I am not related to that dog. Or any dog," Albert said. "I don't even like dogs."

"Impossible," I said, as he stayed one step ahead of Keats down the front stairs and along the paving stones to the barn. "There's no way I could love animals as much as I do without having it built right into my genes."

"Those came from your father's side," he said. "That Polly Fable was a— Ow!"

"Keats," I said, "he's allowed to have an opinion about Calvin's mom. And he's not wrong that she was a pet lover. But the vein is so strong in me that I'm quite sure both you and Mrs. Swingle like animals, too."

"Don't call her Mrs. Swingle," he said. "Call her Grandma."

Cori and Edna faded into the shadows outside as Keats swept the old man into the barn ahead of Janelle and me. "It seems overly familiar on short acquaintance," I told him. "I barely know her, sir."

"Well, we know you," he said. "It's hard not to, with all the news coverage. Poor Gardenia's been living in terror that you'll be killed during your daredevil antics."

"I must have inherited that from my father's side," I said. "Because I certainly didn't learn it at home."

Janelle eased in front of me and offered a tour of the barn that turned out to be quite comical. She introduced Clippers as a pony, Alvina as a llama, and Bocelli as a mule.

Albert frowned, seemingly impervious to her appeal. "That's a donkey, young lady. You're obviously a city girl."

"I was a city girl until recently," I said. "I still have a lot to learn here."

He crossed his arms over the top of the stall Bocelli shared with Clippers. "What's wrong with that donkey? He looks ill."

"Bocelli gets depressed if there's too much turmoil," I said. "Clippers normally settles his nerves but since he started training as a service horse, there's too much hubbub for Bocelli's liking."

Albert turned to me with a mix of confusion and disapproval in his hazel eyes. "This is all very strange, Ivy. I'm familiar with newfangled homesteader notions, but you take it to the extreme. Next thing you'll tell me your donkey sees a therapist."

"What a great idea," I said. "Are there donkey therapists?"

"All therapists are donkeys if you ask me." He tried frowning but it turned into a smile. Janelle and I both laughed out loud, so he tried to take back the joke. "We didn't believe in such foolishness in our time. You fought stress with hard work."

"I hear you," I said. "I spend a lot of time turning manure for that very reason."

"A sensible choice," he said. "Plus you get good fertilizer, when all you get from therapists is… manure."

This time Keats joined in the laugh with a hearty ha-ha-ha and my grandfather stared down at him. Then the old man shook his head, resisting my dog's allure, too.

"What service will this horse be performing?" Albert asked.

"If he does well in training, he could help a woman I met who has a physical disability," I said. "There's a trainer in Twin Points who wants to groom Clippers for that role."

"The trainer who tried to steal him?" Janelle said.

I nodded. "The former owner signed a contract and I'm trying to break it. The man is dead now. Vinnie Swenson."

Albert looked away from the horse and his wiry eyebrows rose. "Of the infamous Swenson family?"

"I'm afraid so. Vinnie was the last of his line and the lawyers are still trying to sort out his estate, so this could take a while. That's why I'm trying to appease the trainer by playing along." I reached over and stroked the horse's muzzle. "Besides, Clippers might want the job."

Janelle touched his forelock and shook her head. "He doesn't."

"I suppose he just told you that?" Albert said. His smile had become more genuine.

"This wee horse doesn't want to work that hard, Albert," she said. "All he wants to do is dance."

"Dance?" He shook his head. "He may be small but he's still a horse. All they want to do is run."

"That's where you're wrong, sir," I said, walking over to the portable speakers that had arrived that day. I scrolled through the music playlists till I found Abba's greatest hits, considering the options. Finally I settled on "Take a Chance on Me."

It was a favorite of both Clippers and our resident Dancing

Queen, Alvina. Sure enough, her big eyes appeared over her stall and she let out her delighted bleat. She wouldn't always dance for strangers, but tonight she was in the mood to cut a rug for Albert.

I offered her a deep bow in the open space between the neighboring stalls. She returned the gesture, then offered a twirl. Clippers bucked twice and the three of us started freestyling. The heels hobbled me but I gave it my best.

"What on earth...?" Albert said.

Janelle did a little curtsy in front of him with a coquettish tilt of the head. "May I have this dance, sir?"

"Dance? I don't dance, young lady. Not anymore."

"Who's here to see?" She fixed him with her magnetic green eyes. "You can't turn a lady down... can you?"

Sighing, Albert took her hand and then gave her a surprisingly vigorous spin. Maybe he hoped to throw her off balance, but Janelle was as good at dancing as she was anything else. Her skills seemed to galvanize him and it soon became apparent that he had been a very good dancer indeed.

One Abba song led to another and all of us danced like there was no tomorrow. Clippers kept kicking the stall, which annoyed Bocelli so much that he let out a heartrending wail.

Suddenly all the air seemed to get sucked out of the barn and everyone froze. Then Alvina sunk to her knees and Clippers slid behind his big friend.

"Albert Phineas Swingle. What is going on here?" Gardenia was in the doorway, scowling. "Have you been drinking?"

"Not a drop," he said, releasing Janelle's hand. "Just discovering some of the talents of Ivy's animals."

"What foolishness," she said. "Come up to the house right now."

He turned meekly to follow. "Yes, dear."

Janelle darted ahead and caught up with Gardenia. She used the soothing tone I recognized from her interactions with difficult residents at the Briars. Even before Albert and I left the barn, my grand-mother was responding to questions.

Letting out a long breath, he turned to me. "She means well, Ivy. This has all been quite a shock for us. Your mother said we'd never see our grandchildren again and for decades she made good on her word."

"All because of my father, I presume?"

He gave a single nod. "We wanted more for Dahlia, our only surviving child, than to be sucked into the hill country cesspool of crime. The Galloways were in over their heads. Couldn't begin to compete with the more skilled criminals like Frank Swenson or the Milloy family."

"I know a bit about that," I said. "I've been researching. That's why I wondered if you knew more about Morris Tubbs, and why the decent, honorable man you knew would kill someone."

From the doorway, he watched my grandmother walk up the front stairs. When she didn't turn back, he gave a resigned sigh and asked, "Did the bones belong to Earl Spratt?"

"It appears so, based on Myrtle McCain's opinion. There was a horsehair toupee in the grave." I pulled my phone out of my pocket and showed him the photos.

"Ah, yes. Earl was a vain, arrogant man. He preferred being ridiculous over looking old and possibly diminished. What's in the mason jar?"

"The lab results aren't back yet. It had mostly disintegrated."

"It had to be something important to the killer," Albert said. "Important to Morris, if indeed he was the killer. There's a chance he was covering for someone."

"I suppose so. But then why the deathbed confession?"

"Time does strange things. Makes us question our strongest beliefs," he said. "But it hasn't changed my view of Earl Spratt. He deserved what he got, in my opinion."

"Yet I keep hearing he was well liked and respected," I said.

"You can't judge a man by his press or even community memory. Earl bought off anyone who'd take the money and threatened the rest."

"I wish that surprised me," I said. "Those were dangerous times in hill country. Do you have any idea why Morris might have come to blows with Earl?"

My grandfather pressed his lips together and I thought the flow of information would stop. But when he looked down, Keats caught him with a blue-eyed probe. Albert took a step backward, into the barn, and the dog followed, trying to transfix him with the sheepdog stare and succeeding fairly well.

"All I know for sure is that *I* wanted to deliver some blows to Earl Spratt," Albert said, at last. "But I couldn't. Not with a child on the way. We'd lost a couple already. Bringing the law into it would only make things worse. They were in bed with him, too."

"What did Earl do?" I asked. "Embezzle money? Sully your reputation?"

"Worse. Far worse." There was such deep sadness in Albert's voice that Keats turned his brown eye toward him. "He stole Creedence."

"Creedence?" I said. "You mean credibility?"

"I mean Creedence, my dog. The most loyal and lovable mastiff ever to grace the planet. That animal was my solace through hard times, and his strength helped me support Gardenia in the way she deserved. And then he was gone."

"How did you know Earl stole him?" I asked. "And why would he do something like that? Did he take him hostage to bribe you?"

"Albert!" The strident voice soared from the front porch. "Come up here, please."

"I knew, Ivy. That's all I can say, and when I tried to rescue Creedence, Earl put me off his land with a rifle. There was nothing more I could do. Even if the police had backed me, no one valued dogs properly back then. I decided to move Gardenia out of harm's way. And then again and again. I couldn't escape the memory, but finally I heard Earl had left, too, and found some relief. Thanks to you, I know exactly where he moved."

Keats whined and I realized I was holding my breath. "That's awful. I'm so sorry."

"Don't pity an old man," he said. "Just value the dog you have. He seems like a good one."

"The best dog to grace the planet," I said. "Tied with Creedence."

I looked up at his stern face and saw the pain of that loss was still very much alive. Keats leaned into the pant leg of his funeral suit. We knew Albert didn't dislike dogs or any animal; he just preferred to avoid stirring up old memories. Although it had seemed like we had nothing in common, we shared something vital.

"I'm going to figure this out, sir," I said. "I'm getting closer every day."

"For heaven's sake, call me Grandpa. Or Granddad. Or just Albert. Anything other than sir." His smile was strangely familiar until I realized it was an older version of my brother's. "And be careful, Ivy. You know crime boils up like lava whenever there's a rift in the land. You opened one with that grave."

I nodded, touching Keats' ears. "We'll try to stuff the evil genie back into the bottle before anyone gets hurt."

Gardenia came down the front stairs and Albert started trotting. "I'm about to take a beating and I'm blaming it on you, Ivy."

I laughed. "I've shouldered worse, sir. I mean Grandpa Albert."

CHAPTER TWENTY-THREE

The party lasted into the wee hours. Once everyone had gone and we'd done some of the cleanup, I found myself wide awake, mind spinning. Keats and Percy were on high alert, too. The dog paced under my bedroom window and stood on his hind legs to peer out. The cat parked on my chest purring in a loud roar intended not to calm but rouse me. Before the clock struck five I gave up and got up. I couldn't evade my pets' plans indefinitely. There was exploring to do.

Dressing quickly, I crept down the stairs and out the front door, averting my eyes from the remaining mess I was leaving for others. What was the point of a large, annoying family if you couldn't allocate work to many hands?

I didn't speak till we got to the barn. "We need to load up Clippers and Bocelli. We're due at the Sutcliffe Academy at nine and I bet you're taking me too far afield to swing back and collect them."

Percy leapt onto their stall while Keats took a dive at my cuffs.

"Give me a break. It's not fair to rush them just because you're impatient." He grumbled and I grumbled back. "I assume you know that sneaking around is a lot tougher with a trailer in tow. People notice things like that, even at the crack of dawn."

Dawn still hadn't cracked when we pulled onto the highway, and both Keats and Percy lined up with paws on dashboard and tails raised. It would have made a cute social media post for viewers who didn't know the pets had murder on their minds.

I had a good idea where we were going and wasn't too thrilled about it.

"I'm not saying you're wrong, but I can think of a better time for a trip like this," I said, taking the turn onto the highway slowly, out of respect for my hoofed passengers. "Furthermore, you know I'm going to catch it from Jilly and Kellan for coming alone."

Keats mumbled at me without turning from the road.

"Alone without humans, I mean. Ideally humans with weapons." I drove another mile before adding, "Although I doubt anyone except Imogen and Albert care too much about this case anymore. I can't stop thinking about what happened to poor Creedence. I can only assume Earl Spratt wanted to use the dog as leverage for something. And whatever it was, Albert couldn't or wouldn't yield, no matter how much he loved his dog."

Now Keats' mumble was more sympathetic.

"I know. There's basically nothing I wouldn't surrender for you two."

The next mumble confirmed he felt the same. I knew that of course because he'd surrendered everything for me plenty of times.

"But I can see why Albert would hesitate, given the circumstances. They'd lost child after child and hoped the next would live. Plus a proud man like Albert wouldn't sell out easily. Especially to the likes of Earl Spratt in his man wig."

I followed the directions Keats thumped out with his white paws. It wasn't the route I'd expected. Maybe I was wrong about where we were headed. Or maybe he had a faster way. Regardless, I did as I was told. Right now, I was just the driver.

"Albert has never allowed himself to have another dog, poor

man. I suppose he felt he betrayed Creedence when he really didn't have a choice. His family needed to come first."

Keats turned his brown eye on me and gave a pant-laugh.

"I know, right? A dog would have been way more comfort than Mom. Once she eloped with Dad, Albert should have got a border collie."

The dog agreed and then we both simmered down until we reached Bluffers Ridge. Keats had indeed found a shorter route there, but it also wasn't our final destination. He lashed me on with urgent mumbles for another few miles and then directed me to turn into an overgrown lane. I could barely make out the entrance but I took his word for it that it was there and pushed through.

By now the sun was up and its rays were a strange and eerie pink. A forest fire down the range had cloaked much of hill country in smoke that blurred all the usual lines. Nothing looked quite as I figured it should, although I had never been here to know better.

"Another abandoned property," I said. "There are far more of them around than realtors let on. I guess eager homesteaders know bad vibes when they feel them."

I pulled up in front of the derelict house and shivered as I opened the door. There were bad vibes aplenty here. Keats hit the ground already puffed from head to tail and Percy doubled in size on contact.

"So, this is where Earl Spratt lived, I presume. He ruled the region with an iron fist and a horsehair toupee. What a strange combination."

Leaving Bocelli and Clippers in the trailer, I circled the house quickly with Keats and Percy. The place had been elegant and lavish in its day, built no doubt on the proceeds of crime. Given its advanced state of decay, I wondered if its corrupt origins had sped its ruin.

"Criminals should build tasteless, ugly homes, don't you think?" I said, circling back to the truck. "Stately manors are just another deception. Regardless, there's really nothing to see here, boys. It's too far gone to poke around inside without falling through the boards. I don't care to be impaled up here."

Keats lifted his white paw and pointed at the lane. My heart gave a little stutter as headlights appeared, but both animals deflated visibly as the vehicle advanced. The driver apparently meant us no harm.

"Oh my gosh, it's Albert," I said, as my grandfather's spiffy new truck came into view. "How cool is it that he tailed us and wants to help?"

It wasn't Albert who jumped out of the truck, however, but Janelle Brighton. She was almost unrecognizable in a pair of my overalls, my second best work boots and a baseball cap over curly pigtails.

"Morning," she called. "Great day for a road trip."

"Janelle, did you steal my grandfather's truck?"

"Of course not," she said, joining me. "If he didn't want me to borrow it, he wouldn't have let me lift the keys from his pocket during our dance. Like Abba says, he took a chance on me."

I couldn't help returning her grin. "You're incorrigible. Albert's going to have a fit and Gardenia a bigger one."

"I'll be back before they know it's gone." She turned and gave the truck an appraising look. "That thing is a dream machine. I love driving stick and it's been ages."

"Well, I can't deny I'm glad to see you," I said. "Even if you lifted my clothes as well."

"If you didn't want me to borrow them you wouldn't have left them in a heap on the floor," she said. "And you would have noticed they were gone last night. You should have warned me to pack for adventure."

"I don't plan for this sort of thing. It just happens."

"Yeah? Well, I figured this sort of thing might happen so I planned ahead."

"And you tailed me?"

"Tailing implies a challenge," she said, laughing. "The hardest part was staying far enough behind the parade float to evade your notice."

"Keats didn't give you away," I said, as she walked around the trailer and unlatched it. "I'm sure he knew you were there. No wonder they were in good spirits."

"We had a word last night and agreed backup was a good idea." She stepped away from the trailer door. "I'll let you unload Bocelli and Clippers. Farm animals are outside my purview."

"Finally... something Janelle Brighton hasn't done."

"Yet," she said, grinning. "I could farm. I probably won't because I like nice shoes. But I could."

I leaned against the trailer door. "Care to explain why I should offload my animals here? In case you haven't noticed, there's a bad vibe."

"Oh, I noticed. That's why I'm forfeiting my beauty sleep."

"But why expose my animals to that?" I looked down at Keats and Percy. "These two volunteered, but Clippers in particular is a flight animal."

"That's precisely why we need him. Animals are so sensitive to changes in atmosphere that with four of them along we'll be done in no time. Besides, we don't want to leave them here alone. Do we?"

I shook my head. "Would you care to say what exactly we're looking for?"

One strap of my overalls fell off her shoulder and she looked deceptively sweet and naïve. My country bumpkin façade was a good choice, but the pigtails pushed it over the top.

"Hard to say, Ivy, but it's not good and I think you know that. How about we all figure it out together?"

Keats looked up at me and mumbled. "Yeah, I am having second thoughts, buddy. This place is so creepy. But second thoughts mean I'm maturing, right?"

"Sounds more like Jilly," Janelle said. "Or Gardenia. The Ivy I met didn't waste time on second thoughts."

"A panel of judges would decree that you and I are a bad team, Janelle," I said, opening the trailer doors. "I'm rash and you're reckless."

"Sounds ideal," she said, moving aside for Clippers to disembark. "Rash and reckless get things done."

Bocelli needed some persuading to leave the trailer. Keats got in and offered encouragement in a brusque tone. The dog was getting impatient.

"Give him a break," I said. "This is a lot to ask of Bocelli."

Once the donkey was out, Keats and Percy took the lead and Janelle fell in behind them. The pets soon found the entry to a trail into what seemed like impenetrable bush.

"How am I to get Clippers and Bocelli through that tangle?" I asked.

"We go single file," Janelle said, taking Clippers' lead rope from my hand. "You get the sad sack."

Bocelli threw back his head and bawled, and I could hardly blame him. I didn't want to take a jaunt through aggressive bush in murky light either.

Humming "Mamma Mia," Janelle flipped on her phone light and pushed into the trail. She sounded cheery, but it may have been a front. I'd already learned she was a chameleon. She knew how to handle herself in a crisis, though, and I felt as safe with her as I did with Edna and Gertie. That said, all of them were wild cards. Keats mumbled something ahead of me, possibly suggesting I was a wild card, too.

The further we went, the less safe I felt and a fleet of police officers wouldn't have helped. Pistols and pepper spray couldn't protect me from the cold creeping into my very bones. Something terrible had happened out here and it left a permanent imprint in the atmosphere. At least, that's how it seemed to my sleep-deprived brain.

We passed through two large clearings in succession, but Keats, Percy, Janelle and Clippers kept walking. I fell further and further behind with reluctant Bocelli, who needed a fair bit of coaxing. Leaving him in the trailer may have been the better choice, but he would have been distraught there, too.

"Get a move on it, Ivy," Janelle called. "We're almost there."

"Where is 'there,' exactly?" I called back.

"Here, I guess. There's no welcome sign but this feels like it."

The large clearing she'd reached had been deliberately cleared decades ago. There were dozens upon dozens of decayed stumps among the more current growth. Still, the smoky sky was quite visible through the foliage.

I pulled Bocelli out into the open and he pranced around like a high-strung racehorse. When I turned around, I saw Clippers shuddering convulsively. The fact that Keats was doing the same surprised me most. Normally only bodies of water generated such a strong response in my dog, yet we were certainly standing on dry land.

But what was *under* that dry land? What was making Percy compulsively claw at the soil with the erratic movements of a broken toy? He started in one place and moved onto the next. And then the next.

"What is that cat doing?" Janelle asked.

"Telling me something died here," I said. "That's his litterbox maneuver." I watched him for a few more minutes. "I've never seen him keep going like that. If I had to guess, I'd say there are multiple bodies."

"Sounds about right," Janelle said, turning to meet my eyes. "Ivy, you know I sense things others might not?"

Without Jilly around to be disgruntled about her strange family, I could be honest. "Yeah. Sometimes, I do, too. Or at least I read my animals sensing things, which they are most certainly doing right now."

"Exactly. They all know something dreadful happened here. Many dreadful things." She shuddered as the animals had and then beckoned me to turn around and head back. "More than I could count. If I could bear to count. You'll need to get Kellan up here with equipment that can find remains."

"Maybe we should make a start," I said. "There's a spade in the truck."

"Nope," she said. "I'm good at loads of things. Digging isn't one of them."

"Keats can…"

"Nope." She came back a few steps, reached out and stopped short of touching my arm. "Leave it, Ivy. As tough as you are, you're going to be upset by what you find here. Can you take my word for it?"

Normally I wouldn't. Not when there was something I could do to move a situation along. In this case, I capitulated. Janelle had gifts and insights far beyond mine, and if she thought I should stand down, I'd go along with her.

Clippers nickered in what sounded like relief and Bocelli let out a heartrending wail. Percy stopped scraping and jumped onto the donkey's back to lick the dirt off his paws. Everyone was glad to move on, even Keats, who hated to leave a job undone.

We were almost out of the clearing when Keats went into a point. On the ground, nearly hidden in the bush, was a huge, ornate bouquet. It looked like a funeral arrangement but there was nothing to indicate where it was from. The flowers were barely wilted, suggesting it was only a few days old.

I took a few photos for Kellan. "Someone else knows about this place and what happened here, Janelle."

"Yeah. It will all become obvious at the right time." She started moving through the bush, falling behind Keats and leading Clippers. "That's how these things work. It doesn't pay to force them."

"I don't know about that," I said. "I force them plenty."

"That could be why you're always in trouble," she called back. "Just saying. Maybe try my strategy. Namely, running in the opposite direction."

I laughed. "I spent a decade running from my old life. Now I stand my ground. No regrets, but I do take some hits for it."

"I know," she said as we emerged near the trucks. "And I admire your courage, Ivy, I really do. I hope to be like you when I grow up."

"Aim a little higher, Janelle," I said, letting Keats load the big animals back in the trailer. "Be like Jilly. Full of courage *and* common sense."

"I'll add a photo of her to my vision board along with my dream dog," she said, trying to grin and not quite succeeding. After I closed the trailer door, she hugged me. "It's going to be okay. You can take my word for it."

That reassurance sunk into my bones and countered the deep chill. "I believe you. And thanks."

"None required," she said, heading over to my grandfather's truck. "I'll follow you home so you don't get any big ideas."

"I'm going on to Clippers' service training class," I said. "Although I hate to miss my grandfather's face when you roll onto the farm."

She got into the truck and rolled down the window. "It's going to be so fun." There was the faintest glimmer of her old self in her smile. "As for Clippers, I gotta say, I don't see it happening with the horse-thief trainer."

"Trelise has a contract right now," I said.

Her fingers fluttered dismissively. "Contracts break down and this one will." She paused for a second, staring up at the smoky sky. "I do see him in service, though. Just not where you expect it."

That sent a little pang through my chest. I didn't want to lose this horse. Not to anyone. In fact, I wanted to hoard all my animals forever. "Are you ever wrong?" I asked.

A genuine laugh spilled out of Albert's natty truck. "Oh yeah. Too often." She gestured to my truck more forcefully now. "Not this time. But it's going to turn out all right."

I nodded and got into my truck. "You'll be back for the wedding in the fall?"

"Wouldn't miss it," she called, pulling aside to make way for me to pass.

I thought I heard her add, "If I live that long," but the words faded under the twin roar of truck engines.

Keats' tail sank to tell me I wasn't wrong about that. Not this time.

But maybe that would turn out all right, too.

CHAPTER TWENTY-FOUR

B y the time I reached the Sutcliffe Academy, I was starting to wonder if I'd imagined some of what happened at Earl Spratt's derelict homestead. Janelle was unusual... a little spooky. Maybe the animals had picked up on that and their senses shorted out. I'd seen many strange things with my pets, but it seemed impossible even to me that Percy could detect a body count that high. I'd stopped counting at 20 and his paws were still flashing. If that many people had gone missing over the years in Clover Grove, Kellan would most certainly have said so. The pile of cold cases would be much higher and while not all of his predecessors were ethical men, there were some good ones. They couldn't all have been bribed or blackmailed into looking the other way. Could they? Was Earl Spratt a wigged serial killer?

I tried calling Kellan but it went to voicemail, so I texted instead. It was too strange a story to tell that way, so I sent him a photo of the flowers and the location and asked him to send someone up to look for a body. I didn't say 20 bodies or more. No need to alarm him. One body was plenty to contemplate over his morning coffee.

Keats gave me a warning mumble before we walked into the training ring. His ears were back and his tail at half mast, as was typical at the academy. He hadn't forgiven Trelise for her audacious siege on his property and he continually let her know it. When we approached today, she tried to frown at him but the Botox worked against her. I knew it irked her that any dog could hold her in such contempt. No professional trainer would want to be spurned by one of the smartest breeds, especially someone with ambitions. Keats and I would never be asked to guest star on her TV show.

Clippers seemed determined to rule himself out of that opportunity, too. He tugged at the end of his lead rope, with erratic leaps, sudden stops and a wild-eyed stare. I had to coax him forward to join the group at the far side of the ring. Meanwhile, Bocelli put his brakes on, and Keats had to drive him from behind. Maybe my nerves hadn't settled as much as I thought and the animals were reading my agitation. Even, Percy, normally the calmest of the lot, arched his back and took dancing sideways lunges at our human classmates. Most were dog people to the core and the fluffy feline tarantula moves unnerved them.

"Trelise, this is unacceptable," Sylvia Vesper said. "How can our dogs focus while surrounded by this hubbub?"

I stared at her hard enough that she pulled down the brim of her Sutcliffe Academy cap. "Isn't that what training is all about?" I said. "Exposing our animals to stimuli and keeping them calm?"

Hawk Bustard shook his head. "Maybe, but the ring itself is supposed to be a safety zone. Clippers should always look forward to coming here."

I was surprised to see Hawk and Sylvia after Kellan had called them both in to discuss their visit to the Hoggins place. Apparently, Hawk hadn't been the least bit fazed. He said he was simply paying his respects to Prudence because the funeral had been postponed. Sylvia Vesper had been along for the ride and backed him up. There was probably more to the story but since there was no evidence to the contrary, and no other obvious motivation, Kellan said it was a watch-and-wait situation.

I wanted to watch and wait now, but managing my crew made observation difficult. Edna and Gertie would have happily joined me, but I wasn't ready to share information about what happened at Earl Spratt's that morning. Edna wasn't one to trust in "bad vibes" or woo-woo readings by possible psychics. It was better to let the police do some initial exploration. Otherwise, my prepper friends would head up there with a spade to find out for themselves.

Clippers pranced to the end of his lead rope, not with his usual joyful spirit, but an unease that told me to watch my step. Most animals in a state of anxiety could lash out, and while Clippers wasn't huge he was capable of breaking bones. Keats left Bocelli and circled the little horse, transfixing him with a stare. That seemed to settle Clippers somewhat. Keats mumbled reassurance either to the horse or to me that he had things under control.

Trelise was silent, observing, but Sylvia cleared her throat to start whining again. "It isn't fair that Ivy's disrupting the whole class," she said. "Maybe I should bring a pig or some chickens along next time and see how *she* fares."

I made a show of looking around the group. "It's not the whole class, Sylvia. Six dogs are taking this in stride but not yours, and not Hawk's. Do you think something else could be setting them off?"

"Like what?" She swept off her baseball cap and the gesture made her dog's tail drop. "My dog is unflappable. Everything a service animal should be."

"Then I guess you have nothing to worry about," I said. "I just wondered if he might be reacting to your state of mind. Isn't that what Trelise always tells us? That our feelings transmit through the leash, or in my case, lead rope?"

"If you're suggesting we're annoyed by your behavior and our dogs are picking up on it, then you're probably right," Hawk said. "How about you stop provoking us?"

I gave them a shrug intended to provoke them further. It seemed likely they were more concerned about Kellan's questioning than about my animals. After all, we'd been provoking them since day one and today was no different. In fact, without Gertie and Edna, it might even be calmer.

Trelise walked into the center of the circle and brought her palms together in a silent clap. Every trainer had some way to grab attention without startling the animals, it seemed. With Cori, it was her black gloves with the orange-fingered flare.

"Settle, everyone," she said. "Ivy's not wrong. Your dogs should be able to handle whatever's thrown at them, even if it is a traveling sideshow."

"Thank you," I said, taking satisfaction in being right despite the ridicule. "My critters will settle soon enough if you just give them some space. None of us likes morning classes. Getting everyone fed, loaded and on the road starts the day on a rushed note."

"Sorry if I can't plan my schedule around yours," Trelise said, coming over to circle me. "I'm a busy woman with clients and meetings all day."

"Oh, I understand completely," I said, clucking to keep Clippers' attention. As Trelise circled, the horse tried to do the same, and Keats did his best to hold him in position. "I'm just noting that most people don't have a farm to run, as I do."

"That's my point exactly," Trelise said. "You have a farm to run and you can't give this horse the attention he deserves. He'll be the main event in *my* circus."

Her acolytes chuckled but there was no real humor in the sound. It was like a laugh track that wasn't quite synced with the visuals.

"My lawyer is still waiting for yours to deliver what we need," I said. "I'm sure we'd both like this resolved for Clippers' sake. Not to mention Bocelli's."

"I've decided against taking the donkey, by the way," Trelise said. "They're totally useless to a trainer and cost money to feed."

"Clippers needs Bocelli," I said. "They're inseparable and I've been clear about that since day one."

"He only needs the donkey in *your* world, where there's a constant state of disruption and stress," Trelise said. "The horse will calm down beautifully at my facility, where he'll have both the rest and the work he needs to fulfill his destiny. No donkeys required."

I kept turning to keep my eyes on her and she circled yet again. "Trelise, it sounds like you have *your* best interests at heart, not my horse's."

"Let me explain this again since you're determined to play the rube," she said. "My interest is in turning your horse into a quality service animal who can support Monica Branham to live a full life again. It's a worthy goal." She gave Bocelli a scornful look. "If a donkey suffers for it, I'm fine with that."

Clippers wasn't, judging by his wild eyes. Keats wasn't either, although he tried very hard to hold the horse in position by moving in short, steady arcs. The dog might have prevailed if Bocelli hadn't eased between the dog and the horse with more grace than a donkey usually showed. That gave Clippers the freedom he needed to reach for Trelise's sleeve. She jerked her arm out of reach in time but as she staggered, the little horse turned, gathered himself, and bucked.

The kick was quite restrained really. I had seen him show more height and flash any number of times during our improv dance numbers. But this move wasn't about Abba and Clippers wasn't going to take a chance on Trelise. Instead, he hoofed her in the shin.

The trainer went down with a howl and Keats immediately drove both Clippers and Bocelli across the ring to the entrance. While he kept them there, I turned to help Trelise.

She was on her back, surrounded by groupies. "Did you get that?" she asked.

Sylvia and Hawk held up their phones, grinning.

It turned out Clippers and I had been played. She'd goaded us into offering more evidence of my unworthiness as a leader. Proof for lawyers and the world that I was ruining this horse's disposition.

Churning my hand through my hair, I sighed. She might very

well be right about that. It was a farmer's responsibility to do no harm, yet two of my charges were unhappy right now.

Percy came back and rubbed against my leg. I picked him up and stared at Trelise, who was making a meal out of her injury. The groans and squeals had to make up for the lack of facial expression.

"Are you okay, Trelise?" I said. "It sounds terminal."

"What a terrible choice of words, Ivy," Sylvia said. "She's in pain."

It didn't surprise me at all that Trelise was willing to take it on the shin to defeat me. But I did wonder why she'd let Clippers demonstrate he wasn't ideal service material. Maybe she expected her equine makeover to be all the more awe-inducing once accomplished.

Either way, she'd miscalculated, because I was more determined than ever to keep the horse from falling into her hands.

"You should get that checked out," I said, turning to leave with my herd. "Clippers may be small, but he's mighty."

CHAPTER TWENTY-FIVE

"My mother was livid," Mom said with barely concealed delight as we drove into town a few hours later. Far from being distressed, Mom had already moved her things back into the best suite, giving it a thorough cleaning to rid "her" room of parental contaminants after Albert and Gardenia left in a huff. "Too livid to spend a single second sharing a roof with a truck thief."

"Yet not livid enough to drive straight back to Mt. Wilshire," I said. "Instead, they only drove ten minutes to the Summit Hotel in town."

"Far enough that I can take a deep breath," Mom said. "My mother sucks all the air out of a room like an industrial vacuum. You have no idea."

I had a pretty good idea what it was like to compete for oxygen with a strong-willed matriarch. In my case, I also had five other siblings gasping for the same air. I kept my mouth shut now to preserve what was left in my lungs.

"I just wish I had a chance to thank Jilly's cousin before she left," Mom said, without noticing I hadn't replied to her last comment. "She slipped away like a spy in a James Bond movie. What an impressive young woman, and so well put together. You'd do well to—"

"Mom? There's only so much air in this truck. Leave some for the rest of us."

"Well, that's just rude, Ivy Rose Galloway." She trailed off into a grumble. Whatever she said, I missed it because of Keats' happy pant. After a few minutes she piped up again. "I'll be glad when you change your name to Harper. The fewer of us with your father's last name, the better."

I tried to resist the goading and failed. "You should change yours back to Swingle. Maybe your parents would like that."

She stared at the side of my head. "Are you trying to annoy me? Because if you are, you're succeeding."

I couldn't help grinning. "Gold star for Ivy Rose."

Easing her seat back, she crossed her legs and knocked Keats off balance. "You got more gold stars at school than the rest of my kids combined. Never a moment's trouble as a girl. Look at you now."

Keats adjusted himself on her lap until she yelped from his claws, and Percy draped himself over her headrest, resisting her attempts to dissuade him.

"Look at me now," I echoed, cruising down the main drag and turning right onto a smaller street that usually had spacious parking spots. "Able to park a horse trailer with ease."

"Can you explain why you brought equines on a trip to see Teri Mason? They can't join us in the art store."

"Well, they could. She's invited them."

"Ivy, please. They'll break her original creations. Or relieve themselves."

"Clippers is potty trained and Bocelli well on the way."

She wrung her hands. "Please tell me you're joking."

"Not about the potty training," I said, grinning. "But no, I won't take them into the art store. Teri can come out and have a quick word about Imogen."

"And you really couldn't leave them at the farm with so many people still around?"

"I could but I won't. The situation with that trainer escalated this morning and I have no idea what she might do. I don't trust Clippers out of my care, and wherever he goes, the donkey goes."

"So you'll sleep in the barn tonight?"

I turned off the truck. "Tonight and every night till the matter is resolved. That's no hardship to me."

"I do worry about the chief, darling. Jilly might be the first bride at the farm but don't let her be the last."

"Kellan isn't that easily dissuaded, Mom." I wondered what she'd think of my being a drag race trophy. Romantic or tawdry? It could go either way.

Hopping out, she clicked around the truck. She stepped as lightly as if she wore red, when she'd opted for a surprisingly conservative suit in royal blue. Gardenia's tart comments had apparently led Mom to hide her light under a bushel, at least temporarily.

Still, she strutted ahead of me, perhaps hopeful no one would associate her with the weirdo walking the donkey and mini horse. Keats tried once to bring her back, but she was fleet of foot today and he was more worried about his other charges.

When we got to Main Street, she turned left toward Hill Country Designs, and I turned right. "You'd better collect her, Keats. And prepare for a Main Street meltdown."

"Excuse me," she said, as the dog took a dive at her ankles. "What do you think you're doing, you varmint? Ivy, the store is this way, in case you've completely lost your bearings."

"We'll stop on the way back, Mom. I've got another errand to run."

"Wait a second, we'd better not be— Ow! I will not have any part of this, Ivy—Rose—Galloway."

Each pause was punctuated by a hop to escape the indignity of a very public herding.

When Keats brought her within range, I grabbed her arm with my free hand. "Let's just get on with it, Mom. Your parents moved into the Summit Hotel hoping we'd come after them. That *you'd* come after them."

"I'm sure they're just too tired from the party to drive home. Ow! Stop it, Keats. I'm moving in the right direction. Now you're just being a jerk."

The dog pranced around her, owning it.

"I doubt Albert would pay for a room when the drive is quite manageable for his spiffy truck," I said. "He seems frugal."

I kept my eyes straight ahead. People were gawking, of course, and there was no reason to acknowledge them when I'd need my fake smile allotment at the hotel.

"My mother is the cheapskate, and I'm surprised she let him buy that truck," she said. "Why do you think she taught me to sew? So she could avoid buying me anything fashionable, that's why."

"Now here you are, creating some of the most original designs in hill country."

"Far beyond the hills. My designs wouldn't be out of place on a New York runway."

"I believe it," I said. "And Gardenia looked proud if you ask me. She stood a little taller when you mentioned it."

Mom stepped ahead of me again, with the swishing tuft of white at her hem. "I don't want to know about that. About either of them. They threw me to the dogs—pardon the expression, Keats—after your father came along."

"They know. And they regret it."

"What makes you say that? I'm quite sure they never said so."

I smiled, and she must have felt it because she turned with raised eyebrows.

"I know because I know *you* regret things," I said. "Sometimes you say so, mostly you don't. And guess what? I'm okay with that. You were doing the best you could at the time."

"You bet I was." She clicked ahead furiously. "And they could have helped."

"Sounds like they did when they were allowed. You sent them six Santa letters every year. I wondered how you pulled off a nice Christmas when you weren't making the big bucks."

Her heels slowed till she fell in step with me. "I refused to cash your father's checks, but I wasn't too proud to ask my parents for a little help at Christmas. Kids remember that more than anything else."

"It helped that Santa came through for us," I said, slowing as she fell further behind. "Mom, we want to get to know your parents before they pass. It's especially important to Asher."

"I don't know why. His father's back and they're terrific pals."

"He wants to have a family of his own and do the best he can by Jilly. Role models help." She started to protest, and I raised my hand. "*More* role models. Lots of them." I walked on and she followed. "I want to know them, too. Know my roots, no matter how twisted they are." I grinned over my shoulder. "Maybe I can unknot some of them."

"How about I wait outside while you work on your knots?" she asked.

"Two choices," I said, when we reached the hotel. "You can come in under your own steam and pretend it's a New York runway. Or you can be brought in like a stray cow."

"Like a cow?" she muttered. "The nerve. An alpaca, maybe. Alvina has presence."

"So does Clippers. You'll see. Your mother will be putty in his hooves."

She walked up a couple of stairs and then turned to pat my head. "You poor dear. Don't mistake my parents for sweet rescues. They'll fly off with you in their talons."

A snicker and a swagger told me she was ready for her next act.

CHAPTER TWENTY-SIX

I was afraid one small hotel room wouldn't be able to contain decades of thwarted love and resentment, so I had the young woman at the front desk call my grandparents and ask them to come down and take a walk. It took a couple of tries to get the clerk to focus. She'd probably never seen four animals in the lobby before. Once my grandparents agreed to come down, I led everyone back outside.

Albert and Gardenia were wearing what probably constituted casual clothing for them. My grandfather wore the same denim sports jacket he had on at our first meeting, my grandmother another black dress that was less funereal and slightly more stylish. I wouldn't have been at all surprised to learn she'd stitched that little number herself. At one point it may have been another color entirely. That was Mom's favorite trick—to dye thrift store finds her favorite shade. In her case, the red was often meant to disguise her real state of mind. Gardenia chose to show her insides on the outside.

"Please tell me you're not going to make us walk down the main street of Clover Grove with a horse and a donkey, Ivy," my grandmother said. "In case you haven't noticed, Albert and I like to blend in."

"Me too," I said, and my words sent a smile around the group. The biggest of course was on Keats' face. "I know that's hard to believe but it's true. You can learn far more when you merge with the crowd, and that was my M.O. in human resources. These days, it's much harder when one animal or another needs special attention."

"This donkey just wants to relax in his pasture, Ivy," Albert said. "He's depressed."

"Depressed?" Gardenia said. "What are you talking about? It's a donkey."

"An introverted donkey who's been forced into being an extrovert because someone is trying to steal his best friend," Albert said. "He's doing his best but it's taking a toll."

Bocelli released a sorrowful, deafening bray that made my grandmother jump and move behind her husband and away from the donkey.

"For goodness sake, do something about that, Ivy," Gardenia said. "He sounds so mournful."

"I'm trying," I said. "Nerves are fraying. Clippers kicked the trainer this morning and she still wouldn't back down on her plans to conscript him as a service animal. She's trying to get a TV deal and my guess is a miniature horse—or at least *my* miniature horse—has magnetic appeal to viewers. There are other horses around but she's stuck on mine."

Gardenia reached out tentatively to stroke Clippers' forelock. He responded with a little whinny and then nuzzled her hand. I thought she'd pull her fingers away but instead she smiled—a genuine smile that looked very much like my mom's.

"He is special," she said. "Gorgeous and spirited. I had a pony as a girl, you know. Your grandfather kept trying to buy me another but there's no point in having a pony as a grown-up."

"There's always a point in having a pet to love," I said. "At least, that's my view."

Her smile vanished. "In my time, you saved your affection for children, so that's what I did."

Mom had dropped far enough back that she could hear but not be expected to participate in the conversation. Keats let her lag and focused on the rest of our strange pack as we headed for the town square. I hadn't been there since choir practice at Christmas and it looked very pretty now, with an array of flowers almost as extensive as Clover Grove Gardens. Bocelli picked up the pace once he realized where we were going, but Clippers had decided to fall in step with Gardenia. I was being pulled in two directions at once. That was nothing new, but it was uncomfortable and I was happy when Albert offered to take Bocelli.

The donkey stepped off briskly without so much as a look back at his little friend. Percy raced after them and leapt aboard, making Albert laugh.

"Bocelli trusts him," I said. "Normally he trusts no one but me."

Gardenia nodded. "He had a gift for animal husbandry and was always happiest puttering in his barn." She gave me a look. "Rather like you, I suppose. What delight he took assembling that farm set. You probably never realized most of the animals were hand carved and painted."

"I didn't, no." Turning, I called to my mother, "I hope we still have that farm set. It's one of a kind and I want to pass it to my own children."

"I've moved it several times for exactly that reason," she called back. "Daisy wanted it for her hooligans but I kept it safe for you."

There was a visible softening in Gardenia's posture as we acknowledged that gift as the treasure it was, even decades later. She let out a little sigh and rested her hand on Clippers' back. He was just about the right height for it and his head came up. There was more pep in his step and his mane lifted in the light afternoon breeze.

"Be careful," Mom called, closing the gap. "That horse kicked someone today."

"He won't kick me," Gardenia said. "He can tell I welcome a little support. My hip bothers me more some days than others. We're due for some rain later."

Albert was far ahead of us now and I guessed from the angle of his head and the twitch of Bocelli's ears that they were having a conversation. Then a few stray notes reached me and I realized my grandfather was actually singing to the donkey. Abba's "Take a Chance on Me," to be precise. It was working like a charm, it seemed, because Bocelli let out a sonorous blast that sounded much happier.

"Is he singing to that beast?" Gardenia asked. "My hearing isn't what it used to be."

"He's singing," Mom said, right behind us now. "Dad always had a nice voice."

My grandmother nodded. "He was a good dancer, too. You got that from him, Dahlia."

"I guess so. Although dancing got me into trouble. Back then, and again recently."

"That's no reason to stop," her mother said. "If it brings you joy."

"It does," Mom said. "Sewing and dancing are my favorite pastimes."

The exchange was so subtle yet so immense that I held my breath, hoping neither would ruin the moment. Gardenia had shown her acceptance of the person Mom had become, and Mom acknowledged the gifts they'd given her.

Mom had the sense to savor the moment, too, and to keep her from pulling it back, I decided to change the subject. I knew well from my own dealings with big emotions that it was best to eat the monster one bite at a time rather than swallow it whole and risk choking.

"Grandma Gardenia," I said, trying that title on for size, "Do you mind if I ask why my grandfather stopped keeping livestock, when he was clearly an animal lover?"

"Creedence," she said, simply. "When that dog vanished, the heart went out of him. We'd been rocked by so many disappointments and the dog had become his comfort. His confidante."

"He told me about Creedence. That he was stolen."

Gardenia nodded. "Earl Spratt, by all accounts. There was bad blood between Earl and your grandfather over business and I guess that was Earl's way of punishing him. Albert had too much integrity to fall in with anyone's dubious dealings but that cost him the love of his life." She found a small smile. "After me, of course, and later, your mother."

"And that's why you moved?" I asked. "Because of Earl?"

"Albert didn't say, and a woman didn't ask too many questions in those days." She ran her hand lightly over Clippers again and again, as if he were a cat, and his hooves lifted proudly. "A wife always knows what's troubling her husband if she watches carefully enough. Your grandfather became restless and vigilant after the dog vanished and I figured he felt we weren't safe in Clover Grove. So I was happy to go. And happier with the next move. The further we got from this town the better. It was a dangerous time."

"Then and now," Mom added. "The criminal element just hibernates."

Gardenia nodded. "Albert was in and out of people's homes all the time as a builder and contractor. I suspect he has information that could incriminate many families, which is probably why Earl left us alone after we got out from under his nose."

"What was Earl's deal?" I asked. "He sounds like a horrible man."

"A horrible boy, first, from what my own mother said. He was known for pulling the legs off frogs and throwing them at girls. Then he grew up and threw misery around instead." She leaned more and more on Clippers to the point I worried he'd do something silly and she'd collapse right there on the sidewalk. Keats walked on the opposite side of the horse and kept him walking a straight line.

"And then Earl vanished, too," I said. "Died without ever accounting for his crimes."

"Oh, he got a taste of misery, if he was capable of feeling it," she said. "His wife passed away very early, and his daughter ran off when she was no more than thirteen."

"A daughter? That's the first I've heard of her."

"He made sure the public record was wiped clean and no one dared speak of her," Gardenia said. "We wondered if he'd killed her. Or she'd killed herself to escape him." Stopping, she pressed a hand to her heart. "Poor child couldn't have survived on her own in the bush. Either way, it didn't teach him a thing. He just got meaner, from what we heard. Until he finally crossed the wrong man."

"Morris Tubbs," I said. "Voted least likely to kill."

"He really was a sweet man," Gardenia said. "I can't imagine what provoked him but the town should put a monument right here in the town square to commemorate his service."

"A monument for a murderer?" Mom asked.

"If you knew Earl Spratt you'd agree," Gardenia said.

Clippers let out a long, shrill whinny as we walked into the square. It startled Bocelli, who ripped out a wail. Keats added his eerie howl to the cacophony, and not to be outdone, Percy yowled.

"Sounds like they've come to an agreement," Albert said, shaking his head.

There was no doubt about that. I only wished I knew what it was about.

CHAPTER TWENTY-SEVEN

I left Mom with her parents at The Berry Good Café to catch up on decades of news, and then walked back along Main Street to have a chat with Teri Mason about Imogen. It felt like I was circling closer to the truth about why Earl died, but Ima couldn't hold on forever while I pondered random clues.

"Remind me not to make big promises to dying people in the future, Keats," I said. "The stakes are too high."

The dog mumbled something encouraging and I sighed. "Normally I work well under pressure, but it's getting harder and harder to focus. Protecting Clippers is a full-time job, and getting Mom to make peace with her parents is a big project, too."

He weighed in with a comment that brought back my smile. "That's one item off the list, so let's tackle another. What else could we do today to move things along?"

Stopping at the next intersection, the dog went into a point. I followed his gaze and my eyebrows rose. "The library? Good idea. Let's give Dottie Bridges the shock of her life. She had a conniption when I took you in to do some research. Imagine her face when I arrive with Percy, Clippers and Bocelli." Keats trotted ahead with his tail up. "Don't worry. If she goes down hard, I know CPR."

His ha-ha-ha carried back as he picked up speed. It seemed like he thought there was a clue waiting for us in the stacks and I felt the prickle of excitement that often preceded an important discovery. Call it sleuth's intuition. I'd searched the records at Town Hall but perhaps my negative experience with the librarian had kept me from doing all due diligence. Dottie Bridges acted like the place was her own personal information kingdom and I suspected she curated everything it contained. Nothing was on the up-and-up in Clover Grove, even the tiny public library.

Mrs. Bridges barred the door with her cane as we came up the walk. "Don't even think about it, Ivy Galloway," she said from the open doorway. "If you'd like to come inside, all of your animals need to be roped up off my property."

"It's not your property but the town's, Mrs. Bridges, and I've earned the right to take a few liberties. I'm sure the mayor won't mind if I come inside with my therapy animals."

Dottie held her ground. "No one needs four therapy animals, no matter how much therapy she actually needs. Admittedly, you probably need more than most."

Crossing my arms, I stared her down. "If I do, it's because of you."

"I beg your pardon!" She bristled with such indignation that she missed Keats and Percy slipping past her.

"Well, you're the one who nearly got me killed for the first time in Clover Grove," I said.

"I am a well-respected citizen and historian in this town," she said. "I won't have you slandering my name like that."

"Have you forgotten the last time I came in? I was looking for old newspaper mentions of Runaway Farm. I only realized after I left that I'd discovered who killed the dogcatcher. By the time I found the proof I needed, you'd checked my browser history and alerted Myrtle McCain."

"That's ridiculous," Dottie said, although her pale cheeks got blotchy. "Pure speculation."

"Actually, Myrtle told me herself," I said. "As she was chaining me up behind my tractor to drag me to the dump and choke me."

Dottie's hand went to her own throat and the color drained from her face. "I didn't know why she wanted us to keep an eye on you. We help our friends here without asking questions. It's the beauty of a small community."

"That's beautiful all right. You and the other sheep-herding harpies covered for a murderer." I tugged at the lead ropes of the horse and donkey. "As far as I'm concerned, you're guilty, too, and that gives me a free pass into your archives."

Clippers got to her first and grabbed the cane in his teeth. There was a brief tussle and the old woman gave up. "Fine. Come inside. But if either one of those beasts drops a load, you are cleaning it up."

"Deal. I love manure, Mrs. Bridges." I grinned at her. "I guess I can call you Dottie since you almost got me killed."

"Stop saying that. I'm the keeper of public information and sometimes it gets into the wrong hands. I've done plenty of good for this town."

"Myrtle still thinks of you fondly," I said. "Friends like you are hard to find, especially in lockup. It's nice you've kept in touch."

It was a guess but it landed with an emotional punch for Dottie, who'd forfeited her cane. I took it back from Clippers and handed it to the librarian. It would do me no good if she fell and passed out before I could find what I needed.

"It's not like that," she said, steadying herself. "Just an email now and then."

"Plus a free pass into the library's resources," I said. "Which I'm pretty sure the chief of police wouldn't approve. All I want is the same access you give a killer."

"There's nothing here that can help you with Earl Spratt's murder," Dottie said, now backed against the checkout desk by the horse. "He made sure of that by going over everything in my collection and expunging what he didn't like. It took days but he was meticulous." She set down the cane and hugged herself with thin arms. "I was young and easily intimidated. Yet it felt like such a violation. He sat right here rifling through papers with his toupee askew. I have no idea what he found because he took it all."

"But you're an avid historian and even more meticulous," I said. "I bet you could read into the gaps in your records."

"Ivy, do you want to get yourself attacked again? What if this case isn't as cold as everyone thinks? Nothing stays dead in this town but the bodies."

I stared at the old woman pinned by a pony. "Sounds like I've come to exactly the right place to sort things out. With your help."

"I won't get you into trouble like that again," she said. "I learned my lesson."

"Dottie, if you have any information, it's a chance to clear your record."

Hoisting herself onto the desk, she spun around with surprising ease and landed on the other side. It made me wonder if she had joined Edna's survival course. Then she brandished her cane. "I already told you. Earl went over the records with a fine-tooth comb. There was very little he didn't touch."

Keats' paw came up in a point and his blue eye gleamed.

"*Very little?*" I said. "That means he left something behind, Dottie. What did he miss?"

Pride competed with fear on her face. She had foiled Earl somehow, that much was clear.

"It was just a small pet project," she said at last. "Earl Spratt didn't seem to notice or care about it, and I guess that was his loss."

"I look forward to seeing your private collection," I said. "It's not for me, Dottie, but for Imogen Pigeon, who wants to clear her conscience before passing. Even Myrtle tried to do the right thing by sending me your way. Maybe she's doing some emotional cleanup, too."

I doubted that, given Myrtle's demeanor, but my HR smile was firmly in place and my neutral voice gave nothing away. I sensed I was working with another flight animal in the common librarian. If I put too much pressure on her she'd bolt.

"You're expecting too much of my little collection," she said. "It's really nothing more than a digital scrapbook of old signs."

"Signs? What kinds of signs?"

"Posters. The kind of thing people tacked to trees and poles when a goat or cow went missing. Or they wanted to hire a farmhand. It's nothing much, but to me they tell a story about this town."

"That's what historians do," I said. "There's an art to it."

Clippers wedged himself into the space between the desk and the wall and her fingers touched his velvety muzzle.

"That's how I see it," she said. "One day, after I've passed, someone could do an exhibition."

"My sister Iris worked in museums before opening the salon. I bet she could stage an exhibition of your signs. I'll tell her about them."

"Only after I've passed, mind you," Dottie said, edging her way past Clippers. He followed as she walked into the stacks and Bocelli fell in behind. I came last, while Keats and Percy darted into another row and met us at the door to a back room that said, "Keep Out."

Dottie paused with her hand on the knob and I saw it was trembling. "Like I said, it's just old signs. They may not lead to anything."

"Or maybe they'll change history in this town," I said.

She groped for the right key from the long chain around her neck, seemingly unaware that Clippers had shoved his muzzle under her fingers with an encouraging nicker.

Finally she unlocked the door and stepped inside. The room was so small only Keats and Percy could join us.

There was an old desktop computer on a battered oak desk. "I'll set you up and leave you to it," she said, as someone tapped the bell out front half a dozen times. "People get so impatient. As if the latest mystery novel were life or death."

Keats gave a polite pant-laugh, and Percy hopped off the desk to lead Dottie away when she was done. Clippers and Bocelli stuck their heads into the doorway, as I sat down to examine the librarian's so-called pet project.

At first, it seemed like a pet project, quite literally. Image after image showed signs townspeople had posted about missing livestock and pets over the decades Dottie had run the library. The early signs were hand-scrawled. Lost dog. Lost cow. Lost ram. Lost mare. Lost lamb. Lost mule. There were no photos, just a few words of description and an address or phone number. Sometimes there were notices of things that had blown off in a storm, like a weather vane or porch swing. At a certain point, however, a pattern became very clear. Lost dog. Lost dog. Lost rooster. Lost dog. Lost dog. Lost dog. Lost rooster. The signs with details described the missing canines as large, powerful breeds, like mastiffs. No sheepdogs or retrievers or lapdogs in the bunch. Either those breeds didn't go missing or the owners weren't too fussed about getting them back.

"Oh, boys," I said, flipping faster and faster through the file, "this is making me very sad. So many lost dogs."

Keats mumbled something and when I didn't pay attention, pawed at my foot.

"What? There's nothing here but heartbreak, buddy."

That's when horrible heartbreak came into view. It was a sign for a missing mastiff named Creedence. What made this entry different from others in the collection is that there were many signs for the same dog, posted over a period of months. Maybe it was my imagination, but it seemed like my grandfather's penmanship faltered as time went on. At the bottom of the last one, he'd written: Reward if found, dead or alive.

Tears filled my eyes and blurred my vision until Keats mumbled again, urging me on.

Wiping my eyes on my sleeve, I kept clicking until I came upon a sign for a lost rottweiler named Hermione, who belonged to Morris Tubbs. There were three signs over as many weeks, and then the sad story continued with other missing dogs bearing contact information for many names I recognized, including Hazel Bingham's family.

Interspersed in all the pet signs were a few for missing people. Mostly farmhands, who presumably slipped off unnoticed. But some names I knew from cold cases Kellan had mentioned. A few had photos, and every single sign was about a man. Surely women went missing too. Didn't they warrant a sign?

"I've had it," I said. "I'm feeling nauseated and the air's so stale in here."

Clippers whinnied loud enough to startle me and the bray that followed made the hair rise on the back of my neck.

"Fine. I'll keep going," I said, clicking on. "This is torture."

My finger got slower and slower on the mouse until I felt like I could click no more.

Then a sign for a missing person appeared on screen. An old photo of a sullen girl, who looked little more than 12, had been tacked to the poster.

Missing: Geneva Spratt. Contact Earl Spratt with information. Generous reward guaranteed.

Keats was standing very still in a point, while many hooves stomped assertively outside the file room door.

"Message received, loud and clear," I said, as a shiver ran up my spine. "There's something strangely familiar about that poor girl's face."

Taking a screen shot with my phone, I sent it to Kellan. I had no doubt Earl had bought off the corrupt police force of his day to disappear Geneva from every public record after he realized she was gone for good. Only Dottie Bridges' tireless commitment to telling the story of our town kept this girl alive in memory. In her way, Dottie was a hero, despite nearly getting me killed.

I followed Keats out through the stacks and paused by the checkout desk just long enough to catch Dottie's eye and give her a nod to say we were square. Percy was sitting on the desk at her side, and he jumped down to join us.

The old man signing out a pile of books turned, and his mouth dropped open as he saw the donkey and horse. I raised my hand in a wave but couldn't linger to enjoy the moment. If I was right about that girl, we had no time to spare.

Outside, I started running back to the truck surrounded by animals going at various speeds and vocalizing according to species.

"I couldn't agree more, boys," I panted. "We need to get to Imogen. Fast."

CHAPTER TWENTY-EIGHT

I drove across town through the back streets hoping that Clippers and Bocelli would forgive the rough and rapid ride, replete with speed bumps and stop signs.

"We might be too late," I said, turning down Imogen's lane. It wasn't the first time I'd said it, or the first time Keats had reassured me that it wasn't. His mumbles didn't ease my worry because he was puffed from neck to tail and Percy had inflated even more. There was something going on at the Pigeon manor, I was sure of that. I texted Kellan and then remembered there was always an officer on duty in Imogen's front hall. No one could get to her unless they got in the window, as Edna had. Would the killer go to such lengths to silence her after she'd already shared her secrets?

"It was a leash, boys," I said. "That's what was in the mason jar in the grave. The remnants of a leather leash. Morris used it to strangle Earl over the stolen dog. Hermione. I think I know why he was driven to that, and even how the old mystery is tied to Prudence. The only problem is that her killer knows we're getting closer and may go after Imogen again."

Keats mumbled a warning.

"Us, too, yes. We'll need to be on guard until Kellan can tie things up. The best thing to do is stand guard at Ima's bedside to make sure she gets to depart this crazy mixed-up world on her own terms."

Dropping the phone into my pocket, I jumped out of the truck and started to run to the stairs. Keats dashed in front to block my path and then escorted me back to the trailer. Clearly it was a bigger risk to leave the equines out here unattended than to take them inside.

"Bocelli, I'm sorry," I said. "I know you hate all this tension."

If he did, he didn't show it as he stepped briskly up the porch stairs and waited for me to open the front door. I didn't get a chance because it was already ajar, and Clippers gave it a good nudge that sent it back on its hinges.

"So much for the element of surprise," I said, following three of the animals in and leading Bocelli. "Although stealth is impossible with a pair of equines."

Keats stopped in his tracks, threw back his head and howled. The eerie, sorrowful sound sent a chill up my spine and made me feel as puffed as the dog and cat looked. I expected the others to join him but this time, they didn't.

"What is it, buddy?" I said, pulling out my phone again. It seemed unlikely the dog would be so distressed over Imogen, no matter what had happened. They didn't have a long acquaintance and Keats only showed that much emotion for people he loved.

He lifted his forepaw in a point that was no longer necessary. I'd already noticed the police officer slumped over the desk. His hair was unmistakable. No one else on the force had blond hair, or at least that much of it.

"Asher!" I dropped the lead ropes and ran over to shake my brother's shoulder. His head lolled back, and for a moment I thought he was dead. It spun out in my mind long enough for me to regret our recent tiff over Calvin's homecoming. If Asher had passed, I'd never know if all was truly forgiven and forgotten with my favorite sibling. Too little time had passed since we cleared the air down south.

I shook his shoulder again, and when he didn't respond, rubbed my knuckles hard against his sternum through his uniform. That was enough to elicit a groan and his lids cracked open to blue slits. "Ivy," he murmured. "Little sis."

Tears sprang to my eyes at the endearment, and the slur in his voice sent such relief through my limbs that I nearly collapsed.

Holding him upright, I pressed the communication button on his uniform pocket and said, "Officer down at the Pigeon manor. Asher Galloway's been drugged and the intruder may still be here."

My brother was a large man who'd seemingly become boneless. He slid out of my grasp and flopped clumsily to the floor. All I could do was adjust his head and limbs until help arrived.

Meanwhile, there were more pressing matters, at least according to my menagerie. Percy and Clippers were already standing outside Imogen's bedroom door, and Bocelli was picking his way up the stairs with careful deliberation. I wouldn't have given him credit for such courage but where Clippers led, he followed. Keats circled me and delivered a nip to my leg just above my boot.

I responded to orders, and he raced ahead of me to join the crew now blocking the bedroom door entirely.

I reached between the equines and knocked firmly, calling, "Imogen? Are you okay? Can we come in?"

Perhaps I held back out of an excess of courtesy, or maybe it was reluctance to find out that she was not, in fact, okay. Keats fell back to deliver another prompt, but I elbowed through the equines and grabbed the door handle.

"We're coming in, Ima," I called, holding up my phone as if it were a weapon. Too bad it didn't shoot out death rays or lightning bolts. "I hope you're decent."

If someone happened to be inside with her, they were now duly warned and needn't react in haste. Maybe they'd take a hint and leave by the window and break a limb or two in the fall, making for easy pickings when Kellan arrived.

I kicked the door open and saw the window was closed. My eyes scanned the room, noting that Ima was propped up in bed as usual, hair nicely coiffed and eyes closed. Nothing at all seemed amiss.

Then her eyes popped open. I thought she was playing another joke on me, but she lifted one gaunt index finger to her lips and then used it to point.

Keats was already pointing to the large oak wardrobe in the corner and Percy jumped from the windowsill to sit on top of it. Clippers picked his way around the bed and blocked the wardrobe's double doors, and Bocelli took up most of the bedroom doorway. There was little chance of the fugitive escaping before the police arrived.

"Ima, how are you?" I said, stepping into the room. "You nearly gave me my death with your fake deep sleep. I asked you not to do that."

"And I told you I didn't take orders from you or anyone else," she said. "I came back from the brink to sort out a problem and the books are still open."

"Almost closed," I said. "I know what happened to Earl Spratt and why, Imogen. He was strangled with a leather dog leash. That's what's in the mason jar. Earl stole Hermione, Morris Tubbs' dog. And many more, including my grandfather's mastiff. He held loving owners in a chokehold, until Morris finally choked him."

Confusion crossed Imogen's features. "But why? Why on earth would Earl Spratt steal dogs? Did he love them that much? Or was he trying to gain even more power over the community?"

"It most certainly wasn't because he loved dogs," I said. "Killing them was recreation."

"Recreation?" Her hoarse voice faded. "He abused them?"

I nodded and then remembered I had to speak up for the benefit of the killer in the closet. "Yes, sadly. There is a big gravesite full of dog bones, along with plenty of roosters, in Earl's back forty. We found them this morning and Kellan will confirm it shortly, no doubt."

"Earl just killed all these animals?" Ima asked, still befuddled. "For sport?"

"Sport of a sort. For some miscreants." I walked over to the closet to deliver the truth from close range. "Earl ran a dogfighting ring, with some cockfighting on the side. He recruited the most powerful dogs from Clover Grove and far beyond, I'm sure. It's a terrible form of abuse—abuse for the purposes of entertainment and gambling."

"How horrible," Ima said. "No wonder Morris Tubbs was moved to violence. At least now we know the truth."

"And likely the truth about Prudence, too," I said. "If I'm right, she overheard you talking about Morris Tubbs and was silenced so that this story would never come out."

"Before you, I only told Teri," Ima said. "Unless... unless..."

I patted the foot of the bed. "Unless someone eavesdropped. Or heard you mumbling in your sleep."

"Or in my lost state." Imogen's voice was no more than a whisper. "My dementia."

"Either way, you couldn't have known Prudence would pass information along. She was bound to respect patient confidentiality. I guess she wasn't as professional as everyone thought."

"So the killer was coming after both of us that day?"

"I would think so, yes. We got here in time to save you but they managed to flee by the back door. Lucky for us, there's no escape today."

The wardrobe door cracked open a hair as someone decided to give it a try.

"Uh-oh," Ima said. "Someone doesn't want to take a telling."

"Don't worry, Ima. There's a brave little horse blocking the exit. Help is on the way and the killer is trapped."

Unfortunately, I was wrong about the last part.

CHAPTER TWENTY-NINE

A loud crack of splitting wood released the killer from the back of the wardrobe. What looked like an impossibly small space between the closet and the wall allowed someone to wriggle out.

The muzzle of the gun emerged first and waved around.

"Don't shoot," I said, pressing record on my phone. "There are animals in this room and I know you won't harm them."

There was grunting and cursing as the killer pushed the last couple of inches, rocking the entire wardrobe.

"Stop! Don't add to the crimes of your family," I said, as the gun waggled wildly. "Your mom, Geneva, ran away to escape the carnage and you've spent your life benefiting animals. There's no way you'd shoot four trapped, helpless creatures now."

"Not the animals, no." Trelise Sutcliffe finally managed to squeeze out the rest of the way. She looked more rumpled than I'd ever seen her, but her face was still utterly impassive. "But I have no issue harming humans that get in the way of my benefiting animals."

"Oh, for pity's sake," Imogen said. "Why take out an old lady who's about to die anyway?"

"You talk too much," Trelise said. "So did Prudence. Eventually someone would piece things together, and of course it had to be Ivy 'the snoop' Galloway."

"Is that why you went after Clippers?" I said. "To distract me?"

Trelise gave a single nod. "I tried to keep Ima from speaking to you and when that didn't work, I hoped that diversion would at least slow you down until Ima kicked the bucket and you lost your sleuthing mojo."

"The contract with Vinnie Swenson?" I asked. "A fake?"

"Yeah," she said. "I did try to buy the horse last year, but Vinnie wouldn't sell. He wanted to twist Bailey's arm enough so that she'd come back."

"Like I figured," I said. "Vinnie was a—"

"Dirtbag," Trelise said. "Like all the Swensons." She sighed. "Obviously the Spratts weren't any better."

"But you escaped all that," I said. "Your mother was just a child when she left."

"I don't know how she did it," Trelise said. "Somehow she managed to cross the country safely to her mom's cousin in California. They went into hiding until long after Earl disappeared. No one believed he was really dead."

"Geneva sounds like a remarkable woman," I said.

Trelise nodded again. "She was, but she never got over what happened. The men gathering on Saturday nights. The drunken laughter. The sounds of the—"

"Please don't," Ima said. "I can't bear it. I didn't come back to hear this."

"I'm sorry," Trelise said.

"We understand the trauma," I said. "Truly we do."

Trelise stared down at the gun and I thought it was over. That she was going to surrender. But when her amber eyes rose again, they had the crazed glint I'd seen before.

"Truly, you *don't*, Ivy. You can't possibly understand what it was like, knowing all this and loving animals the way we did."

"It's not Ivy's fault," Ima said. "It's mine, for digging that old story up again. I'm the one who's sorry. I didn't know about you."

"Your grandfather deleted your mother," I said. "He expunged records. He bought people off. He threatened them. People wanted to forget ever knowing Geneva's name."

"Like *she* was the guilty one," Trelise said. "Poor sweet girl, just deleted like that."

"Terrible," Ima said. "You were a poor sweet girl, too."

Trelise's eyes blinked rapidly, and I wondered if the Botox was an attempt to hide the emotions she'd been repressing her whole life.

"I tried so hard to make up for... for what Earl Spratt did," she said. "And it was all going to come crumbling down."

"But you didn't run that fight ring," Ima said. "Everyone will understand that."

"No one will understand that," Trelise said. "You can't possibly be that naïve, having lived in hill country this long."

"I suppose," Imogen said. "But you could work to redeem your family one critter at a time."

I watched Percy get into position. He planned to jump down to deliver his trademark 10-claw scalp massage but I gave a slight shake of my head to dissuade him. That gun could rain bullets at random targets in this small space.

"Ima," I said, "Trelise has a huge new academy and a mortgage to match. That can only be paid with the proceeds of the TV show producers are fighting over now. A show in which Clippers would have a starring role."

"Ivy for the win," Trelise said, bending at the knee to pick up the horse's lead rope while keeping the gun trained on me. "Those TV offers would dry up if they learned about my past."

"Not if you shared your remorse," I said. "I know you left those flowers at the burial site. This could add emotional depth to a reality TV show, and I know from experience how much they love drama."

She backed toward the door, pulling Clippers with her. "Imogen might be on her way out, but you'd keep on flapping those lips, Ivy. Even if I took your entire menagerie hostage. You just never shut up."

"It's true," Imogen said. "I almost wanted to die early to escape the barrage."

Trelise gave a bark of laughter. "I'll save you the trouble and put you both out of your misery. Clippers and I will be off, but I'll leave the rest of the animals in safety. Ivy. It's the least I can do when my grandfather killed your grandfather's dog."

"Creedence," I said. "I don't want to think about that dog's final days. My grandfather still cries, you know. It's the kind of pain that never goes away."

A tremor passed through Trelise's body. The pain she felt over the past was obviously very genuine. In fact, she was tortured by the tales and in her own warped way, was trying to address her grandfather's sins. "Get on the bed, Ivy, and prepare for takeoff. At least you'll have company for the ride."

I glanced around for a way out of this bind. Always before, there had been an escape hatch if I looked hard enough. This time there was nothing I could do without jeopardizing my human and animal friends.

Guns made things so much harder.

Guns made things impossible.

Until now.

WHEN THE SHOT FIRED, I dropped into a crouch and grabbed the only animal I could reach. But Keats slipped out of my grip and charged right at Trelise. He took a leap at the same time Percy catapulted off the top of the wardrobe.

It wasn't a huge challenge to take Trelise down, because she was already staggering and howling in pain. Her finger must have twitched like her face couldn't, and she shot herself in the leg by accident.

She toppled to the floor with Keats attached to her earlobe and Percy clawing her head. Once she was flat on her back, Clippers planted his front hooves on her midriff.

I unclipped Bocelli's lead rope and ran over to Trelise's prone form. The gun was beside her on the hardwood floor, and I kicked it gently away. It spun around and then slipped out of sight under the wardrobe.

While she moaned, I tethered her like a wayward animal to the heavy oak bed frame.

"I'll run down and get Asher's handcuffs," I said, standing and turning to Imogen.

"Don't worry about that," Ima said. "I've got you covered." She waved a small handgun in my general direction. "This little lady pistol I got from Edna packs a good punch."

My mouth dropped open and I blinked at her a few times. "*You* shot Trelise?"

She made a show of looking around the room. "Do you see anyone else with prehensile thumbs? Your animals are gifted but they fall short in that regard."

"Oh my gosh, I can't believe Edna gave you a gun."

"I'm grateful she did, and that Carl taught me to shoot fifty years ago." She held it steady on Trelise now. "After Prudence passed, I felt so vulnerable until I tucked this trifle under the mattress. I wanted to join Edna's survivalist course but that seemed too ambitious."

"It was a good shot," I said. "Grazed the thigh. Enough to disable but not kill."

"Exactly. This woman needs to stick around long enough to pay for what she did."

I heard the sirens in the distance and my pounding heart slowed ever so slightly. Trelise was trussed up securely, the animals had her anchored and a wise woman planned to go out fighting.

"Ima, you amaze me. I can't believe you're actually—"

"Dying?" she said. "There's no doubt about that, Ivy, so don't go making plans. It's my time."

"You don't know that," I said.

"I do, because I feel it coming," she said. "I stuck around to see the end of this situation and thanks to you, I have." She gave me a huge grin. "Getting to shoot a bad guy was such a bonus!"

I perched on the side of the bed, keeping my feet well clear of Trelise. She couldn't do much with Keats still holding her earlobe, ready to remove it if necessary. That probably hurt more than the bullet wound. The pressure of hooves on her chest kept her pretty quiet, too. Clippers pulled one back to make sure there was something for the police to take into custody.

"You did something heroic today, Ima, and I can't thank you enough for saving my animals and me."

"It was a good way to go," she said. "All anyone could want, really."

"Not everyone wants a shootout at the end," I said, smiling. "Edna and Gertie, maybe."

Outside there was a crunch of gravel as emergency vehicles pulled in. In moments, Asher would be carried out and boots would thud up the stairs to collect Trelise.

"Oh, there's Carl," Imogen said, gesturing to the window. A gorgeous, colorful bird was sitting on the sill and tapping at the glass. "It's a painted bunting, and it's come every day since I woke up. So I tell myself it's Carl, signaling for me to come over."

"What a beautiful bird," I said. "I've never seen a painted bunting."

"I've always been a bird lover," she said. "Used to keep a canary in a cage until I realized how it must feel to be trapped. Once I let it loose in the house, that little bird sang like an angel and rode around on my shoulder for years."

Several police officers eased around Bocelli and came into the room. Ima and I continued to chat about the bird outside, as if Trelise weren't being carried out wailing.

Pulling her eyes away from the window, Ima said, "If I could come back from beyond, it would be as a bird. Maybe I'll have that chance to fly, someday. You keep your eyes open. I'll try to help you with your work."

"You're known for spectacular comebacks, Ima, so you can bet I'll be on the lookout." I got up when Kellan came into the room. He tried to step around Clippers to hug me but failed, because Keats was worrying his police-issue bootlaces. There was a real risk of Kellan tripping over the horse and landing in Imogen's lap.

"I know you want to chat with me, Chief, but I'm terribly tired," Ima said, handing him the little pistol. "Can you take this for me? I won't be needing it anymore. Take your lady and her animals outside for some fresh air. By the time you're back I'll be ready to fill you in on this glorious encounter."

"Glorious?" Kellan hopped out of Keats' reach. "Someone was shot here."

She flicked frail fingers, but it was like her hand had become heavy suddenly. "Justice was served in this bedroom, and I don't need to tell you how satisfying that feels."

Kellan met Imogen's eyes and gave her a reluctant nod.

I bent to squeeze Ima's hand, knowing I'd never see her again. "Thank you," I whispered, "for a wonderful, albeit short, friendship."

She pulled her hand away and eased the wedding ring off her finger. It was a platinum band with sapphires like tiny tiles embedded all the way around. The deep blue reminded me of Kellan's eyes. Pressing it into my palm, she folded my fingers around it. "Too conventional for Teri's tastes, so you take it." I started to protest and she shook her head, settling into the pillows. "May it bring you the happiness it did me. See you again, my friend."

Keats circled to get me moving and then collected Clippers and Bocelli. Percy leapt onto the bed. Instead of sitting on Ima this time, the cat curled in the crook of her arm, purring.

"Percy can stay as long as you like," I said, as I left. "Kellan can bring him home later."

"Just what the nurse ordered," she said, smiling as she closed her eyes.

CHAPTER THIRTY

G ardenia wore a red dress to Imogen Pigeon's funeral.

"I can't believe she even owns a red dress," I told Jilly, as my entire family lined up on hard wooden chairs in the large yard behind the house.

"She didn't," Jilly said. "Dahlia's sewing machine roared all night as she pulled something together. Apparently, Gardenia was quite specific. No satin, no feathers, no sequins, no glitter. The opalescent buttons passed inspection."

"Why red?" I said, looking down at my own suit, the dour gray one left over from my days at Flordale Corporation.

"Imogen wanted everyone to celebrate her life with color." She looked down at her own black suit. "Somehow we missed the memo."

"Well, it is our second funeral of the day," I said. "The first wasn't exactly a red dress affair. My suit barely made it out of that forest alive."

Everyone in my inner circle who was able to make the trek had joined me earlier for a brief ceremony at Earl Spratt's property, near the site of the dogfighting ring. Gardenia went as far as the house with Albert and waited there with Clippers and Bocelli. My grandfather had been well supported, however, with the pirate cat on his shoulder and a dedicated sheepdog escort. Percy had eased into Albert's arms when his head bowed with grief over Creedence once more, and my grandfather didn't put the cat down until we got back and Gardenia pulled out a lint roller.

I had been surprised and dismayed to see some of Trelise's followers join what I considered a private service. Jilly gave me an entreating look and I decided to let it go. Hawk Bustard and Sylvia Vesper may have known something about what Trelise had been doing, but there was no evidence they covered up Prudence's murder. Still, their arrival broke up our service early and we headed on to Imogen's, where nearly a hundred people gathered.

Soon, Jilly and I gave up our seats to some of the many seniors. Edna was pacing in new fatigues, but Gertie had doffed her poncho in favor of a nice dress, with her braid twisted into a heavy coronet. She was nearly unrecognizable.

"Do you think Edna will wear fatigues to your wedding?" I asked Jilly.

"I hope not," she said. "Because I'm thinking of asking her to join the bridal party."

"Sounds fun," I said. "Janelle on one side, me on the other, and Edna in the middle."

"A prepper sandwich," she said, laughing. "Gertie and Cori can take care of security that day."

We walked to the sidelines where we could watch everyone without being overheard. "Isn't it a shame we need to consider security as part of your wedding planning?"

"It's just a fact of life," Jilly said. "And remember, the risks started for me long before I met you." Glancing at Asher, who was hovering attentively over Gardenia, she smiled. "I can't imagine being happier than I am today, despite two back-to-back funerals."

"Right? I miss Imogen already but I'm still happy. Life is so strange."

She squeezed my arm. "I'm glad Clippers is safe. He's one of our best and brightest, isn't he?"

"Very much so. I felt bad about Monica Branham, Trelise's client, but Cori is lining up another service horse for her. With Hannah's backing, she'll have her own little helper much sooner."

"Perfect," Jilly said. "Now all we need to do is convince your grandparents to move here, so we can help them out."

"I bet they will eventually," I said. "Asher won't stop till he wears them down."

Teri got on the podium in her most flamboyant caftan, and I imagined Imogen smiling from beyond. Her granddaughter looked like the human incarnation of the brilliant painted bunting Ima had loved.

The itinerary was short on speeches and long on music. After the second song, I made my way over to collect Clippers and Bocelli from Poppy. The little horse was starting to shuffle in time to the music and I didn't want to draw attention away from the ceremony. At any moment, Bocelli could start braying and then all bets would be off.

Walking the two around the front of the house, I said, "Go ahead and cut loose, Clippers. You've outdone yourself and I'm proud of you. No one can ever take you away from me now."

"Are you sure of that?" The deep voice behind me held a note of bemusement. "Because I was just going to make you an offer you can't refuse."

I turned to see Albert and Gardenia, arms linked. "You want to buy my horse?"

"No one mentioned money," Gardenia said. "Although technically you'll save money by losing two mouths to feed."

"Which she'll spend on feeding two new mouths, no doubt," Kellan said, joining us. "I'm still waiting for the pachyderms to arrive."

"First the pond, then the hippos," I said.

"The winters here are too harsh for hippos," Albert said.

His wife poked him in the ribs. "You don't know hippos. But you do know horses, so convince that girl to part with Clippers."

"She won't do it, Grandma G," Asher said, coming around the corner with Jilly and Mom. "It's all about the dancing."

"It *is* about the dancing," I said, grinning. "Clippers and I have a thing."

"You can dance with Alvina," my grandfather said. "I need to dance, too. And sing. Maybe we'll take our show on the road and earn some extra cash."

"You'll do no such thing, Albert. Clippers is for me, remember?"

I stared at her as Kellan's arm tightened around my shoulders. "You really want my little horse?"

She pressed her lips together and I knew it was hard for her to ask. "I do, Ivy. He's a wonderful support and I've been a little shaky since my hip surgery."

"Too proud to use a cane or a walker," said Albert. "But not too proud to use a teeny-tiny horse, apparently."

"Clippers has barely begun training," I said. "He's so easily distracted. Look at what just happened in the funeral. His hooves got tapping and he was in an imaginary disco. If that happened while you were leaning on him, your hip could get much worse."

Her blue eyes narrowed. "I'm not a fool, young lady. I intend to train him properly, just as I did the ponies of my youth. I already had a word with your friend. The small one with the rude gloves."

"Cori Hogan? And she endorsed this?"

"After a grueling interrogation that aged me ten years, yes," she said.

"Huh." I glanced at Jilly and she gave me an almost imperceptible shrug. Kellan's arm relaxed. The decision of whether or not to part with my sweet horse and his sweeter donkey pal rested on me alone.

Of course, I was never truly alone in my decisions. My black-

and-white exterior brain snagged two lead ropes from my hand and delivered them into Gardenia's.

Everyone laughed, including me, although my heart squeezed so tight it hurt. These two were special to me among many beloved animals.

"Oh darling, it's your grandparents," Mom said. "They gave you the farm set that got this whole thing started."

"I'll carve more animals for you, starting with an alpaca," Albert said. He pointed at Kellan and added, "For my great-grandchildren."

"That's a nice offer," I said, as heat rose in my cheeks. "Ultimately, I defer to Clippers and Bocelli."

"All right, if you want to play hardball, we'll compete for them," my grandfather said.

"Oh yeah?" I laughed again. "How is that going to go? A drag race in the back country trails?"

"There's an idea," he said. "It's been nearly eighty years but I could give it a go."

"I have a better idea," Gardenia said. She took the phone out of my grandfather's breast pocket and tapped until Abba's "Take a Chance on Me" started up.

Albert stepped forward and sang, "If you change your mind, I'm the first in line."

"Honey, I'm still free, take a chance on me," Gardenia picked up.

They carried on for a few more lines until Clippers started his signature shuffle.

Then I stepped forward and belted out, "If you're all alone, when the pretty birds have flown, honey I'm still free, take a chance on me."

The rest of my sisters came around the corner and everyone joined in the song. Asher grabbed Mom's hand and twirled her several times. Turned out he'd been hiding some moves—or learning new ones.

Albert grabbed Jilly's hand and did the same, and when Kellan took my hands, there was nothing I could do but whirl and laugh.

"We're going to be the butt of terrible gossip," he said, lifting me right off my feet in a spin. "The chief of police dancing at the funeral of a woman who shot someone right before dying."

"Ima is singing along somewhere," I said. "This is exactly what she wanted."

He set me down again and turned me to face Gardenia. In the midst of the frivolity, the little horse had gone to stand quietly beside the one person who *couldn't* dance. Bocelli moved into position beside Clippers as the last strains died and he brayed their final decision.

"I believe that means we won," Albert said.

I nodded. "Clippers and Bocelli have chosen their destiny. I've lost two family members and gained two more."

"Don't compare your grandparents to equines, darling," Mom said.

Keats silenced Mom by tying her up with her parents in an elaborate sheepdog love knot. There was an ouch or two as the trio tried unsuccessfully to evade hooves, but other than that it was a beautiful sight.

Then the dog gathered Kellan and me into a separate loop and started herding us to my truck. Both seemed to sense without my saying a word that I needed to go somewhere else to deal with the sorrow of parting with my animals on top of everything else. Jilly gave me a nod as I left, letting me know she'd stick around to support Teri.

"Ivy, wait," Edna called after me.

Keats kept us moving. He still wasn't "speaking" to Edna.

Heavy boots thumped after us and she demanded, "Hey, what gives?"

I gestured to the dog, who was sweeping us through the parking lot. "Talk to my manager. If he'll grant you an audience."

He didn't give Edna the benefit of either eye, blue or brown.

"Are you suggesting I need to apologize to your dog?" she said.

"Things work much better without friction on the team," I said.

Edna stopped and crossed her arms. "Chief, can you—?"

"Miss Evans, I wasted no time making peace with Officer Keats," he said. "This dog is a valuable member of my team, too."

"Fine," she said, boots thumping after us again. "I apologize, Keats. That lead was a bust, and I shouldn't have doubted or teased you."

He offered a grudging mumble of acknowledgment.

"How about I let you drive back to the farm?" she said. "Paws on the wheel."

There was a flash of his white tuft as he turned. Now she had his attention.

And Kellan's. "What exactly will you and Keats be driving without licenses, Miss Evans?"

She gave him a cocky grin. "Albert's shiny new truck. He asked me to load up the animals to save Ivy the trouble. I already unhitched the trailer, and obviously I need Keats on the job."

Keats trotted toward her without a backward glance.

"I did not hear any of that," Kellan said, shaking his head. "Good thing I'm off duty."

"Rematch anytime, Chief McSnobalot," she shouted.

When she was out of earshot, I said, "What if Jilly pairs you with Edna at the wedding? You're both attendants."

"Jilly would *never* do that," he said, helping me into the passenger seat. "You know why?"

"Why?" I asked, as a black-and-white blur charged toward us. In the end, Keats couldn't abandon me, even for a sweet ride.

"Because it's the one day she'll want to avoid a murder," Kellan said, letting the two pets pile in on top of me. "Somebody wouldn't survive that pairing."

I was still smiling over the possible wedding photos when he slid behind the wheel and asked, "Any particular destination, fair maiden?"

"Surprise me," I said. "Pedal down. Kellan for the win."

"Now you're singing *my* song."

Once he was out of sight of the crowd, Kellan geared up fast and roared down a side road past green pastures filled with animals like my childhood toys. Keats stuck his muzzle out a crack in the window, trying to gobble the wind.

Laughter eased the ache in my heart. I focused on Kellan's hand on my knee, gathered my dog and cat in a joint hug despite their squirming, and didn't look back.

Have you joined Ellen Riggs' author newsletter at **ellenriggs.com/opt-in**? You'll receive two books free, including *The Cat and the Riddle*, which is EXCLUSIVE to subscribers. The story takes place after *Swine and Punishment* and sets the stage for the next book in the series, *Tweet Revenge*. Don't miss out! Plus, you'll hear some fun stories and see great photos of my adorable dogs.

Do you enjoy a little magic with your twisty & witty cozy mysteries? Welcome to the Mystic Mutts Mysteries, a paranormal spinoff series featuring some of the characters you already know and love. Try the **short prequel**, starring Janelle Brighton and her sassy dachshund, Mr. Bixby.

RUNAWAY FARM & INN RECIPES

Gardenia's Pucker-up Lemon Bars

Ingredients

Crust:

- 1 cup flour
- 1/4 cup white sugar
- 1/2 tsp salt
- 1/2 cup butter, melted and slightly cooled

Filling:

- 2 eggs, beaten
- 1 cup white sugar
- ½ tsp baking powder
- Zest of 2 lemons, grated
- 1/4 cup lemon juice

Instructions

- Heat oven to 350°F. Line an 8-inch pan with one piece of parchment paper, with ends hanging over sides of the pan.
- Combine flour, sugar and salt, and then stir in butter. Press firmly into prepared pan.
- Bake about 18 minutes, until edges slightly browned.

Filling

- Beat eggs, then add remaining ingredients. Beat until frothy, 2-3 minutes.
- Pour filling onto hot crust.
- Bake for 22-25 minutes, or until filling is set.

Cool and refrigerate overnight. Remove from pan using parchment edges and cut into squares.

More Books by Ellen Riggs

Bought-the-Farm Cozy Mystery Series

- A Dog with Two Tales (*prequel*)
- Dogcatcher in the Rye
- Dark Side of the Moo

- A Streak of Bad Cluck
- Till the Cat Lady Sings
- Alpaca Lies
- Twas the Bite Before Christmas
- Swine and Punishment
- The Cat and the Riddle
- Don't Rock the Goat
- Swan with the Wind
- How to Get a Neigh with Murder
- Tweet Revenge
- For Love Or Bunny
- Between a Squawk and a Hard Place
- Double Dog Dare
- Deerly Departed
- Think Outside the FoxMouse of Ill Repute
- Bee All and End All
- Sheep with One Eye Open
- Roo the Day
- Till Death Zoo Us Part

Bought-the-Farm Mysteries - Boxed Sets

- Bought the Farm Mysteries - Books 1-3
- Bought the Farm Mysteries - Books 4-6
- Bought the Farm Mysteries - Books 7-9
- Bought the Farm Mysteries - Books 1-10

Mystic Mutt Mysteries Paranormal Cozy

- I Want You to Haunt Me
- You Can't Always Get What You Haunt
- Any Way You Haunt It
- I Only Haunt to be with You

- All I Haunt Is You (Novella)
- Do You Haunt to Know a Secret?
- All I Haunt for Christmas

Books by Ellen Riggs and Sandy Rideout

Dog Town Series

- Ready or Not in Dog Town (The Beginning)
- Bitter and Sweet in Dog Town (Labor Day)
- A Match Made in Dog Town (Thanksgiving)
- Lost and Found in Dog Town (Christmas)
- Calm and Bright in Dog Town (Christmas)
- Tried and True in Dog Town (New Year's)
- Yours and Mine in Dog Town (Valentine's Day)
- Nine Lives in Dog Town (Easter)
- Great and Small in Dog Town (Memorial Day)
- Bold and Blue in Dog Town (Independence Day)
- Better or Worse in Dog Town (Labor Day)

Dog Town Boxed Sets

- Mischief in Dog Town - Books 1-3
- Mischief in Dog Town - Books 4-7
- Mischief in Dog Town - Books 8-10
- Mischief in Dog Town - The Complete Series

www.ingramcontent.com/pod-product-compliance
Lightning Source LLC
Chambersburg PA
CBHW060536260626
47161CB00003B/921